THE NUMB

Printed in the United States of America

First Printing, 2013

ISBN 978-0-9910456-0-0

Editing by Emily Kokoll and Lauren Kehoe

Cover and Book Formatting by,

Les Van Pelt
lvanpelt.wix.com/site

The Numb

Lauren Kehoe

CHAPTER 1

"Duck!"

Muscles tensed, I obeyed the command and crouched in the dirt.

An enormous black garbage bag flew through the air and landed on the back of the truck, missing my head by inches.

I frowned and grabbed onto the rusting metal of the dumpster, lifting myself up and climbing onto the edge. I picked up a bulging sack and launched it the few feet into the back of the truck, reaching down immediately for another.

Todd flung the bags beside me at warp speed, making the job seem effortless. His face was cold and focused. He didn't look at me as he finished his side of the dumpster and moved closer to pick up my slack.

I heaved another one up towards my chest and tossed it in with the others; indifferent to the fact I was lagging behind. My head pounded. All I wanted was to go home and sleep.

Every day I woke up at seven, got to work by eight,

and collected garbage until five. Afterwards I would go home, sit with a cup of coffee in my chair, and listen to music on the radio until I was tired enough to go to sleep. I had to force myself to work this morning.

So what if my supervisor notices I'm slacking? I've got nothing to lose.

Todd grabbed the last bag and jumped onto the back of the truck. "We're done," he yelled.

I glanced up at the vast sky, noticing gray clouds spreading before my eyes. Thunder rumbled in the distance, a warning to take cover from the coming storm.

Todd dropped the bag and strode briskly to the front of the truck, flinging the door of the driver's side open and jumping inside. "Come on, Vic. Let's go."

I sighed, slowly dropping to the ground. The gravel crunched beneath my boots, a shock reverberating up my legs. A light rain began to fall as I padded over to the passenger's side. I clambered up and sunk into the torn brown seat, slamming the door behind me.

The second it shut, Todd jammed his foot on the gas and spun out of the parking lot.

"Where we gettin' lunch?" he asked, pulling out onto the road.

I shrugged, staring out the window as the drizzle turned into a pounding rain. "Wherever." The food we received was always the same. Since farming space was so limited, the lower working class ate whatever food was left over.

Todd swerved around a piece of debris in the middle of the street and turned up the windshield wipers. He sped past the rows of decrepit gray apartment buildings and cracking sidewalks. Jamming onto the accelerator, he turned onto the highway. The buildings blurred together as we drove, melting into one gray block.

After a few minutes on the highway, he exited onto a bumpy road. The gray apartments were replaced with a small square of shops. The stores were jammed together to fit in as many as possible. He pulled into the nearest convenience store parking lot and switched off the engine, hurrying inside to avoid the rain.

I lingered, listening to the raindrops beating the roof. The smell of the garbage caused my stomach to churn, making the idea of lunch extremely unappetizing. The hammering pain in my head drove me to follow Todd. Maybe something to eat would alleviate the throbbing.

A rush of wind greeted me as I opened the door and stepped down, cold rain dousing my body. I shivered and dipped under the front of the building, slipping inside. Convenience stores for workers were nearly identical. Rows of boxes containing powdered and "just-add-water foods" lined the shelves. A set of freezers held meals that had long ago crossed their expiration date. The storm caused the dim lights overhead to flicker. The walls were a dull shade of gray, matching the dirty gray tiles beneath my feet. They were covered with The Signs. The Signs were a reminder for citizens to obey The City's laws. You couldn't walk into a public place without seeing a collection of them. Some of the most common were "No Physical Contact" and "Remember Your LVs".

I stepped behind Todd at the counter and ordered a meal when he was finished. A bottle of hand sanitizer caught my eye and I squirted some into my hands, trying to rub away the awful stench that seemed to accompany me everywhere.

"Here." The girl behind the counter nodded, sliding me a round white food container and a small pocket of pills.

I pressed my thumb to the reader to pay for my lunch. The machine beeped in recognition as it subtracted the money from my bank. I grabbed the box of food and the pills and sat down in the small eating area in the front of the store. Tables barely bigger than the food cartons themselves were lined up in front of the window, each with a single chair forcing you to stare at the cars driving by while you ate.

The container felt warm in my hands, which was pleasantly surprising. Hot food was a rarity. I wondered what it could be. My fingernails dug under the lid to pop it open, and I peered inside.

An unpleasant aroma greeted me, causing my nose to crinkle in disgust. The thin brown noodles floating in a thick yellow sauce looked as bad as they smelled, but the rumbling in my stomach made me raise the food to my lips and try to eat it.

My tongue cringed as the sourness and oddly chunky consistency suffocated my taste buds. I gagged slightly and spit it back out, wiping my mouth with the back of my hand. The disgusting taste remained in my mouth. I wasn't hungry enough to eat that.

I glanced at the Life Vitamins resting next to my hand and rolled my eyes. It was a citywide law to take the LVs with breakfast, lunch, and dinner. They are guaranteed to lengthen your life span and keep you healthy.

I tore open the pouch and fingered the little white pills. Three pills. Three times a day. Three more years on your life at least. The rain splashed against the window and the wind wailed like a banshee, but I didn't take my eyes off of the three white ovals in my hand. They were small and smooth, with the letters "LV" stamped across the front in white lettering. Little capsules guaranteed to ensure that you kept living your wonderful life in The City. We wake up, go to work, come home from work, go to sleep, and repeat. What a wonderful life. Before I knew what I was doing, I dropped the pills into the rancid brown muck in front of me and tightly closed the lid.

My head snapped up and I glanced around me to see if anyone saw.

Todd was busy slurping up the remains of his lunch. He finished his slop and dropped the empty cylinder onto the table, letting out a satisfied belch. The girl at the counter had her back to me and was busy on the computer.

The only other person in the store was a woman seated at the table closest to the door. She held her lunch in her dark hands, but she raised her gaze to mine as if she could feel me staring at her. Her dark brown eyes locked onto me, causing me to sweat. Had she seen me?

My hand shook as I gripped the container and forced my eyes away from the woman.

Calm down. She was probably concentrating on her food and just happened to look up. There's no way she saw you.

My palms got clammy, the self-talk failing to soothe my nerves. I considered eating the food in case she had seen me drop the LVs, but stopped myself. The deed was done. I didn't need LVs. I didn't want to keep pushing the replay button every morning of my life. What was the point? What was the worst thing that could happen if she had seen me? She could report me to the authorities and I would be taken into custody and then who knows what. It would most likely be a horrible experience, but so was the day I was having.

I tightened my grip and stood up, throwing out my lunch and the LVs inside. The weight of the full container hitting the bottom of the garbage can seemed to echo through the store.

Todd appeared beside me, noticing nothing. He tossed his garbage into the can and headed for the door. "Back to work."

I started to follow slowly, glancing over my shoulder to take one last look at the woman. She was still watching me. My throat felt dry as I exited the store. Her icy eyes burned a hole in the back of my skull.

I didn't know why she was staring at me. That could get her in trouble.

It's not even a big deal if you get reported, I told myself. *What is The City really going to take away from you? There's nothing to take.*

I relaxed a little and straightened my shoulders. I shouldn't be worried about The City. As far as I was concerned, it couldn't touch me. I was a young, lowly worker. I was unimportant. They couldn't punish me because I was nothing. I had nothing, I knew nothing, I was worth nothing.

To my surprise, the pounding in my head was gone. I wondered what effects not taking the LVs would have on me. I had taken them for as long as I could remember. Would not taking them give me some kind of withdrawal symptoms?

Honk!

The horn of our truck startled me out of my thoughts. Todd sat impatiently behind the wheel, waiting to finish the rest of our work.

I hadn't realized I'd been standing in the rain for so long. My thin clothes clung to my body as droplets washed over my face. I tilted my head back to look at the shower plummeting from the sky. Water poured into my eyes, burning and making me blink.

Honk!

The deafening noise wrapped around my skull, swimming through my eardrums and finally rocking me back into reality. I rubbed my eyes with dripping hands and shook my head before darting forward and grabbing the door handle. I hopped back inside, making a puddle with my soaked clothes.

"Damn it," Todd muttered. "We better not be behind schedule," he muttered. He put the truck in reserve as I wrung out my shirt over the car mat. Slamming on the gas, we sped out of the lot.

I leaned against the window, fogging up the glass as I breathed. The cars sped by, blurring together into a mass of gray. They were all the same. Hurrying to get to their destination, despite the lack of meaning behind it. Scratchy clothes stuck to my flesh and water droplets dripped from my hair, stubbornly keeping me awake. I only had a few more hours. I would make it. I always did.

* * *

"Last stop," Todd murmured as we pulled up behind the arena.

My nose crinkled as we hopped out of the truck and headed towards the dumpster. The trash collection at West Point Winner's Circle was one of my least favorite due to the pungent odor. The garbage was always filled with dog shit and the occasional

7

abandoned dog carcass. West Point was an enormous arena for Dog Shows, where the upper class citizens would take their prize winning pups to compete. Dogs were only for show and competition, not kept in homes as they were rumored to have been in the past. When they got too old or were defective and no longer won ribbons, they were usually thrown into the dumpster and left to die. Throwing out little dogs was easy, but the big ones that topped a hundred pounds were a pain in the ass. Either way, the odor stuck with me the rest of the night.

We heaved the bags into the truck quickly. I wanted to match Todd's pace so we could finish as soon as possible. The stench was already burning my nostrils, making me nauseous. The rain had let up, but the garbage bags were still covered in runny dog waste. Within seconds my hands were covered in brown glop.

My arms were starting to ache after hours of tossing heavy bags into the truck. Another one of The City's laws was exercising three times a week to promote good health. I didn't mind working out; weight lifting usually was the only bright spot in my life. But no matter how much I seemed to lift, working never failed to take its toll on my body.

I raised the last bag over my head and launched it into the back of the truck among the others. I held my hands up in attempt to rinse them clean of some of the dog feces, dropping to the ground beside the dumpster

The sound of a whimper made me jump. I craned my neck downwards to see what the noise was coming from. Two brown furry paws poked out from beneath the dumpster.

I looked at Todd and he shrugged at me. "It'll be

dead by the time we come back next week. We can get it then."

Something in the pit of my stomach churned, and I was overcome with a sick sensation different than the one caused by the horrible odors of the waste. My hands flew to my stomach, afraid of what was to follow. The stir passed as quickly as it had come, leaving me dazed.

My face twitched into a frown for a minute before forcing my lips back into a tight line. I glanced around for Todd. He had his back to me and was already on his way to the front of the truck; oblivious.

I wiped my still dirty hands on my soaking wet pants and dashed after him. Whatever the sensation was, it was gone. I was finally finished and it was time to go home.

* * *

Wind whipped outside the window as I curled up beneath my covers. The howling breeze mixed with the pounding droplets echoed throughout my dark bedroom. I glanced through the glass at the horrible storm and shuddered. The glowing clock read 1:03 am. To save energy, The City shut off all major lights at eleven o'clock. Usually I went to sleep around then, but the deafening noises outside denied me of any sleep. I hugged my pillow over my ears, letting out a frustrated groan.

Why can't I just fall asleep?

Giving up, I tossed the covers off of my body and hopped out of bed. I trudged into the kitchen and fumbled around in the drawers for my flashlight. My hand closed triumphantly on the cylinder and flicked it on.

9

The light illuminated the sink a few feet away. I stared longingly at the faucet, my throat dry. The City placed a limit on the amount of water we used. Sinks could only be used between the hours of 7:00 am and 11:00 pm and only produced eighty ounces of water a day.

I felt something beneath my left foot, blocking the cold kitchen tile. I looked down and spotted the LVs I hadn't taken at dinner. I bent to the floor and scooped them up. My foot had reduced them to a dusty, white powder. Dropping to the floor, I swept the powder into my hand. I opened my garbage pail and stuffed them inside. I looked around, paranoid. Of course I was alone in my apartment. It was just me. It always was.

Annoyed, I paced around my small high-rise. I went from room to room, trying to think of something to keep me occupied. In minutes I'd been in the kitchen, bathroom, bedroom, and living room five times each. My home was small; after all, I was only a garbage collector. I collapsed in the easy chair in the living room, tapping my fingers against the armrest.

A whimpering noise caused me to jump a few inches.

"Who's there?" I whispered, shining my light around the room wildly. The beam danced from corner to corner, but everything sat in its usual place.

The whimpering died down before picking up again.

Relax. It's just the wind.

A branch scratched against the window, sending shivers down my spine. The wind morphed from a whimper into a wail, as if were about to blast down the walls of my apartment and blow me away.

Whimpering. My thoughts flashed back to that

afternoon at the dumpster behind West Point. The odd sensation deep in my stomach returned, as if my muscles were twisting into a giant knot.

Thunder rumbled. I grimaced—the poor creature was stuck. I couldn't imagine how terrified, cold, and miserable it must be. Nothing deserved that.

I froze. Where were these thoughts coming from? Feelings toward another living creature were strictly forbidden, and frankly had never existed before. At least I'd never felt anything towards another person. Especially not towards a dog.

It's just a stupid dog, I told myself. *You've gotten rid of hundreds of bodies before. That's just the way it is.*

As hard as I tried to forget about the creature and convince myself leaving it there was no big deal, the bad feeling in my gut refused to disappear.

I shuddered as a flash of lightning lit up the room. I wasn't sure what had brought up these sudden emotions, but I was getting a little scared. Realistically I knew that The City couldn't read my mind. Of course if they found out I was having these feelings, something would be done. Though The City couldn't take anything from me, they could still torture me somehow. If I didn't get rid of them, they could be hard to hide. I had never felt such strong urges in my life. Well, I'd never felt anything. Conveniently, I had always operated just as The City wished; oblivious to other living creatures except when I had to work with them. Being alone was not enjoyable, but I'd never desired anything else either.

I'd certainly never cared about anyone else or what happened to them. I'd seen countless dead dogs in my lifetime, and disposed of them without a second thought. I'd even come across a few dead bodies, which had also failed to stir up any sort of feelings

11

inside me.

Feelings.

Is that what this was? This unwelcome, unhappy feeling for this dog? Was this a feeling? If so, I could see why The City forbade such "feelings". It was uncomfortable, to say the least. All that I could think about were the two brown paws and the horrible whimpering sounds that had come from the dog. And how it was outside in the storm right now, cold and wet. How it was left to die.

STOP! I ordered myself, my eyes darting around nervously as if The City was somehow watching me at this very moment.

The City continuously preached about how relationships had ruined civilizations in the past. All the history books from school explained the horrors and complications associated with having any kind of relationships whether they are friend, family, or even animals. We interacted with others when we needed to and that was it; end of story.

There's nothing you can do, I reasoned, battling the thoughts as hard as I could. *It's not your problem. It's just a dog.*

"Just a dog," I whispered, my voice barely audible above the wind. "It's out of my control." I wasn't the one to dump the dog and leave it to die. It was just an unfortunate circumstance. Todd was right; in a few weeks we'd get rid of its body and continue on as if nothing had happened.

But something would happen. The innocent dog would die. It would never get to see another day, never get to do whatever it was dogs liked to do.

It obviously was a loser at the dog shows. It could achieve nothing, so was completely useless. The purpose of dogs was to compete. They went to shows, and if they won they were praised. If they got nowhere, they were done for. That's how it worked.

Did it deserve to die because of the way it looked or performed? Surely there could be some other use for the poor thing. It could do some sort of manual labor, or possibly be trained for the police force? Of course if it couldn't win a measly dog show, there was no place for it on the canine unit.

It couldn't be completely useless could it? There had to be something that I could do that could save it from its horrible fate. Something . . . hell I could even take it in if I could save it from death.

WHAT? Me? Take in a dog?

I didn't have the money to show the dog, and surely if I brought it back to the shows its owner would recognize it and get suspicious. It's not like I could keep it in my home as the history books said they used to do with dogs. What did they call them? Peeps? Peets?

Pets! That was it.

A pet. That was ludicrous. Pets had been banned decades ago due to the intense amount of grief they had caused their owners when their lives ended. Some owners never got over the loss of the animal and had to live the rest of their lives with the weight of the pet's death on their heart.

Grief? Was that this "feeling" I was experiencing? I could only recall bits and pieces of what they had made us read in school. I had never really tried to reach into my memory for anything from it until now.

I shook my head. If that's what it was, then grief was definitely not something I enjoyed. And thinking any further about this dog was sure to only bring me more of this grief.

I stood up and went back to the kitchen to put away

the flashlight. I was exhausted, confused, and needed sleep.

My eyes landed on my muddy boots beside the front door. I glanced at my dark bedroom, then back at the boots.

I was paralyzed. My brain told me one thing, while something somewhere else inside of me screamed another. It felt like I was being pulled apart inside, a piece of rope on the verge of snapping.

I took a deep breath and closed my eyes.

You are going insane. Stop these illogical thoughts. Go back to bed.

I started towards my bedroom and reached the doorway before I stopped once more. My heart pounding in my chest, I whirled around. Before I could stop myself, I was kneeling on the floor lacing up my boots.

This *feeling* wasn't going to go away, and I wasn't going to sleep or get any peace until I attempted to appease it.

Despite the cold air in the apartment, a river of sweat cascaded down my face. Flashlight in my shaking hand, I thrust open the door to the hallway and slipped outside. What I was about to do was ridiculous. If I was caught, I would be condemned for sure. But as I ran down the steps and out into the freezing cold rain, there was not a doubt in my mind it was exactly what I wanted.

Chapter 2

Once outside, I broke into a run. My boots pulled down on my legs, extra heavy from the rain. I kept going, splashing through the puddles covering the sidewalk. The City turned into a different world at night. Since all lights shut down at eleven, so did the citizens. Every apartment and building I passed was dark. My flashlight was dim in the blackness, but it allowed me to see the necessary few feet in front of me so I didn't fall.

I shined the light up at the street sign to get my bearings. Twelve. I turned to my right and trudged on. My lungs burned as the cold rain beat against my body. The thin pajamas I wore offered little protection from the storm, but I tried to keep the focus on my mission. Only a few more blocks and I'd be there.

Breathing hard, I tried to keep my mind busy to distract myself from the burning sensation in my chest. Running was one of my least favorite activities, but at least now there was a purpose behind it. As my legs pumped furiously back and forth, I realized for the first time in my life I wasn't being forced to run. The City wasn't checking off my weekly activity or ensuring that I exercised. I was running because I wanted to, and the more I thought about it, the faster I moved.

I charged across the pavement to the next block, the sidewalks and streets vacant. It was only me, the rain and the sound of my shallow breathing.

A flash of lightning lit up the road, the clap of thunder following driving me on. The pain in my chest lessened as I focused on the sidewalk. My feet hit the ground in a steady rhythm. Left, right, left, right. I rubbed my eyes to clear my vision as a gust of wind flooded them with icy water.

I peeked over my shoulder for a minute to make sure I wasn't being followed. There was no one there of course. Everything was shut down. I was in a ghost town.

Suddenly I was on my hands and knees. I cried out in pain and fumbled around for my flashlight. My arm stretched as far as it could until my fingers closed over it. I pulled it close and aimed it behind me, looking to see if I had tripped over anything.

The sidewalk was empty; I must have just slipped. My work boots were definitely not meant for running. I moved the light so it illuminated my hands, wincing as I saw that they were cut up and bleeding. I rose to a crouch to examine my knees. My left pajama had split open, blood dripping from the hole.

I groaned and stood up slowly, wrapping my hands around my shirt to wipe off some of the blood. Another burst of lightning reminded me where I was going. I broke into a light jog, trying to be more careful. Stopping had given me a chance to catch my

16

breath, allowing me to keep up a steady pace for the last few blocks.

I slowed to a stop in front of the looming arena. A quick scan of my flashlight over the sign assured me that I was at the right place, though I'd been there hundreds of times. The dark blue sign bore the words "West Point: Dog Show Spectaculars." I used the back of my hand to wipe more water from my eyes before turning to the left and heading towards the more familiar part of the property.

I jogged along the edge of the chain link fence and stopped when I reached the gate, shaking the lock as if somehow it would open. I should have thought that they would lock things up at night.

Even in the murky darkness I could see the towering outline of the dumpster. I kicked the fence in frustration. There had to be some way in. The fence was at least seven feet tall. There was no way I could scale it, especially with my hands already torn up.

I slammed it again with my boot and cursed, walking back and forth to try and stir an idea in my brain. Fences were made to keep people out, but they also existed to keep things in. Surely there had to be some dog that had escaped from here at one point or another. I just had to think like a dog.

I ran my flashlight over the bottom of the fence, searching for any break in the chain link. To my dismay, the fence was all perfectly in tact. What was I thinking? Of course a dog couldn't chew through The City's chain link. It was way too strong.

I continued pacing, running my left hand along the side of the fence.

Think Vic. You didn't come all this way for nothing.

Suddenly my foot slipped on unlevel ground. I

17

reached out and grabbed onto the fence to prevent myself from falling again. My hands throbbed as the metal pressed against my fresh wounds. Letting go, I aimed the flashlight at my foot to see where I had lost my balance. A triumphant whoop escaped my lips. A hole!

I bent down to examine the gap between the mud and the bottom of the fence. The space was small, too small for me to fit through. But it was definitely big enough for a dog.

Instinctively I began to dig at the dirt with my hands, trying to widen the opening. Mud stuck under my fingernails and stung at my cuts, but I kept digging. I was so close. I flung mud behind me as fast as I could.

Lowering myself onto my stomach, I shimmied into the hole. The chain link tugged at my clothes and scraped along my back. I winced, realizing I was stuck. Grunting and squishing myself into the dirt, I mustered my determination to wiggle through. The fence clung to my jacket. I dropped the flashlight and fumbled around for something solid to hold onto, my right hand closing over a decent-sized rock.

Holding onto the stone with both hands, I tried to pull myself forwards. I exhaled to make myself as small as possible, rolling around in the mud until I finally felt my body slide forward a few inches. The fence cut into my spine as I squirmed forwards like a worm. All of a sudden, I felt the metal give way and unhook itself from my jacket. I slid forward through the mud and sighed with relief. I made it!

My back burned slightly as the wind blew through the new hole in my jacket. After wiggling my ankles and boots through the opening, I struggled to my feet. I grabbed the mud-covered flashlight and surveyed my surroundings, trying to ignore the raw pain in my palms. The dumpster was just a few feet to my left.

I darted towards it then slowed, as my feet sank into the mud with each step. I put the flashlight down to free my hands and crouched beside the dumpster. Hopefully the creature was still here. And if it was still here, hopefully it was still alive.

I shook the bad thoughts away and peered under the dumpster, staring into the darkness. My eyes were useless without the flashlight.

I sat down and tried to think of the best way to approach the situation. I didn't know much about dogs. I'd read a little about them in the history books, but none of them focused on their personalities.

A chill ran through my body as a burst of wind blasted my face with cold rain. Frowning, I grabbed my flashlight again. I wasn't going to get anywhere without it. At least it would help me find this thing.

I flicked it on and set it flat on the ground, lowering myself until I was lying on my stomach. Eye level with the bottom of the dumpster, I moved the light so I could see what lie beneath.

"Ahh!" I screamed. Two eyes stared back at me, glowing in the soft light. I sat up, taking a few seconds to realize that it had to be the dog. Though I'd dealt with dogs before, none of them had been living.

What if it's vicious?

My heart beating faster than a speeding car, I crouched and flattened onto my stomach once more. The eyes remained in the exact same spot they had before. They were locked onto me, observing every twitch of expression that crossed my face.

A low whimper rose from the animal, sending

19

shivers down my stinging spine.

"It's okay," I whispered softly. Too afraid to stick my hands under in case it would bite them off, I continued talking to it in a quiet voice.

"I'm not going to hurt you. I promise. I want to help you. I came to save you."

The eyes held their unwavering stare, unblinking. The whimpering only increased as I futilely attempted to soothe the animal.

I sat up and tried to wipe the mud off my face, but my hands were too dirty. I leaned against the cold dumpster, tired and cold. The urge to whimper myself washed over me, but I bit my lip and lowered my head to rest it on my knees. I had come here for nothing. This dog was going to die and I couldn't change it.

My eyes began to sting and a droplet of moisture ran down my cheek, hot and slow. It was different than the icy cold rain. Another drop slid down my face. It was coming from my eye.

"What?" I murmured aloud, raising my head. "What's happening?"

My nose burned slightly and ran a little, the droplets continuing to fall from my eyes.

What was going on?

I sniffled and rubbed the bottom of my nose with the inside of my shirt, overwhelmed with the same "feelings" I had experienced earlier. All I could think about was the dog beneath the dumpster, starving out in the cold. And how I had let it happen because I had failed to do anything about it. And now some water was falling from my eyes and nose? I remembered in the past when I had hurt myself pretty badly I had experienced a similar reaction, but this was different.

20

A noise beside my leg startled me, interrupting my thoughts. My eyes fell to my hip and I gasped. A scruffy dog was slowly emerging from the bottom of the dumpster.

The creature stood up, not taking its eyes off me for a second. It was big and gray, its fur wet and matted. One ear pointed up and the other flopped down. Its eyes were two different shades of brown. Beneath the mud stains I noticed that its paws were white, as if it were wearing socks. Its tail was fluffy, hanging between its legs.

We stared at each other, unmoving and unsure. Another drop rolled down my cheek, seeming to break our face-off.

The dog stepped closer, shaking. Its niffed me, carefully raising its snout to my face.

I was immobilized with fear. *Don't bite me.*

It opened its mouth, revealed rows of sharp white teeth. Its breath felt hot against my face. A pink tongue emerged from between the fangs, slowly reaching out towards my flesh. I closed my eyes and braced myself, fearing the worst. Surprisingly the pain did not come. The tongue felt warm and soft against my face as the dog ran it delicately up my cheek, sweeping away the drops.

Relief flooded my body as all of my tensed muscles slowly relaxed. The slight change in my posture startled the dog, and it backed away.

I stared at it, trying to be as still as possible. "It's okay."

It cautiously crept back towards me and began licking me, steadier this time. It doused me in slobber until it had reached every part of me face, removing the mud mask caked on my skin.

A smile spread across my lips. I almost laughed but

caught myself, not wanting to scare it once more. I had never come in contact with a live dog before, but it had replaced the sick feeling in my stomach with a warm sensation.

It sat down beside me and sniffed the air, not taking its eyes off of me. It had finally stopped whimpering, and now stared silently.

I let out a soft chuckle and it didn't flinch. I wasn't sure what to do next. My body had driven me here, but my mind hadn't really planned on what I would do after I actually arrived.

"I'm Vic," I told it. I don't know where it came from, but it was the only thing I could think of to say. Its tongue hung from its mouth, trembling slightly with each breath. I didn't know if it could understand me, but I felt the need to break the silence.

"Well I guess I need to call you something," I mused. "But I don't know if you're a girl or a boy."

The dog continued to watch me and began flicking its tail slowly back and forth. It seemed to be less jumpy now, its eyes less guarded than before.

The rain had eased up and now fell in a slow drizzle instead of a steady, rough stream. The dog seemed to notice it too, and stood up to shake itself off. Once it was on all fours, it was obvious how large the dog was. As it shook off its entire body, the water and mud from its fur sprayed in every direction.

"Hey!" I cried out, but realized it didn't matter. I was already drenched. A little more water wouldn't wouldn't make a difference.

Its tail swayed back and forth faster, causing its whole backside to wiggle. It moved in closer and licked my face again.

"Okay, okay." I reached out cautiously and held out my hand for it to sniff. After its nose had given me a thorough once-over, I mustered my courage to do the same. I slowly reached to touch its wet fur below his neck.

Its body tensed when I tapped it, but then relaxed and its tail began to wave again. I exhaled with relief, stroking it as gently as I could. Its fur was soaked and muddy, bugs and dirt twisted through the knots. Despite all the muck and grime, it was beautiful. The mess of fluff was unlike anything I'd ever seen before; even in the darkness it was mesmerizing.

The dog lowered its head and bumped my chest. I moved my hand to scratch behind its ear, and its back leg began to thump in time to its tail. Despite the cold in the air, my entire body felt warm. I felt indescribably good.

I felt. I was feeling. My mind wanted to race and attempt to analyze what was going on. It questioned why I had some kind of connection with the dog, but for a moment I quieted it. I wanted to savor this good feeling for as long as I could. I had never felt so happy in my life. The dog was so sweet, and it liked me too. And I was happy.

The dog seemed to lose its balance, but wasn't bothered. It rolled onto its side and rested its head against my knee, slipping in the mud onto its back.

Carefully, I moved my fingers above its stomach and reached down to scratch it. Its tail continued shaking, which I took as a sign of pleasure since it didn't try to stop me from petting it.

Once it was on its back, I was able to see that it was a girl.

"Good girl," I whispered. Her tail moved faster when I spoke to her, and her eyes now seemed to gaze at me instead of stare.

"What should I call you?" I'd never been to a dog

23

show, so I didn't know what kind of names people gave their dogs. I assumed it could be like people names, or anything I really wanted it to be.

I noticed the rain had completely stopped. I looked up at the dark sky. It was cloudy out, but my eyes spotted one star peeking out from behind the clouds.

"You made it stop raining!" I told her. She rolled back over onto her stomach, covered in mud. She showered me in more licks, her tail in constant motion. I tried to think back to school time. Had they mentioned what the tail movement was called? I couldn't remember.

My brain drifted back to the thought of a name. She was certainly big. She was also beautiful, so full of light and life. But everything that crossed my mind seemed unfitting for her.

My legs had fallen asleep, and I struggled to get to my feet. She hopped up beside me, staying close to my side.

I tried to think of names of women I had met in the past. Nothing caught my attention. This dog was special. She was magical. Her eyes remained locked on me, their expression soft.

"Amber," I murmured. I wasn't sure where it came from; it had just popped into my head. I had always liked the color amber. I wasn't sure if it was a name, but it was something.

"I'm calling you Amber," I declared.

Amber let out a woof and waved her tail at the sound of my voice.

"You like it?" I asked her, reaching to ruffle her fur.

She put her front paws on my side and licked my arm, which I decided to take as a yes.

"Good!" I smiled, the warm feeling still surging throughout my body. "Well . . . I can't leave you here.

24

I guess you'll have to come home with me."

She woofed again and dropped back to the ground. Though she had been abandoned, it must have been recently. She was stocky and didn't show signs of malnutrition.

"I'm going to have to keep you quiet somehow," I said. Someone like me would never have a show dog. The other tenants in my apartment building probably wouldn't care enough to report the strange event of me getting a dog, but they might care if she barked and kept them awake. The authorities also did patrol every once and awhile, and if they found her they would be suspicious. Dogs were for show, not for these feelings I was experiencing. I'd never shown a dog, but I couldn't imagine that it could be better than the way I felt now. It was like I was floating on a cloud. Like anything was possible.

Amber barked and I shook my head. "No!"

She looked startled, circling a few times before barking again. She grabbed my pant leg in her mouth, shaking it gently back and forth.

"What are you doing?" I exclaimed. I surveyed the ground quickly and grabbed a rock, desperate for something else to put in her mouth. I threw it a few feet away. "Go get it!"

Delighted, Amber galloped over and pulled the rock out of the mud. She hurried back over and dropped it at my feet, her tail moving faster.

"Wagging!" I exclaimed. That's what the tail motion was called. She was wagging her tail because she was happy!

I threw the rock farther this time, accidentally throwing it too close to the dumpster. She barreled into the side, not having enough time to stop. Seeming unfazed, she grabbed the rock eagerly.

25

As she dropped it at my feet I couldn't help but laugh. "You know you'd be a lot easier to keep under the radar if you were a little smaller. And more graceful."

Amber barked and leapt up, putting her paws on my shoulders. "Whoa! You're pretty heavy there," I cried, staggered backwards, "How much do you weigh?"

In response, she barked louder and picked up the rock again. She ran circles around me, her tail wagging like a windshield wiper. I could picture her in my apartment knocking everything over.

"Shh!" I ordered. "You have to be a quiet dog, remember? Come on, let's go home."

I started to walk towards the fence, afraid she wouldn't follow. She stood still for a moment, then hurtled over and pressed up against my side.

"Ahh!" I cried as the force almost knocked me over. "Easy!"

Reaching the hole in the fence, I exhaled slowly. "All right. If I can do this, so can you."

She looked at me expectantly, as if waiting for my next move. The look in her eyes was definitely free of fear now. If I wasn't mistaken, it looked a lot like it had been replaced with trust.

I dropped to the mud, sinking into the muck. She immediately followed my lead. Using my elbows to propel myself towards the hole, I pressed as low into the ground as I could. It seemed easier this time, perhaps because there was no rain falling in my eyes. It still was a tight squeeze, but I wiggled through without too much pain.

Before I even stood up, Amber had wriggled through the opening and was at my side.

"You're a pro," I told her. I struggled to my feet

26

and rubbed the fur behind her ears. The black watch on my wrist caught my eye. Eager to see the time, I used the inside of my shirt to scrape off the mud that had become caked on it. My finger pressed a button on the top to light up the screen. It was almost three thirty!

"Come on! We gotta go!" I whispered. In an hour and a half, some people would already be getting up to go to work. My apartment wasn't too far, but I was too exhausted to run.

Amber followed my lead as I began a fast walk down the puddle-ridden sidewalk, keeping close to my side. Her eagerness and attentive trust gave me a second wind, pushing me to march faster. She splashed through the water joyfully as we walked, dipping her nose into the puddles from time to time.

It was hard to believe that she could be so happy. After all, someone had left her to die because they hadn't wanted her. She wasn't perfect enough to be show dog. How anyone could do something so cruel and heartless was beyond me. She was so full of life; the fact that someone would want to deprive her of that was unthinkable.

Though I hated to admit it, if I had been her owner the day before, I might have done the same thing. No, I would have done the same thing. *What happened to me?*

I was overcome with everything The City deemed horrible and against the law. I didn't know why I had started feeling things toward Amber, but I was confused. I felt better than I could ever remember. Usually I didn't feel much of anything at all; it wasn't even an option. But now it seemed like my whole world was flipped around. I felt happy, something I hadn't felt in as long as I could remember. I felt connected to another living thing. I felt accepted. And it felt good!

We walked fast and made good time. When we reached my apartment, I stopped and looked up to make sure it was quiet. I wasn't sure when my neighbors got up for work. I hadn't really thought twice about them until today.

"What is going on?" I blurted, covering my mouth with my hands.

As quietly as I could, I opened up the door and headed for the staircase. Amber stuck to my heels, the low whine rising from her throat again.

"Shh!" I whispered. "It's okay. You'll be safe here I promise. I'm not going to let anything happen to you. Just follow me and be quiet!"

Hearing my voice, the noise surprisingly stopped. She followed me quickly and silently, sitting behind me when I stopped in front of my door. I rubbed my finger off the best I could on the inside of my shirt, which now wasn't much cleaner than the rest of me. The scanner beside my door beeped as I pressed my finger against it, recognizing me as the resident. I pushed open the door and stepped inside. Amber hesitated before cautiously following me.

I closed the door and crinkled my nose. We reeked like stale rain and garbage. I glanced at my watch: it was four am. The water wouldn't be back on for another three hours. We would have to be stinky and dirty until then.

I opened the closet and grabbed a few bath towels, tossing one onto Amber's back. I rubbed her vigorously with it, attempting to get off some of the mud, dirt, bugs and waste that clung to her fur. After a good ten minutes of work she was a little cleaner, but still in desperate need of a bath. Most of the muck had dried. I used the other towel to clean off myself as best as I could.

Exhaustion swept over my body as I collapsed into my chair. Finding Amber had given me adrenaline to keep going for a few hours, but it was wearing off. My eyelids drooped and I leaned my head on my hand, allowing them to close.

"Oof!" I let out a groan as I felt a blow to my stomach. I struggled to open my eyes, greeted with a blurry Amber on my lap.

"Really?" I grunted. "You are too big for this."

Amber stared at me with her big brown eyes and wagged her tail, flicking her tongue across my chin. She stood up on my legs and sat down again, trying to make herself comfortable. A sigh escaped her as she lay down, resting her head on the arm of the chair.

I fidgeted out from under her and curled up on what was left of the cushion, pulling the chair's pillow out from under her. Moving it so I was able to lean my head against it, I closed my eyes once more. Amber's warm body heat and slow, steady breathing soothed me. I felt myself slipping into a trance, and the rhythm of my breathing fell into time with hers. My mind began to cloud. Before I knew it the world was dark.

CHAPTER 3

Sunlight streamed through the window and cast its rays across the pale blue living room carpet. I rubbed the sleep out of my eyes, letting out a big yawn. Reaching my arms up, I stretched as far as I could. The room was still cloudy, and I felt tired and achy.

A bang startled me out of my sleepy state. I sat up straighter in the chair and looked around the apartment anxiously. "Who's there?"

I heard another crash and realized that the sound was coming from the kitchen. Memories of the following night flashed through my brain as if it were on fast forward. Amber!

I hurried into the kitchen, finding Amber squeezed onto the counter. Her legs flopped over the side; she was crouched to avoid being squished by the cabinets above. Upon seeing me, she tried to leap up and hit her head on the bottom of the wood. She let out a yelp before sweeping her tail across the counter and knocking off my stack of napkins.

"What are you doing?" I squeaked, my voice still

30

not fully awake.

Amber slid off of the counter, crashing to the floor beside my feet before putting her paws on my shoulders. She immediately got to work on covering my entire face with slobbery licks.

"Shh!" I exclaimed, but couldn't help but laugh as she showered me with affection. Her tail continued to wag furiously, beating against the bottom cabinets like a drum. She still reeked of garbage and poop, and her fur had dried into a solid, brown covered mess.

"You must be hungry," I reasoned. I had no dog food in my house, and barely any human food. I was going to have to figure out something to feed her . . . but what?

"What time is it?" I wondered, looking at the digital clock above the stove. "7:05!" I only had slept for around two hours, and had to leave for work in less than an hour. No wonder I was so exhausted.

Amber whined and paced around the kitchen, stopping to look at me from time to time. She was panting, and I figured she must be thirsty also.

I grabbed a tattered plastic bowl from the cabinet and filled it with water, placing it on the ground in front of her nose. She eagerly lapped it up and waited while I filled it once more. She slurped the second batch and looked at me again.

"Not right now," I told her, filling a glass of water for myself. The cool liquid drifted over my cracked lips and soothed my dry throat.

"I need to think of what you can eat for breakfast," I said. "But first, let's take a shower and clean the rest of this mud off of us."

She followed me into the bathroom, her nails clicking along the tile floor. Showers were also limited to thirty minutes of running a day. I was going to have to do some adjusting to my normal schedule.

"Let's see . . ." I thought aloud, tapping my foot to help me with my math. "If I take a ten minute shower now instead of my usual fifteen minutes, then I can clean you off for ten minutes and squeeze in another ten minute shower for me before bed."

I hopped in the shower and set the timer on my watch to ten minutes, scrubbing, soaping, and shampooing as fast and as best as I could. The muddy runoff turned the bottom of my tub temporarily brown. It felt so good to feel the warm water washing over me, and I felt the urge to linger longer when my watch went off. Amber's nails clicked along the tile as she waited for me, as if she was reminding me that she needed a turn as well.

I begrudgingly turned off the water and wrapped a towel around myself. I slid the shower curtain to the side, revealing Amber's face staring at me.

"Ah!" I yelled. I had known Amber would be there, but didn't expect her to be so close. I stepped out of the shower and tapped the side of it. "Come on girl. Your turn!"

Amber just stared at me, her tail thumping on the floor. Either she didn't like water, or didn't understand what I was trying to get her to do. I had been talking to her as if she was a human. Could she understand a word I said?

"You wanna take a shower?" I asked. I tried to pick her up and lift her in, but she squirmed around and evaded my grip. She licked my face once she saw that I had given up. Crouching down, she leapt into the shower and slid along the bottom.

Breathing a sigh of relief, I switched on the water. I tossed my towel on top of the closed toilet, sure that I would need more drying off after Amber's rinse.

The stream startled her at first, but after a few seconds she was jumping around and playing. She leaned her head back and opened her mouth, trying to catch what she could. Then she tossed her head back and forth, spraying water in my face.

"Easy!" I grabbed the soap and shampoo from the side and poured it generously over her fur. Using my fingers, I massaged it along her back and legs. Water poured over us, sending a fresh stream of mud and waste down the drain. She stood obediently and allowed me to clean her off, though she looked as if she would be happier splashing and playing.

When my watch beeped signaling the ten minutes was up, I turned off the water and covered her up in a towel. I gave her a good rub down while she wiggled around, her tail drumming against my arm. Her fur was still messy with knots, but nearly all of the mud and other garbage was out of it. Upon closer inspection, her coat seemed to dazzle with different shades of silver and gray despite all of the mats. It was beautiful. She was beautiful.

"Time to find you some breakfast!" I grabbed the towels and gave myself a final wipe down before tossing them in the hamper. Amber tried to catch them but missed. Confused when the lid snapped shut and they disappeared, she bounded after me into the kitchen. She seemed to like staying pinned to my leg.

I rummaged through the cabinets, frowning at the boxes of instant this and powdered that. I was pretty sure dogs were supposed to eat meat, which I usually could only afford to eat a few times a week. A light bulb went off in my brain as I remembered the almost expired sausages I'd snagged for half price at the store. I opened the freezer and took them out, holding them down so Amber could see them.

"You want these?"

Amber looked at me expectantly. She whipped her tail against the cabinets, her pink tongue lolling out of the side of her mouth. She didn't take her eyes off of me as I took out a plate and put the sausages into the microwave.

I took a bowl out and poured two packets of instant oatmeal into it, waiting for the sausage to be cooked so I could heat up water. The microwave beeped and I put the plate down on the floor. Amber dove for the sausages, gobbling them up in seconds. She had licked the plate clean before I even finished pouring the hot water into my oats.

Her big brown eyes begged for more. My heart sank. I didn't have any decent food in the house, and buying extra food for her was going to clean out my account.

"I hope I can take care of you," I sighed, putting a spoonful of oatmeal into my mouth. I emptied another packet into a bowl and prepared hot water in the microwave, setting this one down for Amber. She seemed to enjoy it, and finished it almost as quickly as the sausages. Her muzzle was covered in sticky oats, making me chuckle despite my worries.

"I'll work something out," I promised her, scratching the top of her head. "But right now I have to get ready for work." I gobbled down the rest of my breakfast and put the bowls and plate in the dishwasher, hurrying to brush my teeth and get dressed.

Amber took the pant leg of my olive green uniform in her teeth as I tried to put it on, moving her head side to side. A playful growl rose in her throat and her tail continued to wag.

"No Amber!" I said sternly, pulling the clothes from her grip. "I need to wear these, they're not a toy."

She sat down next to me, letting out a disappointed whine. Her head moved back and forth, following my every move as I darted around the room to put on my socks and boots.

"I have to go to work now," I told her as she followed me to the front door. She let out another whine as I grabbed my coat, as if she knew this meant I was leaving her alone for hours. "I'll be back later. And maybe I can buy you some dog food."

She let out a louder whine and hunched over, her tail tucked between her legs. She circled the furniture in my living room, stopping at the door that led outside to my fire escape. Tilting her head, she fixed her big brown eyes on my face.

"What?"

Her head turned to the door, her paws pressed against the glass. The whine emitting from her throat was tearing at my soul.

"Do you have to go outside?" Something clicked in my brain, and the words seemed to trigger a sense of excitement in Amber. She leapt to her feet and turned in circles, her tail swaying from side to side.

I walked over to the door, unlocking it. "Now don't run away." Her eyes continued to stare at me.

As soon as I slid the door open, she darted out onto the red metal. She instantly squatted and proceeded to go to the bathroom for about a minute. Once she finished, she trotted back inside.

Relieved, I pulled the door shut and flicked the lock back into place. "All right. Good dog. Now I'm going to be late for work." I walked back to the door at the front of my apartment and gave her a smile.

35

I opened the door and she bolted into the hall.

"Hey! Get back here!" I hissed.

Confused, Amber trotted back inside.

"You can't come!" I exclaimed. Though I doubted she could understand what I was saying, it was comforting to have someone to talk to. She seemed to listen to every word that came out of my mouth.

"Stay here," I told her, grabbing the doorknob and shutting the door slowly behind me. She tried to squeeze after me, but I held her back with my boot. "Stay!" She sat down inside and watched me go, a forlorn expression filling her eyes.

*   *   *

I hopped from the bus, stepping onto the sidewalk in front of the public works building. People hurried off behind me, one nearly running me over as he pushed in front of me.

"Hey!" I exclaimed, shooting a glare at the back of his head. But I got more attention from Amber than any of my fellow workers. That was how it was supposed to be. That was how The City wanted it. Everyone who lived here had accepted it. No questions asked.

I slowly followed the rest of the workers into the building, my feet feeling heavy. The lack of sleep last night was catching up to me. My whole body felt as if it was made of bricks. A sharp pang in my neck reminded me never to sleep on the chair again. The boots on my feet were encrusted with multiple layers of mud. They were always disgusting and dirty, but usually I made an attempt to clean them before I went to work again in the morning. Supervisors sometimes checked to make sure everyone's uniforms were in order, and it would be hard to tell that these boots were the proper pair under all of the grime.

The dim lighting inside the building was a welcome change from the blinding morning sunlight. My eyes were too tired to confront anything so bright. Fellow workers were lined up at the counter, waiting for their work assignments. The room was quiet except for the whirring of an electric fan in the corner and the people at the counter giving workers their daily routes.

I stepped at the end of one line, trying to look straight ahead like everyone else. Something inside of me stirred. Curiosity. For some strange reason I was interested in the other people around me. I noticed the colors of their hair, their posture, and the tired blank looks in their different colored eyes. I wanted to reach out and speak to someone.

I forced my head to look forward once more. If I tried to talk to someone, people would think I was crazy. Besides, I had nothing to discuss with anyone. What would I try to talk about? The weather? The only time workers talked to each other was for work purposes. Period. That was the law, and everyone was okay with that. Why was I trying to change things?

A sign on the wall caught my eye and I took a step back. The sign read "One foot apart." It had always been there, and I had seen it before. Something in me was just off this morning. I had been way too close to the person in front of me.

Trying to appear normal, I stared straight ahead. My brain was racing, and I needed something to focus on. The man in front of me caught my attention. He stood still, slightly hunched over. He held a coffee cup in his hand but didn't drink from it. Light brown hair dusted with streaks of even lighter shades covered his head, falling over his tanned ears. All of his skin matched his ears, glowing in the dim light. The sleeves on his uniform were rolled up so you could see the muscles bulging from his arms.

Even without seeing his face, I thought the man was beautiful. I longed to step closer and break the one foot barrier, but my boots stayed rooted to the spot I was in. I could imagine myself reaching out to take a lock of soft hair in my hand. His hair reminded me of Amber's with the different shades. There were so many colors I had never noticed before. It was breathtaking.

He stepped forward, startling me out of my thoughts. I moved behind him, shaking my head in attempt to rid my mind of these foreign, trespassing contemplations. I glanced around nervously, wondering if anyone had noticed me acting so strangely. Everything remained unchanged in the small dark room. No one was paying any attention to me. They couldn't read my mind. They wouldn't care enough to if they could. I was invisible. I was nothing.

"Next!" The man in front of me stepped up to the counter to receive his papers, nodding as the old woman at the counter reviewed the day for him. They flipped through the paper quickly, and the man with the brown hair took the folder and left.

I stood next to the counter, trying to focus on the assignment that the woman was reading off for me. Her voice was soft and high-pitched, pleasant to listen to. My ears seemed to smile the more that they listened. I wasn't hearing the words any more, just the lovely diverse tones as she read different words and pronounced syllables. Her voice got louder, breaking the pleasant melody that had been drifting over my ears and lightening my body.

"I said you got it?" she demanded, holding out the folder for me to take.

What? We'd finished already.

"Yes," I stammered, grabbing the assignment and hurrying out of the building. A blast of cold air from outside cooled my flushed, red cheeks. I couldn't believe that I had zoned out for so long. The woman's voice was just so mesmerizing.

"Vic!"

I jumped at the sound of my name, a panic rushing over my body. My supervisor strode towards me, someone following closely behind him. I hoped he hadn't noticed my strange behavior. What if he knew that I was having feelings and took me into custody? What if we went somewhere to perform crazy experiments? What would happen to Amber?

I set my mouth in a straight line and tried to rid my eyes of the fear that was surging through my veins. The expression on his face was not angry, not happy. He held nothing behind his eyes.

"The man you were supposed to route with will not be coming today," he told me. We only worked with the same person a few times a month. Perhaps this was to ensure that we did not develop any sort of relationships. I startled myself with this thought. In the past, I never would have made this connection. It made me uneasy.

I snapped back to the conversation as I realized that my supervisor was still talking.

"Just arrived from training," he was saying. "But I'm sure she'll do fine and you two will finish your route with speed and precision. Get to work." He turned around and was gone as quickly as he appeared.

For the first time, I noticed the person who had

been standing behind him. The words "I'm sure she'll do fine" echoed in my brain. She? I'd never had a route with a girl before!

The girl was tall, almost as tall as me. She had shiny, long black hair pulled back into a ponytail that cascaded down her back. Her skin was a deep chocolate color, looking smooth beneath her gray uniform. Even with the loose hanging clothes I noticed the shape of her body. Her chest jutted out past her toned arms, capturing my attention. Her voice drew me out of my thoughts, but not before my heart stopped as I made the startling connection. It was the woman from the convenience store.

"Kim," she spoke, her voice loud. Her dark brown eyes seemed to sparkle, making me now grateful for the sunlight.

"Vic," I replied, wondering if she remembered me.

"Shall we go to our transportation vehicle?" she inquired, holding a stack of papers tightly between her hands. She moved her fingers slightly, crinkling the pages.

"Yeah." I nodded and motioned for her to follow me. "They're over here."

She fell into step next to me. I tried my best to remain quiet; the only sound I produced was the crunching of my boots against the gravel. Inside, I was dying to strike up a conversation about who she was, where she was from, and how she got placed on garbage patrol as a female.

We reached the truck and I stopped. "This is it. Do you know how to drive one of these?"

Kim shrugged. "Kind of. I mean, they taught us in training but I've never actually driven a real one. This is my first day on the job."

I eyed her uncomfortably. That was a lot more

information than I was used to receiving in response to a question.

"Well okay. How about you drive then so you can practice?" I suggested, tossing her the keys.

She caught them with both hands, clutching them tightly for a few seconds before loosening her grip. Her fingers were long and I could see the skin on the bottom was rough and callused.

I climbed up into the passenger side. Driving was not something I did well or often, so I was relieved that she had agreed to do it. Most of the time whoever I was working with was willing to drive. I liked to sit in the passenger seat and relax in between stops instead of constantly having to focus on the road. It was more comfortable when someone else was in control.

We pulled out of the lot and turned onto the road. I kept shooting her sideways glances out of the corner of my eye. I had never worked with a girl on garbage patrol before. Why had she been assigned this job? It was never an honor or a good thing to be on garbage patrol. Could she have done something horrible that landed her here? Even so, why would they send her here if she was a girl? They'd never done so before. Perhaps some sort of change was taking place in The City.

I glanced at her arms beneath her uniform. They looked pretty big, which meant that she was probably strong. It would be useless to give her this job if she couldn't handle the weight of the garbage. I hadn't been around many girls since school. Sure there was the old woman who gave us our morning assignments and the cashiers at the supermarket, but I'd never spent more than a few minutes with any of them.

She kept her eyes on the road, her jaw set as she

concentrated. If she noticed me staring at her, she didn't show it.

"It's going to be your next left," I told her. "We're not doing a residential area, so it's more big stops. That will be easier for your first day." I spoke carefully, trying hard to contain myself. If I said too much, she could become suspicious of me. My desire to communicate more with her was overshadowed by the need to keep Amber safe.

"Here?" she asked.

"Yep," I replied.

She turned onto the side road and pulled to a stop behind a large brick building. I recognized the back of it as East Street Gym. This was the gym that I went to when I was scheduled for weight lifting. It wasn't as clean and fancy as the gyms for people with higher status and careers, but it still had some treadmills and weight machines that would get the job done.

I swatted a fly out of my face and got to work loading the truck up with bags. My cut up palms burned as the plastic rubbed against them. I tried to take my attention off the fiery pain by looking at Kim. To my surprise, she could lift most of the heavy bags. She did have a tight expression pasted on her face, indicating she was having trouble with them. I finished my half of the dumpster and reached over to help her, shocked that for once my role was reversed. No matter who I was paired with for the day, it always seemed that they were faster and stronger than me.

Kim looked up at me as I grabbed the last bag, her eyes piercing my skin. Taking a closer look, I noticed that they weren't just brown. They were an array of beautiful hues of brown that dazzled in the sunlight. The lines jutting out from her pupils were a light color of coffee, accenting the deeper, darker chocolate behind them. They mesmerized me, and I couldn't take my gaze away.

"What?" she demanded, her voice icy and accusing.

"Um . . . nothing." I could feel my face flush and the sweat gather on my forehead. Crap. Why had I stared at her for so long? She must think I was crazy. It was just her eyes . . . they were incredible.

I desperately racked my brain for an excuse, but came up dry. "It's just . . . you'll need to work harder if we want to be done on time. I'm not the best at this job, either, so I don't know if I'll be able to pick up your slack." The words were cold and harsh, and I immediately wished I could take them back. I couldn't think of anything else to say that wouldn't be ridden with emotion.

She nodded. "Okay. You're right. I'm sorry, I'll try harder." She wiped her hands on the back of her uniform, momentarily tightening them around her butt. I felt the desire to stare once more, but I forced myself to walk back to the truck. I tried to focus on the crackling gravel beneath my feet, unable to shake the image of her from my mind.

Footsteps clicked behind me for a few seconds, then faded away as Kim strode along the other side of the truck. I could tell my face was red. I stopped outside the passenger door for a minute to try and calm down. A rush of wind cooled off my face, and I breathed in the air slowly. I had to hide these feelings or else I was going to get in serious trouble.

Kim drove quickly to the next stop, and we completed our work without words. I could tell she was working as hard as she could, but she still was lagging behind. At the rate we were going, we would be working long past five. I longed to say something

43

more to her, but wasn't sure how to phrase my words without increasing her suspicion surrounding me. Instead I directed my concentration to the work at hand and tried to finish as fast as possible.

We went quickly from stop to stop and ate our lunch in the truck in attempt to catch up on lost time. I was again grateful she was driving so that I could slip the LVs into my pocket without her noticing. When we reached the end of the route, my arms were aching and I was exhausted. In addition to the lack of sleep from the night before, I had worked harder than I ever had all day. My whole body stung from soreness and my eyes were burning from being open for so many hours. The scorching pain in my raw hands made me want to scream.

Kim seemed to be in pain as well. Her tight expression changed when she lifted the bags, displaying a flash of discomfort before reverting back to her standard appearance. Despite her efforts, it still wasn't enough.

Dusk was upon us as we reached the last stop. My stomach rumbled and I checked my watch. It was already six. The image of Amber alone in my apartment flashed through my mind. She must be tired, hungry, and lonely. She also probably had to go to the bathroom again, unless she couldn't hold it and already went in my apartment. I still had to pick up dog food for her on my way home.

"Let's go as fast as we can," I told her as we hurried to the piles of garbage. I wanted to add the words *I know it hurts but we're so close,* but knew that the phrase was a product of my newfound feelings and emotions.

She nodded at me, but I could see the fatigue in her face and the sluggish way she climbed up into the dumpster.

We pushed ourselves and finished within ten minutes, dragging our tired legs back to the truck. I squirted hand sanitizer from the dashboard onto my hands and rubbed them together, shoving them in my face. I hoped the aroma of vanilla would wake me up, but it merely increased the burning sensation in my cuts.

"Where are the lights?" she asked me.

"That button," I replied, motioning to a circular button on the right side of the steering wheel.

I bit my lip and tried not to concentrate on her. Instead, I struggled to decide where I would buy Amber's food. There were a few stores I knew of that carried it, but none were in my neighborhood. They were all in more upscale areas where people actually had dogs. I'd have to take the bus about fifteen minutes there and then take it back home. I shifted my gaze over at the speedometer. Kim was already speeding slightly, and I sighed quietly to try and remain patient. I would get home when I got home and there was nothing I could do about it.

Kim pulled the truck into the public works parking lot and killed the engine. I sighed with relief and clambered down onto the pavement. Instead of bustling with workers arriving home from their routes like usual, the parking lot was deserted. The sky was dark, and since no one was around, so was the parking lot. A lone light shined above the door of the building. I'd never been here this late before.

"What do we do now?" Kim asked.

I shrugged. "Well we have to drop off the keys and clock out. But I don't know if anyone is around. Hopefully the building's unlocked." I spoke slowly and carefully, trying to keep my voice in a steady even tone.

Kim nodded and started towards the building, walking quickly. I fell into step behind her, looking around as we went. The lot was eerie in the dark. A sea of inky blackness stretched before me; the two flickering streetlights were useless. The wind rattled pieces of scrap and blew them across the cement. I felt as if I would be swallowed up into the darkness. Looking at the sky, I noticed it was a cloudy night. There were only a few visible stars and half of the crescent moon peeking out from behind a large cloud. A shiver ran through my body, not from the cold but from an uncomfortable feeling washing over me.

"Oof!" I let out a cry as I crashed into Kim. She had stopped in front of the door, and was staring blankly at it.

"Do we just go in? There's no lights on inside," she commented, standing on her tip-toes to peer through the window on top of the door.

"I've never been here this late," I admitted. "It might be locked."

Kim wrapped her fingers around the doorknob, surprising me when it turned and the door opened. She let go and looked back at me for guidance, not taking another step into the inky blackness of the building.

"The lights might be on the timer to shut off," I told her. I took a few steps forward, cautiously entering the building. No lights flickered on, even if the sensors in the floor had recognized my body weight. The room was dark, but I'd been in this building long enough to know where everything was. Even in the blackness I could put the keys back, but I wondered if we could still sign out.

"Give me the keys," I said, turning around to face

Kim. Still standing in the doorway, she carefully took a few steps inside. She squinted, trying to adjust to the deeper darkness. She dropped the keys in my hand, her fingertips brushing my palm.

A shock shot through my hand and up my wrist, heat reverberating throughout my arm. The subtle touch awakened something inside me. Never in my life had I ever had any skin-on-skin contact with another human being. It was a different feeling than touching Amber. It had been too quick for me to really feel her rough fingers against my flesh, and I felt my body yearning for more. Despite the cold, her hand had been warm and inviting. All I wanted to do was reach out and hold onto it so I could experience more of these wonderful feelings inside.

Embarrassed by her mistake, I heard her retreat a few inches in the darkness. She coughed and began to fumble around. "Where is the computer to sign out with?"

My mouth felt dry. I swallowed, trying to stir up saliva so I could answer. I turned to distance myself from her in attempt to slow my racing heart. "I'll find it after I put the keys back."

I ran my hands against the wall, slowly feeling my way towards the key hooks. Leaning against the wall for a moment, I tried in vain to allow its coolness to transfer to my body. My fingers glided over the hooks until they closed on an empty one. I slid the keys over the metal and took a deep breath.

Kim was still shuffling around, not waiting for me to look for the computer.

"It should be over this way, I think," I called out, slowly making my way across the room to the opposite side. "On top of the last counter." My eyes had adjusted slightly to the dark, and I could make

47

out inky silhouettes. I sidestepped to avoid walking into one of the poles that separated the different lines in the morning. Reaching the counter, I groped the square black shape. I was pretty sure this was the computer, but I had no idea how to start it.

Suddenly, I felt a warm breath beside me.

"Ah!" I yelped and jumped a few inches in the air. How did she get over here so fast?

"How do you turn it on?" she asked me.

"Uhh . . . there's a button somewhere," I lied, still feeling around the screen.

She flipped a light on next to me, causing me to nearly cry out. The flame flickering above her fingers was from a lighter. Lighters were used for candles, but no one ever carried them around in public. Back in the olden days, people had used them to light cigarettes. Cigarettes were banned before I was alive, so now there was no point in possessing a lighter outside of ones' home. It wasn't against the law, but it was strange.

Though I was dying to ask her why she had the lighter, I bit my tongue. She moved the light closer to the computer, sending a wavering glow over the screen. There were no visible buttons anywhere. I pressed on the screen to see if that would wake it up, but it remained dark.

Frustrated, I turned away. I wanted to let out my aggravation with a wail, but tried to remain calm to keep Kim's suspicion of me at bay. The image of Amber alone at my apartment remained strong in my mind. All I wanted to do was get home so I could see her.

"This is useless," Kim grumbled. "Can we just forget about it and say it was an error with the computer?"

I shook my head. "I don't know." I gritted my teeth. "This has never happened to me before."

"Well it looks like there's nothing we can do," she reasoned, heading for the door. "I'm going to go home and deal with this in the morning."

Begrudgingly, I followed her to the door. Though I wanted to get home just as much as she did, I was nervous about the consequences. I wasn't sure if not clocking out was unacceptable. Even if it wasn't, we could be thoroughly questioned about what had happened. Would my supervisor believe me if I tried to lie and say that I had clocked out? Did these computers make errors?

As I stepped outside, I could see Kim making her way around the back of the building. Where was she going? All that was back there were the landfills and trash compacting equipment.

Curiosity getting the better of me, I decided to compromise a few minutes of my time to follow her. Keeping a safe distance, I darted through the darkness. She slipped through the doorway in the fence surrounding the landfill.

I carefully opened the gate, trying not to squeak it. A blast of cold wind muffled the sound of the metal, drying out my eyes. I blinked and spotted Kim near the edge of the huge hole in the ground. The pit contained piles of decomposable garbage.

What was she doing over there?

She moved closer to the hole until her toes were leaning over it. She appeared to be interested in something, bending down to get a closer look.

Suddenly, she lost her footing and her leg slid along the edge of the hole.

A scream echoed through the night air. I couldn't tell if it was mine or hers. She tried to grab hold of

49

something, but the only thing around her hands was dirt.

I stood frozen in horror as her body disappeared into the hole.

Chapter 4

I scrambled forward over the dirt, dashing to the spot where I had last seen Kim. I dropped to my knees and leaned carefully over the side of the hole. Kim was holding onto a rock sticking out of the dirt a few feet below. The stone was small; she was only able to fit one hand around it. Her feet dangled helplessly above the pool of blackness, too deep to see the bottom.

"Help me!" she begged, looking up at me. She struggled to adjust her fingers to get a better grip, but the rock was too blunt. Her normally empty eyes held a wild look, her face distorted. "Please help me!"

Panicking, I looked around frantically, searching for anything I could use to try and pull her out. The dirt was bare except for some rocks and short sticks. There was nothing I could throw down to her.

"Hang on!" I yelled. I dashed around the hole, scanning the ground desperately for something she could hold onto. If I couldn't find anything, she would lose her grip and fall. If only I had a rope.

Suddenly, an idea popped into my head. "Genius!" I whispered to myself. I began tearing off my pants. I dropped them in the dirt and pulled off my jacket as well. Grabbing a pant leg, I wound it securely around one of the sleeves of the jacket. I tied a knot as tight as I could, and then ripped off my shirt to add it to the makeshift rope. Securing the fabric as firmly as possible, I stepped on my pants. Pulling the shirt at the other end, I was pleased to see that it stayed together.

"I'm coming!" I cried. I raced to the edge.

"Hurry," she pleaded. "My fingers are slipping! I can't feel my arm."

I threw my clothes over the edge, positioning them so they were suspended a few inches above Kim's head. Making sure I had a good grip, I lowered them even further to brush the top of her hair.

"Okay! Now you're going to need to carefully reach your other hand up and grab onto the end of my clothes!" I called down.

A look of intense concentration spread across her face as she slowly raised a shaking arm up towards the clothes rope. I felt a small tug at the end as her fingers closed around my pant leg.

"Good!" I shouted. "Now you're gonna have to let go of the rock and grab on with your other hand!"

"I can't!" Her voice was shaking, and I could see her eyes glistening. A droplet of water emerged from one and slid down her cheek. "I'll fall! This won't hold me."

"Yes it will!" I replied. "You just have to hang on. Trust me I will pull you out and you'll be okay!" I wasn't fully sure that the clothes could hold her weight, but it was our only option. We had to try.

"I-I . . ." Kim stammered, her eyes shifting to the

rock. I could see her fingers sliding farther to the edge.

"On a count of three!" I said. "One . . . two—"

"Ah!" Kim screamed as her hand slid off of the rock. I felt a jolt as the shock of her weight pulled me forward. My heart pounded as I dug my feet into the dirt and secured my footing. I gritted my teeth and hung onto the clothes with all my might.

She grabbed onto my pants with her other hand and swung slightly from side to side, her arms extended far above her head. Her knuckles were tense and shaking, fingers threatening to slip at any moment.

Sweat trickling down my temple, I began to pull at my clothes with all of my strength. Slowly and cautiously I took a step backwards. My arms burned and screamed at me, but I tried to ignore the pain. Adrenaline surged through my entire body as I heaved the clothes towards me. My muscles strained and my body stalled for a minute. Fear swept over me, and I worried that I had failed. I couldn't pull anymore. Kim would plummet to her death.

The image of Kim falling sent another wave of power pumping through my veins. Harnessing every bit of energy and strength I had left, I yanked the clothes. I wrenched them again, and again, until I could see Kim's fingertips surface over the edge of the hole. The sight of her filled me with even more drive, and I hauled the rest of her body up and over onto the dirt.

I dropped the clothes and let out a triumphant cry. Breathing rushed to her side and grabbed hold of her hand.

She shook violently and gasped for air. Water streamed down her cheeks, erupting from her eyes and nose. She slowly raised her head to look at me.

"It's okay," I murmured when I finally caught my breath. I ran my fingers over the back of her hand and talked to her quietly. "You're safe. It's okay." An unbelievable feeling of warmth rushed over me as I stroked her skin. Her palm was sweating and shaking, but holding onto it gave me an incredible feeling.

She began to quiet down as she calmed herself. She used her other hand to wipe some of the water off of her face. Her lips parted and moved as if she wanted to talk, but no sound came out. Her eyes flicked over my face, the softness and gratitude behind them speaking louder than any words ever could.

Without warning, she pulled herself closer and wrapped her arms around me. Her body emanated heat as she pressed against my bare chest. Another implausible feeling rushed through me. Indescribable warmth and comfort paralyzed me. My knees felt weak, forcing me to drop to the dirt from my crouch. Though having her hold me was the most wonderful feeling I had ever experienced, a part of me felt like something was missing.

A fire seemed to rise in her eyes as she felt me press against her. She reached out to touch my cheek with one hand, dropping her hand in shock as something moved below my waist. Surprised, she let go of me and slid backwards. I looked down in shock as well, then looked back at her. What was that feeling?

I studied her face, but she was looking down at the dirt. "Here." Her voice was barely audible as she passed me my clothes.

I could feel my body sweating despite the chilling wind. I still felt hot and longed for her warmth back against me. Every part of my body seemed to be in overdrive; I had no idea what was going on. All I wanted was to hold her against me. I never wanted the feeling to go away.

The clothes felt rough and unappealing in my hand. Something about not wearing them felt wonderful. I felt freer, and I didn't want to lose hold of the amazing sensation that lingered throughout my body. Even though Kim was no longer touching me, it was like part of her had never left.

Although the insanity and confusion still raced through me, I tried to calm down. I wanted to hold Kim longer, but she obviously didn't. She had given me my clothes; she wanted me to put them back on. Did she not feel the same wonderful feelings that I had when we touched? Did she not feel the happiness and warmth in every part of her body? What had happened seconds ago?

I longed to reach out and touch her again, to ask her for some answers, but she seemed distant. She fidgeted in the dirt, refusing to look at me. Her fingers traced shapes in the earth beside her legs.

Watching her, I was mystified. Her long hair cascaded over her shoulder as she drew, shining in spite of the darkness. The uniform stuck to her, outlining the delicate curves of her body. Her lips looked pink and soft as she inhaled and exhaled. Her beauty was so mesmerizing; my eyes were glued to her.

She slowly raised her head, startling me out of my trance. I looked away and fingered the uniform she had given to me. She wanted me to put them on. Something inside me fell, but I stood up so I could slide back into my clothes. I untied the three articles, reluctantly slipping back into my pants. The rough material suffocated my skin, swallowing me up from the night air.

I fingered my shirt and jacket. Why were we forced

55

to wear these uncomfortable things? It was just another way for The City to make us miserable. They had to know how good one could feel without them.

Kim was still looking at me, waiting.

I sighed and pulled my shirt over my head.

"Thank you." Her voice was soft and gentle, carried to my ears by a sweeping gust of wind.

I nodded. Speechless, I pulled on my jacket and hugged it close to my body. So many feelings and thoughts were racing through me I didn't know what to do. All I could concentrate on was her tantalizing body. I wanted to make her feel the ecstasy that I had, but she had closed herself up. Trying to push the thoughts of her beauty out of my head, I struggled to find an answer.

She spoke before I could muster words. "I knew there was something different about you."

"Huh?" I uttered.

Her eyes locked onto mine. Suddenly feeling shy, I looked away and ran my fingers through my hair.

"From the moment I saw you. I felt it."

Felt. The word sent a shock throughout my body. She had said felt! She had feelings too! My head snapped back to look at her. "What?"

"I sensed it," she continued. "The way you held yourself. The way you walked. The way you talked to me. A curiosity in your eyes. I suspected it since I first saw you in the store."

"But you . . . you feel things too?" I murmured with disbelief.

She nodded at me. "Don't even think of turning me in."

I couldn't stop myself from laughing. "Me? What? Why would I turn you in? I'm just as guilty as you are."

"How long?" she demanded.

"How long what?"

"How long have you been experiencing emotions?" she prodded, her voice serious and flat.

"Two days now," I answered. "I think."

"Why?" she asked, a hint of suspicion in her voice.

"I . . . I don't know," I replied, shrugging my shoulders. "I wish I did know."

"No one else knows, right?" she inquired.

"Of course not," I hissed. "Who would I tell?"

"Good." Seeming satisfied, she rose out of her seated position so she could speak to me face to face.

"What about you?"

"What about me?" She brushed a lock of long hair that had slipped out of her ponytail from her face. A whip of wind blew it right back across her lips.

"How long have you been feeling things?" I asked.

"A few months," she said.

"What?" I murmured in disbelief. "How have you kept it hidden for so long? I've had a hard enough time the past few days!"

She looked down at her hands and fidgeted slightly. "I' have no choice."

"What do you mean?" I pressed.

"I couldn't risk losing this," she said. "These feelings are so precious and so wonderful . . . if The City found out they'd all be gone in the blink of an eye."

"They are incredible," I agreed. "So incredible I wonder why they're forbidden."

She remained silent, biting her lip and looking up towards the sky.

"Do you know why?"

The question seemed to surprise her, though I'd been dancing around it just moments before. Her

57

eyes widened and she stared at me. "You really want to know why?"

"Yes!" I nodded. "I want to know! I want to keep feeling forever."

"Not all feelings are good," she warned me.

"I know," I replied. "But the good ones are so amazing . . . won't they make the bad seem insignificant?"

"At times, yes. At times, no."

"I think it's worth it," I decided.

She allowed a small smile to spread over her lips. "I like your drive."

"You're avoiding my question."

Again, she seemed surprised. "You're right," she chuckled.

"Do you know why?" I repeated, looking her straight in the eye. "Why are there laws against feeling emotions?"

"I don't have all the answers," she admitted.

I waited for her to tell me, to open up further, but she was quiet. She turned away and began walking towards the gate.

"Hey! Wait!" I cried, dashing after her. "You're not going to tell me what you know?"

She shook her head. "Not here. Not now. Things are more complicated than you know."

I narrowed my eyes, offended. "You don't think I will understand?"

Kim turned, opening the gate so it stood between our faces. Pressing against the chain link, she shook her head. "It's not that I don't think you'll understand. I'm just not sure I can trust you."

"That's crazy!" I spat. "Why wouldn't you be able to trust me? Besides, I have emotions too. I'd only be hurting myself by revealing what you tell me."

58

"Maybe." She pulled her face off the chain link and paused. It cast shadows across her face before she continued through the gate. "But I can't take that chance."

"What?" I followed and hurried to walk beside her. "But you let me know you had emotions."

"Yes. But I'm just one person," she started. "If The City finds out about me, I'll probably be killed. But at least it's not endangering anyone else."

"Wait . . . are you saying there's more?"

"I'm not saying anything."

Frustrated, I tried to change the subject to pry more information from her. "What were you doing by that hole anyway?"

"I had to test you," she answered.

"What?" I shrieked. "You did that on purpose!?"

She nodded. "Yes."

"Why?"

"It was a rash, stupid decision," she admitted. "But I wanted to find out if my theory was right. If you really were different."

"So you decided to risk your life *and* almost give me a heart attack?" This night was getting crazier by the minute.

"Well I couldn't ask you about it without revealing myself first."

"So?" I asked, my voice squeaking in disbelief.

"I told you it was stupid," she growled, turning her head to glare at me. "But it seemed like a better idea at the time. If you didn't come get me, then my secret would still be safe."

"Safe? You'd be dead!"

"I didn't know that I wouldn't be able to get back out of the hole on my own. It was meant to be an act . . . but there was nothing to hold onto."

I shook my head, speechless. This girl was truly unbelievable, in more ways than one.

"You're crazy," I blurted, covering my mouth.

I expected her to get angry, but she just laughed. "Maybe. But it worked."

"What do you mean it worked?"

"You saved me, and I was able to test my theory," she said nonchalantly. Her ponytail swung back and forth as she strode across the pavement. My legs worked quickly to keep up with her pace.

"Okay," I said. "So your theory proved right . . . now what?"

She stopped walking so suddenly that I passed her and had to backtrack a few feet. I stood in front of her, waiting for her answer.

"Well . . ." she said slowly, resting her hand on her hip. "You really want to know more about this?"

"Yes!" I replied, exasperated.

"How do I know I can trust you?" she demanded.

"I have a dog!" I said.

"Huh?"

"I found an abandoned dog, and I took her home," I explained. "She's amazing. It might sound dumb, but I think she really likes me."

She smiled at me, her face softening. "It's not stupid. You're probably right."

"Well, either way, I wouldn't do anything to risk her safety," I stated. "She is my number one priority. And I need help keeping her a secret."

Kim laughed, making me narrow my eyes again. "Stop laughing at me!"

"I'm not laughing at you," she replied. "All right . . . maybe a little. But it's a good laughter. I'm not trying to offend you."

"Oh."

Her face reverted back to seriousness. "Fine." She pulled a scrap of paper and pen from her jacket pocket. She quickly scribbled across the paper and held it out to me. I grabbed it, not touching her fingers.

"Memorize this," she ordered. "And destroy it."

I nodded. I recognized the address on the paper. It was an old furniture warehouse not too far from my apartment.

"Friday night. 8 o'clock don't be late."

I wanted to ask more, but I doubted she would answer. She had already started walking again. She reached the end of the lot and turned onto the sidewalk.

"Kim!" I called.

She turned her head to look at me. Her hair blew in the wind, taking my breath away. I couldn't take my eyes of her body.

"Will I see you again?" I asked.

She smiled. "It's a possibility."

I found myself smiling back as I walked towards her. "Can I ask you one more question?"

Kim nodded. "I don't know if I'll answer it."

"Why now?" I asked.

"What?"

"Why these feelings all of a sudden?"

"Have you done anything different lately?" she inquired. "Anything out of the ordinary?"

"Well I picked up Amber."

"The dog? Before that."

"Not really," I answered. "Except I didn't take my LVs the past few days."

She winked at me and vanished around the corner.

"Wait!" I dashed after her, rushing to the sidewalk. I looked in the direction she had gone, but all that

61

remained was a blast of wind.

Chapter 5

"Bye Amber. Have a nice day!" I scratched the top of Amber's soft head as I headed for the front door.

She woofed and wagged her tail, following at my heels.

"No you can't come," I laughed. "Go eat your food." I gestured at the bowl of dog food she had been eating before she noticed I was trying to sneak out. I had managed to pick some up on my way home from work the previous night. When I had returned home there was a nice yellow puddle in my kitchen. I couldn't be mad at her though, since I didn't know anything about dogs or how often they had to relieve themselves. Buying the food made me more nervous, since all purchases were an open book to The City. I kept reassuring myself that they would never take a second look at my activity and the food was definitely worth buying. She seemed to enjoy it much more than oatmeal, but my plan of distracting her with it so that I could slip out the door had failed.

She whined and licked my hand, plopping down between myself and the door. Her eyes gazed intently at me as I grabbed my coat from the hook. The material was still gritty with mud and a long slit ran down the back where the fence had ripped it. I used my knee to try and move her. She begrudgingly stepped to the side and sat down, sadly watching my every move.

"I'll be home in a few hours. I promise." I opened the door and closed it quickly. I wasn't sure if she would attempt to run away, but didn't want to find out.

I hurried down the stairs and hopped on the bus, getting off at the hospital rather than the public works building. Today was the first Wednesday of the month, which meant it was time to donate sperm. Every male citizen between the ages of nineteen and thirty eight was required to give his sperm once a month. The day for each individual to donate always remained the same, and I didn't mind too much because it meant that I didn't have to go to work. I was especially grateful because I didn't have to face my supervisor about the night before.

The air was warmer today, the sun peeking out from behind the clouds. I stopped on the sidewalk to take in the nice weather for a moment. The bit of sunlight was rare; the air was normally clouded and full of smog.

People impatiently darted past me, hurrying through the revolving doors. The hospital loomed overhead, a tall gray building with over twenty-five stories and enormous glass windows. The doors constantly twirled with people rushing in and out. I checked my watch and pushed my way through the revolving glass.

64

Once inside, I was greeted with an even bigger crowd. The sound of shoes on the tile floor and people bustling about filled my ears. The room was stuffed with people, yet no words were exchanged between anyone. I made my way over to the row of computers along the right wall of the lobby, pressing my finger against the screen so it could identify me.

"Vic Mill. Appointment at 9:30, 18th floor, room 297 A." The monotone, automated voice of the computer read the information aloud as it appeared across the screen. I pressed "okay" and headed for the elevator, trying to squeeze my way through the mass of people.

I struggled to avoid eye contact with anyone, focusing on the ground as much as I could without barreling into them. There were so many different sights and smells, I feared becoming overwhelmed. Even brushing past people sent little electric shocks through my body. I had to remind myself this was just a mass of citizens. If I began to notice each person and really look at them, I didn't think I could take it.

Relieved that I had reached the elevator, I stepped quickly inside. I tried to stare at the tower of gleaming buttons before my face. It was crowded but everyone remained a foot apart, not touching one another. Empty stares were aimed straight ahead, echoing hollow souls. I closed my eyes and took a deep breath. I couldn't feel things. Not here.

The doors slid closed and I opened my eyes once more, watching intently as the numbers lit up. We stopped at nearly every floor to drop someone off or pick up someone new. A flash of red hair exited the elevator on floor three. A mass of dark skin entered in its place. A short body squeezed to my left. A briefcase dug into the back of my knees.

The ride to the eighteenth floor seemed to last for days, though it couldn't have been more than two minutes. As the bell dinged and the automated voice from the ceiling blared, "Floor Eighteen," I eagerly pressed myself against the doors. They slid open and I stumbled outside, taking a breath of fresh air as if I had been suffocating.

I straightened my posture and looked around, relieved that this floor was less crowded. A few people entered or exited the doors lining the hallway, but I carefully avoided studying them too closely. My eyes scanned the wall for room 297 A. Since I'd just recently turned nineteen, this was only my third time donating. The past two times I had come I had been in two different rooms, though they were both on the eighteenth floor.

I stopped in front of my assigned room and placed my hand atop the scanner. It beeped in recognition and the door slid to the side, allowing me to enter. The lights flickered on as I stepped inside, revealing a small square room. The walls were silver and bare, matching the silver tile floor. A bench was splayed across the back wall beside a computer mounted on a small counter. A few vials lay alongside the sink atop the white granite surface.

The computer screen whirred to life, showing a picture of a beautiful city on a sunny day. The buildings appeared to be from the nicer, wealthy section of the city, but they had still been cleaned up and overdone. Trees and singing birds had been inserted to make the picture seem more alive. The same voice that had been on the computer in the lobby began its lecture. It reeled off the same story it had the other two times I came to donate.

"Welcome! You're here today to donate your

sperm. What a wonderful thing. Because of you, we are able to produce healthy offspring. These healthy offspring will eventually grow into adult human beings like you. They will take on jobs and roles in our society and carry The City towards further advancement."

I yawned and waited for instructions.

"Please remove your pants and underwear and sit on the bench. Then we can perform the quick, painless, and harmless procedure. Please remain still until I say that we are finished."

I squeezed out of my pants and sat down on the bench. If I remembered correctly, the procedure was fast and pain free. It was just a small pinching feeling and then it was over.

The cabinet door beneath the counter swung open and a little silver, square robotic box slid out. Its wheels whirred as it moved towards me. A little green light on its side lit up as its wheels extended, pushing it upwards so it was level with the bench. A slit in the front opened, revealing a robotic arm. The end of the arm held a long, sharp needle that was used to extract the sperm.

Even though the process hadn't hurt in the past, the sight of the needle made me cringe. I frowned and watched warily as the arm extended farther towards me, the needle pointed at me. I closed my eyes and felt a sharp pang as I felt the point injected between my legs. It didn't hurt, but it made me very uncomfortable. The past two times I hadn't had a problem, but for some reason this was different. I felt violated. I just wanted it to be over so I could get dressed and get out of here.

After what seemed like an eternity, I felt the needle pulling out of my skin. The computer's voice began to speak again, and I slowly opened my eyes. The robotic arm held a vial of my sperm before me, inserting it into a slit in the wall before slowly rolling back under the cabinet.

"You have done a great service to The City, and we want you to know that as a citizen you are important to us. Your sperm will be delivered to the lab and assigned to a carrier. It will eventually turn into a child that will be raised in a Safe House. There they will be educated so they can succeed later in life. At seventeen, they can live on their own and become a productive member of The City. I will print out a card with the date and time of next month's appointment. You are free to go."

Safe Houses were places where all children lived until they were seventeen years old. Then they took a test that would help decide where they would be assigned their career or if they were to be placed in further school. Housing or an apartment depended on the level of the job they received and was given upon employment or university acceptance. They start working, and in return receive credit that can be used towards food, extra clothes, and rent. Since I was assigned a lowly job after scoring badly on the test, I did not receive as much credit as those who scored higher. I often wondered what it would have been like to be able to continue to further schooling and be in a better class. I would be able to live in a nice house in a better neighborhood with superior food, furniture, and clothing. Perhaps I wouldn't have to work a job that was so physically draining.

I didn't have any memories from my Safe House. I knew that I had been raised in one, and I knew that there had been other people there. My memory began that day I received the test results, but it was very fuzzy. I only remembered bits and pieces here and there.

It was the day of my seventeenth birthday. I woke up to snow falling outside my window. The other beds in my room were empty, and I hurried downstairs. I was worried that I had overslept, and was eager to know the results of the test. This was, after all, what I had been studying for my whole life. Though I couldn't recall what had happened when I took it, somewhere inside me I remembered the fact that I had taken it. And I knew that the rest of my life depended on how I scored on my test.

The plush white carpet felt soft and warm on my bare feet as I climbed out of bed and hurried through the hallway. The walls were a soft pink color throughout the house. I entered the kitchen and a voice began talking to me. There was another person in the room. She was a woman. My eyes couldn't seem to focus on what she looked like, but I liked the sound of her voice. It was gentle and pleasant, and she spoke to me like she knew me. She acted like we had known each other for years, but I did not recognize her.

Breakfast was served to me by the woman with the lovely voice. She instructed me to sit at the long, wooden table. I did as I was told, swinging my feet below my chair in anticipation. The kitchen smelled wonderful, and the frying pan on the stove sizzled as she cooked. She placed a platter of food in front of me. It was a feast fit for a king, complete with pancakes, eggs, bacon, hash browns, butter, and syrup. She gave me a glass of cold orange juice on the side. The pancakes had a smile on it, with chocolate chips in place for the eyes and mouth. The food was delicious and the smile on the pancake caused me to grin. In that moment with the woman, her soft voice and the hot food filling my empty stomach, I was in pure bliss. I wanted to pause my life so everything would always be as incredible as it was in those few minutes.

But time cannot be stopped. I finished the food that was in front of me. The woman's tone of voice changed. She still spoke quietly, but something in her speech hardened. She told me it was time to see the results of my test. She handed me a big, soft jacket. I slipped into the warm, brown coat and zipped it up. I pulled the hood over my head, the inside lined with soft white material. She gave me white gloves, socks, and boots. Everything was so soft and dreamy. I felt the urge to stop and feel all the wonderful fabrics she was giving me, but the air was thick with urgency.

I exited through the back door, ready to take the short walk into town and see my destiny unveiled. As I was leaving, the woman called me. She told me to wait, and I listened. The snowflakes swirled around me as I stood on the doorstep, the heat from the open door warming my cheeks. She shoved a thermos into my hands, calling it cocoa. Her voice cracked as she bid me farewell, slamming the door. I found her behavior odd, but continued my mission.

It was slow going through the snow. I left big tracks with my bulky boots as I headed towards town. There must have been a foot of snow on the ground. It slowed my progress, but I sipped my sweet cocoa and daydreamed. When I discovered the results of the test, I would officially become an adult. I couldn't wait to go to a university. I imagined it would be warm and big, bigger than the house. I would learn so many new things and explore areas I had never been before. There would be big, comfy beds and warm, invigorating meals three times a day. The university would have to be beautiful, and in the winter they would have snow. There would also be warmer weather. Days when you could go outside without a jacket and bask in the warm sun as it beat down on your bare arms. There would be lots of trees and the lawns would be green and perfect. The birds we had only just learned about in school would be there. They would provide the students with music as they studied, helping everyone achieve their full potential.

The vision of the university was burning in my brain and driving me onwards. The cold snow suddenly felt warm, and I opened my mouth to let the refreshing flakes spiral down onto my tongue. I broke into a run, stumbling slightly through the fresh white snow. My breath grew labored, panting clouds into the damp air. The snow became shallower and within minutes my shoes were crunching plowed pavement. The buildings surrounding me were a blur. My eyes focused on the large white building at the end of the street: City Hall.

I reached the huge steps and scaled them in seconds.. My heart was pounding as I flew through the revolving doors, slowing once I entered the lobby. It was crowded and I didn't want to bump into the other people around me. I rushed to the computers in the back of the lobby, my fingers shaking as I pressed the screen. I placed my hand to be scanned, attempting to steady it so that it could be identified. I didn't hear the beep of recognition, but it must have happened because the screen lit up. My picture was displayed across the screen. I looked young and my gaze seemed dull. Ignoring the photo, I tapped the screen impatiently. Words scrolled in place of the picture, my eyes flying over them. I was only searching for a few select words. I found them and cried triumphantly. Eager, I pushed the button that read "Next plan of action." The computer made a whirring sign and froze for a minute, causing me to gasp and hold my breath. The screen completely changed, turning a deep olive color. I searched for the results of my test, but they were nowhere. Finally words began to appear across the screen. "Congratulations. You have been chosen for a job in the Public Works System. You will be on Waste Removal Duty. Stay tuned for further instructions."

A sharp pain struck my chest and I could feel something die inside of me. I wasn't going to university. I had done horrible on my test. I must have forgotten to breathe because my vision began to cloud. Black spots crept from the corners of my eyes, my head pounding. Dizziness overcame my body and I reached

out to steady myself. My hands could not find anything to grip.
I found myself falling. The world around me faded away into
nothing.

A shiver ran through my body. It took me a few seconds to remember where I was. I was in the hospital. I had just finished donating sperm. I had never experienced such vivid thoughts, especially from my past. Where had they come from?

The feelings of the haunting memory lingered with me as I left the room, a harsh reminder that I was a failure. I would never be more than what I was today. I would never have another chance to get into university, or obtain a job that I enjoyed. I was nineteen years old, and would be working for the Public Works Department until I was seventy. Things weren't going to change for me.

As I padded down the hallway and glanced around, my attitude began to change. When I saw the people walking by, I no longer saw empty shells. I saw people who were beautiful. I felt things toward them that I had never experienced before. The feelings may have been overwhelming, and they may have been a jumbled mess, but nonetheless they were feelings. I was *feeling*. For a reason beyond my comprehension, The City kept us from these emotions. They had ingrained in everyone's minds that feelings and emotions associated with other living creatures were bad, and we had believed them. We didn't question, we just did what we were told.

I had seen The City make arrests before, but had never given them a second thought. They were few and far between. The arrests were always quick and quiet, and the people under arrest did not concern me. But now I was questioning those arrests. What kind of crimes had those people committed? Had they been feeling emotions, like me? Had they accidentally touched another human being? If so, what was so wrong about it? It's not like feelings were hurting anyone. I had never felt more alive than I did when I was with Amber, or the night before when I had touched Kim. Never before had I appreciated all of the diversity around me. I had never noticed how different people looked, and that everyone had something special about them that intrigued me. Something that made me yearn for more.

I was so caught up in my thoughts that I didn't realize I had reached the end of the hallway. My feet stepped right into the door that led to the stairwell. I pulled it open and bounded down the steps. Alone on the stairs, I felt a rush of adrenaline. The City couldn't stop me from feeling if they didn't know that I was. If I could hide the emotions swirling through me, I would be safe. I could continue to feel joy when Amber licked my face. I could go to the meeting on Friday night, and maybe see Kim there.

Tantalizing as the idea of holding onto these feelings was, the need to keep them hidden was a daunting task. I could no longer look at someone without batting an eye. I noticed people's hair color, their eyes, their skin, the shape of their body, and the way they walked. I noticed how their eyes didn't pause to look at me, and felt a strong desire to make them see I existed. I wanted to talk to people. I wanted to know their stories. What they did and where they came from.

But all of this was impossible. I couldn't allow people to be even the least bit suspicious of me. If anyone was put off enough to report me, I didn't know what would happen. I had a few guesses of course, like losing these new feelings toward other people and animals. I would lose Amber. Worse things would probably happen. I had never heard about what happened after people were arrested. I remembered learning in school about things called prisons, but they had been eliminated decades ago. Prisons had sounded like horrible, scary places. That's probably why they had destroyed them.

There were no other laws except the ones against relationships. This seemed to prove The City's point that relationships caused most of the problems of the world. Without the complications associated with relationships, there were few issues. In the past, there had been murder and stealing. Now, no one had a second thought about another person. Certainly no one wanted to kill anyone else. Now, no one noticed what other people had. They focused on themselves. Perhaps there were lower class people who desired more in life, but because of the credit system it was impossible to take money from anyone else.

I had never given this much thought about The City before. There had been days when I was frustrated with my job, but I didn't show it. I had no one to share my dulled frustrations with, so I kept everything inside and went around with my daily life. Until a few days ago, I was certain there was no way to alter my circumstances.

But something changed inside me as I stopped on a landing of the stairwell. I threw my head back to stare up at the levels and levels of steps above me. The City may be able to choose my job, my home, and the amount of material things I could obtain, but there was now more to life than those things. The feelings inside me were better than any enormous house, or glitzy job, or extravagant feast. I had the ability to feel close to another living creature. Whether it be the love I felt for Amber, or the love I felt for Kim, it didn't matter. They were different but the same.

Love. I didn't know where the word had come from. I had learned about it in school. Fragments of memories were beginning to pass through my brain. I was taught that it was evil. It was a kind of emotion that existed a long time ago. It was felt towards friends, family members, and significant others. We had been told that it complicated one's entire life, and distracted them from their real purpose on this Earth; to serve The City. It would only create a mess of webs in one's life that would eventually cause everything to come crumbling down. It was an emotion that couldn't exist towards another human being or an animal because in the end it caused too much pain. Things that the other person did would hurt you inside, and vice versa. It would destroy one's happiness and one's life completely. Was this why relationships were forbidden?

I was confident that what I was feeling was a type of love. I was also certain that it didn't make me sick and wasn't horrible as The City claimed. Instead I felt free and alive, as if anything was possible. I was no longer alone. I had a furry, four-legged friend that I loved and it loved me back. There was something to look forward to when I came home after a long day, and something that looked forward to seeing me as well.

There was a girl who I felt a different feeling for. I wasn't as certain this was love, but I didn't know what else to call it. I couldn't think about her without wanting to smile and getting an airy, fluttery feeling deep inside my stomach. The thought of seeing her again made my heart beat faster and my palms sweat.

I could picture her shiny black hair cascading down her back and her soft pink lips as clear as fresh snowfall.

Pulling open the heavy metal door, I carefully wiped any indicator of my thoughts off my face and stepped into the lobby. It was as busy as it had been when I first arrived. Everyone was there for a purpose, but no one was here with another person. They didn't give anyone a second glance. The blank expressions and uninterested eyes made me sad. If only everyone knew they were missing out.

I headed for the door, mimicking those around me. Fighting the urge to look at everyone I passed, I stopped outside the door for a minute to let a flock of people from the street inside. The moment of hesitation caused me to falter. I looked out into the lobby, catching the eye of a man stepping away from a computer.

For a second, we held each other's gaze. He turned away and walked towards the elevator. My heart pounded in my chest as I stood frozen. Had that man been staring at me? It could have been a coincidence of course. We must have just happened to glance at each other at the same time. It was nothing more.

I hurried outside, trying to reassure myself it was nothing. I was simply being paranoid. As much as I tried to reassure myself, I couldn't control my imagination. There had to be others out there who felt things like Kim and I. She had given me an address and time of a meeting. I was sure that it was a meeting for people who didn't want to be alone anymore.

The minute the thought crossed my mind, a shock reverberated through my body. I didn't want to be alone anymore. The realization was terrifying in a way, but also liberating. I felt the urge to say it aloud but held my tongue. Thinking was enough. For as long as I could remember, I had been alone. I went to work, went to sleep, and repeated each day. Every one of those days, I was alone. Sure, I had people who I went out on routes with at work, but neither of us was ever really present. We were there to work; two completely separate people. I could be surrounded by people, such as in the lobby, but I was still ultimately alone.

The thought of not being alone was terrifying and seemed out of reach. The idea of being with another person and having an actual conversation with them seemed impossible. It was against the law, and surely we would get caught.

But I'd done it with Kim. If I'd done it once, maybe I could do it again. Perhaps Friday night, I would go to the address Kim had given me and experience the presence of other people for a second time. The thought of me sitting next to someone and feeling the heat from their body sent chills throughout mine. It was going to happen. It had to. I couldn't have these feelings and have no way to fulfill them.

I snapped out of my head at the sound of the bus engine. The big white vehicle had just shut its doors and was pulling away from the sidewalk. I dashed towards the curb, waving my hands in the air.

"Wait!" I cried out, but the bus had already sped away.

Crap. The next bus didn't come by for an hour and a half, and I didn't feel like waiting. There were too many people around. My head spinning, I decided to walk home. I hadn't been in this part of town in a while, and a change of scenery could be a positive thing.

I zipped my coat up to my chin to shelter myself from the wind and started down the sidewalk. The sun from earlier had been replaced with more familiar gray skies and chilly air. A gust of wind whipped at my face, causing my eyes to water. The wetness in my eyes reminded me of the moisture that had fallen from them right before I found Amber.

Amber liked to be outside despite the dismal weather. She seemed to find joy in everything. She loved to follow me around my apartment and stick her nose in whatever I was doing. I wished I could take her outside, but I didn't want to risk any suspicion. I didn't usually see any The City's officials watching my apartment, but they were supposed to be everywhere. The only time I took Amber outside was to go to the bathroom, which she did on the fire escape.

The stinging smell of smoke filled my nose. Wrinkling it in disgust, I looked up to notice that I was passing by factories. I glanced in the windows as I walked. The big glass squares were tinted, but squinting allowed me to see murky figures inside. I hated my job, but the thought of working in a factory wasn't very appealing either. It was another occupation for the low class, with long hours and uncomfortable conditions.

Murky gray smoke emerged from the chimneys atop the roof of the factory, splaying out into the air. The smoke drifted towards the gray clouds, blending into each other. For a second I thought I could see the sun peeking out from behind the clouds and smoke, but it must have been an illusion. I returned my gaze to the sidewalk in front of me, stepping over a hole in the cement.

The City was an ugly place to live. Even the wealthy

parts were not as beautiful as the video had made them seem. Visions of trees, yards, and pretty suburban houses danced through my mind. They must have been images from when I was younger. I didn't remember experiencing the beauty, but I suspected I couldn't make them up on my own. The spotty memories were starting to overwhelm me. After my job assignment, I'd relocated to the city where the only trees were small and dead. They were barely enough to absorb all of the smoke the factories emitted. There were a few parks were dirty and neglected, with trails used for exercise and nothing more.

I never exercised in parks, mainly because I preferred weight-lifting to any kind of cardio activity. The thought of a park was attractive to me now. I imagined being able to take Amber, and showing her the best part of The City. She would like the sticks and rocks. She enjoyed picking things up in her mouth and playing tug-o-war with me. I had even started rolling my socks in little balls and throwing them for her. She'd probably like hunting after things in the park.

Amber was such a happy dog; it was still hard for me to imagine anyone leaving her behind. My logic reminded me that dogs weren't meant to be pets, that they only were used in competitions. I wondered if her previous owner ever petted Amber or scratched her stomach. Probably not, since the only reason her owner had her was to show that she was better than other dogs. And her owner obviously had been unsuccessful in proving that, so she dumped Amber. It must happen all the time, I'd just never thought of it before. All of those dead dogs I disposed of had to come from somewhere. They were all defective show dogs, and with no other purpose in this world, they were useless.

Amber wasn't useless to me. Seeing her beautiful fur and her tail wag back and forth never failed to make me smile. I would bring her everywhere with me if I could.

The factories turned into apartments, signaling that I was nearing my home. The rows of brick buildings blended into each other. They all looked exactly the same. I watched the numbers until mine appeared, pausing on the steps before going in.

A car was parked across the street, the engine still running. The windows were black, matching the dark black exterior. Seeing a car in this neighborhood was odd enough, but even the upper class cars weren't that fancy. The car looked so familiar, but I couldn't place where I'd seen it before.

The engine roared louder as the car slowly rolled forward, then accelerated down the street. As I watched the vehicle turn into a black speck on the horizon, I felt a jolt inside my body. Of course! The car belonged to The City. I remembered seeing them parked outside of the town hall the day I went to get my test results. There had been a whole line of them along the side of the building.

The wind picked up and thrashed against my face, but the shiver I experienced wasn't from the cold. What had the vehicle been doing outside my house? It couldn't have been watching me . . . could it?

CHAPTER 6

Creeeaak! The door squealed as I pushed it open, stepping into the inky darkness behind it. The building was damp and musty, reeking of mildew. Dark, boxy figures lined the walls of the room. As I took another step forward, a dim light flickered to life above my head. The square figures were actually large cardboard crates, some stacked all the way to the ceiling. A dark, wooden door stood at the opposite end of the room, beckoning me closer.

"Hello?" I asked. The only answer I received was the wind. I closed the door behind me and advanced forward, the beat up wooden floorboards wailing like an alarm. Every step I took made me cringe, sabotaging my attempt to be quiet.

I reached the other door and grabbed the brass doorknob. It was locked. I pressed my ear against it to see if I could hear any sounds of activity on the other side. Whatever was in there was quiet, if there was anything at all.

Frustrated, I knocked louder.

Why would Kim send me here for nothing?

I banged until my knuckles hurt, leaning against one of the boxes as I waited. The door remained closed, and I still couldn't hear anything on the other side.

After a good ten minutes of waiting, I let out a loud sigh. It was useless. I didn't know what kind of game Kim was trying to play with me, but the place was deserted. I had seen her in passing the previous day at work, but we were assigned to different routes. My supervisor hadn't mentioned anything to me about failing to sign out, making me even more on edge. I feared that he would be suspicious, but it was more likely that he recognized his mistake in putting two weak links together.

I was becoming more frustrated by the second. I had come to the abandoned warehouse expecting answers for my new feelings, but apparently my expectations had been unrealistic.

I turned, about to leave, as the door opened slightly. In the murky light, I could make out an eye peering through the crack.

"What do you want?" a gruff, scratchy voice demanded.

"I . . . I . . ." I paused for a minute, wondering what I should say. Kim hadn't told me what to do when I came.

"I want information," I said slowly.

"Who are you?"

"My name is Vic."

"Well, go home Vic. You don't belong here."

"Yes I do!" I protested. Hoping Kim wouldn't get mad at me, I dropped her name. "A girl name Kim told me to meet here in ten minutes."

"Kim?" the voice seemed to recognize the name, but didn't open the door any wider. "How do I know you're telling the truth?"

"I'm here aren't I? Why else would I be here if I wasn't one of you?" I tried. I wasn't sure what I meant by saying "one of you", but I assumed the man was there because he felt things toward other people like I did.

"You could be from The City," he pressed.

"If I was from The City, wouldn't I have already busted the door down and arrested you for having *feelings?*"

The eye widened when I said the word feelings, but he seemed satisfied. He opened the door, revealing a short old man. His hair was gray and he wore large eyeglasses. His skin was pale and wrinkled, the texture appearing leathery as if he had spent a lot of time in sun. A short, wooden cane supported his frail body. He struggled to move backwards to create room for me to enter.

I stepped inside cautiously, eyeing the old man.

"Follow me," he murmured. He turned and began walking shakily away.

The door had opened up to a long hallway that was just as dimly lit as the previous room. It sported the same musty odor and creaky floorboards. A lone door stood at the far end.

Although I was eager to continue into the building, I slowed my step to match the old man's. I followed closely, peeking over my shoulder at the sound of a thud. The door had shut automatically behind us, leaving us closed in the narrow hall.

"All right." The man stopped in front of the other door and looked at me closely. "Now you must swear that no matter what happens outside of this building, you will never, under any circumstances, repeat what you have heard inside it."

I nodded, excitement building in my chest. "I swear."

Hand shaking, he pulled a small brass key from the pocket of his dark gray coat. He slowly inserted it into the lock and turned it to the left. The sight of a key made me realize how abandoned this building really was. No one had used keys in years, everything was fingerprint recognition. I wondered why the building had been neglected and not updated into something useful.

"Go ahead. This is as far as I go." He pulled the key from the lock and pushed the door open. The hinges shrieked shrilly as he swung it a few feet, motioning for me to proceed.

"Thank you," I said, slipping through the opening. The man closed the door behind me, a familiar clicking noise filling my ears. Trying the knob, I found that he had locked it again.

"Hey!" I pounded on the door. "How am I supposed to get out?"

There was no answer from the other side. The excitement that had been brewing turned to nervousness, my stomach clenching tightly. With no other option, I turned away from the door. I found myself in another dim hall. At the far end stood a small archway.

I padded over to the entrance and found a set of spiral metal stairs leading downwards. Another faint light hung from the ceiling in the stairwell, but it wasn't bright enough to reveal the bottom of the steps. Taking a deep breath, I stepped onto the top rung.

The metal let out a loud clang. The sound echoed in the otherwise silent stairwell. I took another step, creating an equally loud clink. Giving up on trying to be quiet, I thumped down the stairs. A cacophony of bangs flooded the space. If anyone else was in the building, surely they would have already heard me coming.

When I reached the final step, I found another wooden door inches away from my face. Gripping the knob with my sweating hand, I turned it slowly. To my surprise it was unlocked. I pushed it open and gasped as I emerged into another room.

The area was large and full of people. There was a long table with a dozen or so seated around it, all engaged in conversation. A few people sat on couches in the back of the room. Some were seated awfully close to one another; one man even had his arm draped around a woman. As soon as I entered, the conversations stopped. Everyone stared at me in shock.

"Who are you?" A tall man leapt up from the table and started towards me, his hands clenched in fists at his sides. He wore faded jeans and a tight blue t-shirt that accentuated his toned biceps. Ice blue eyes glared at me accusingly, his eyebrows turned down.

"Wait!" A girl cried out. Kim's familiar face rose up from the table and hurried after the man. She reached out and grabbed his hand, lowering her voice. "I know him. It's okay."

The man stopped in his tracks and turned to Kim, his face red. "Who is he? And why the hell have you brought him here?" Anger dripped from the edges of his voice. Kim's hand was still enclosed in his, causing something inside of me to twitch.

"I found him during the search," she protested, looking up into the man's glowering eyes. "I think we can trust him." She stood only inches away from his body, her head tilted back so she could meet his gaze.

"You *think*?" The man had raised his voice so loudly that everyone at the tables and on the couches stopped their hushed whispering. They watched silently, their eyes shifting from the man and Kim to me.

"You can't bring someone back from a search if you merely *think* he supports the rebellion! Are you crazy? You put us all in danger!"

Kim bit her lip, her fiery persona dampened. "He saved my life."

"What?" The man snapped his head to look at me.

"He saved my life." Kim spoke louder this time, giving me an apologetic look. "I should have told you about him. I was going to . . . we just didn't get to it yet. I told him to come at eight . . . it's early."

My face flushed as all eyes focused on me. The wheels in my brain were spinning in confusion and disbelief. The man had said rebellion. What was he talking about? And what did Kim mean when she said search? I tried to open my mouth and say something but my tongue was a block of sandpaper. Even if I wasn't so nervous, I wouldn't have known what to say or where to start.

The man shook off Kim's hand and started towards me again. He unclenched his hand and held it out to me. "Adam."

I stared at his hand, then back at his pale face. "Hi."

Kim let out a laugh from behind him. "Adam, he's new at this."

"Oh, right. You're supposed to shake it . . . it's just something we do. It means welcome." Adam's voice was deep and softer now, as if the anger had evaporated. He ran his free hand through his light, reddish brown hair, the other one still extended toward me.

86

Wrinkling my brow, I reached out and took his hand. His fingers closed firmly around mine and he raised his arm up and down, moving my hand with his. His touch was warm but different than Kim's. There was stiffness in his manner, or perhaps the stiffness was in me. Either way, the contact we shared was unusual compared to contact with Kim. Without warning he let go of my hand, causing it to flop back against my side.

"And you are?" Adam pressed, waiting for me to introduce myself.

"Sorry," I mumbled. "I'm Vic."

"Thank you," he told me.

"For what?" I shifted awkwardly. All eyes remained glued to me; an alien in their sacred space.

"For saving her life," he said. "Sometimes we have to resort to desperate measures to complete our searches, and they can put us in grave danger."

I nodded, not sure what to say. I was dying to ask him what kind of searches they kept referring to, but my mouth refused to open. Beads of sweat gathered on the edges of my forehead and I felt my temperature rising. I looked to Kim, hoping she would say something.

She remained silent until Adam turned and addressed her once more.

"What happened?" he asked.

I studied Adam's expression as Kim relayed the events at the dump. He kept his face flat and unrevealing; as if it was something he had been trained to do his entire life. I pondered how much practice he had at hiding emotions. When Kim finished explaining how I had pulled her out of the hole, he nodded.

"So are you ready? This is what you want?"

He was staring at Kim, but when she failed to answer I wondered if he was speaking to me. Though I was a few feet away, I could feel the heat between the two of them. I wasn't sure what it meant, but there was some kind of connection there.

"You want to join the rebellion?" This time Adam turned to me, his eyes burning a hole through my flesh.

"I . . . I didn't know there was a rebellion," I stammered. "A rebellion against who or what?"

Kim opened her mouth to talk, but Adam spoke first. "I guess we have a lot of explaining to do."

I swallowed and tried to steady my voice. "If you would be so kind, I would be eager to listen. That's why I came here tonight. I want to keep feeling more of these emotions. Emotions toward other human beings and living things."

"Living things?" Adam raised an eyebrow at me, crossing his arms across his chest.

"I found a dog . . ." I began.

"Say no more," he interrupted. "I get it. We've done research on that. Terry had a dog." He raised his arm and motioned towards a small, brown-haired girl on the couch.

"Research?" I blurted, biting my lip as the words escaped my mouth. I was trying to remain calm and keep my composure, but it seemed that I was not doing a very good job.

"Would you like to have a seat?" Adam grabbed a wooden chair from the corner of the room and pulled it up to the side of the table.

"Okay." As I went to take a step toward the table a wave of dizziness washed over me. I stumbled forward and steadied myself before falling too far.

"Guys, I think he's a little overwhelmed." Kim

hurried over to me. She grabbed my arm, sending electric shocks through it. "Maybe we should take things slow."

Adam nodded. "All right. How about just the three of us talk?"

Kim led me over toward the left side of the room, easing me down onto a deep maroon mat. She slid down to sit beside me, Adam dropping next to her.

"This is the first time in months that one of our searches has been successful in finding an anomaly," Adam said.

Unsure of what he meant, I kept my mouth shut. I turned my head from him to Kim, then back to him, hoping he would continue with some sort of explanation. Sitting down had calmed my dizziness. In addition, when I discovered that many of the others in the room had stopped staring at me I felt my body temperature drop. They returned to the conversations they had been having, though every few minutes I caught someone glance over at me.

Unable to contain my curiosity and unsatisfied with the Kim and Adam's pause in speech, I piped up. "What's an anomaly? And what are you searching for?"

"An anomaly is what we're searching for," Kim began. "Periodically we send members of the rebellion out to see if we can find anyone who is different. People like you, who have begun to have feelings regarding others. When I saw you in the store, I thought you were different."

She took a deep breath before speaking again. "Why did you stop taking your LVs?"

The question surprised me. I wracked my brain but found it difficult to come up with a response.

"I don't know," I answered honestly. "I was really

sick of the same routine in my life. I didn't know what to do. I figured any change from the life I was living would be a positive one, even if I became sick or worse."

"That's pretty deep," she observed.

I shrugged.

"The LVs, as I hinted at the other night, quell any bit of feelings that you may have for another living creature. These feelings, whether it be a mental or physical attraction, are impossible to have when taking LVs. It could be something as simple as eliminating the desire to speak a few extra words to someone. Any kind of connection that could later turn into a relationship of any kind or stir up more feelings is prevented using LVs."

"Wow," I murmured.

"The LVs don't only eliminate these feelings, but they are supposed to lessen all of someone's other emotions as well. That's why I'm surprised that you had such serious feelings that lead you to stop taking them in the first place. Somehow the LVs may have not had as strong an effect on you as intended. It's strange."

"Why aren't we supposed to be connected with other people?" I inquired, asking the question that had been blazing in my brain for the last few days. "I remember being taught in school that relationships were bad, but I don't think so. Most of what I've felt so far has been . . . incredible."

Adam and Kim exchanged a glance. Adam turned his gaze back to me.

"The City does not want us to have relationships but doesn't provide significant evidence against them. That's why we call ourselves a rebellion. We are against The City because we disagree with what they are doing. They are keeping us separate to keep us weak."

"But they say that relationships are evil . . . do they not believe that is true?" I wondered, thinking aloud.

"It's possible," Adam continued. "Affiliations with other people do complicate things at times, but the negatives are outweighed by the positives. Our theory is that The City keeps us apart with the cover that relationships are evil because they don't want any excess problems. They want to keep us operating, working, and staying simple. They want robots, not human beings, this way nothing ever gets too out of control."

"Why?"

Adam shook his head. "We don't know."

"It's the magic question that has us going crazy," Kim admitted.

"So really . . . you don't know any more than I do?" I accused, perhaps a bit too harshly. I had come expecting to leave with answers, but was disappointed that I hadn't received many.

Adam scowled at me. "That's not true. We know how to conceal our desires."

"Huh?"

"We were all in your spot at one time," Kim explained. "When we first stopped taking the LVs, we were just as overwhelmed as you."

"Why'd you stop?" I prodded.

"Well, I used to work in a factory about thirty minutes away. It burned down, and since then The City has been bouncing me from job to job trying to find the best match. That's why I was at the dump. I've worked a bunch of jobs since then, which is why I perform most of the searches. It was pretty dumb luck that we were assigned to the same route. It was pretty tough to hide my surprise when I recognized you from the store."

"Why didn't they just put you in another factory? And factories don't burn down! Fire accidents are a thing of the past. And what does that have to do with the LVs?" I blurted out, unable to contain the thoughts that were rushing through my brain like a windstorm.

Kim narrowed her eyes and pursed her lips. "Maybe I'd be able to explain it if you didn't keep interrupting me."

"Sorry." I blushed and looked at my boots.

"First off, factories do burn down. Most factories have very unsafe and harmful conditions, but only the people who work there know the horrors. That's why they didn't put me in another factory. I had developed lung cancer, and they said they wanted to keep me alive for a long time. I thought it was nice of them at the time, moving me to a better job where the work wouldn't be so difficult, but since then I've changed my mind."

"Cancer?" I exclaimed. The word sailed through my brain, triggering another memory from school. Cancer was a horrible disease that had plagued the population decades ago, but scientists were said to have found the cure. It was one of the things that LVs were supposed to protect against.

"Yes," she continued. "Cancer, like fires, does exist. The City keeps things quiet so they don't ruin their mask of perfection. We keep things quiet as well, not discussing personal matters with other human beings. There are no doubt thousands walking around. I was lucky enough to be cured. There are also many other accidents such as the factory fire that just don't get passed around to citizens."

She paused for a breath and looked at me as if waiting for me to interject with something, but I remained silent. This new stream of information left me speechless and ravenous for more.

Seeing I had no response, she kept talking. "Many people died in that fire. I was one of the few lucky to survive. There were five of us. We were kept in a truck together to be taken to the hospital. The fire and the immediate rush to the hospital caused us to skip lunch and dinner, which meant two sets of LVs missed. We waited in the hospital for hours, getting bandaged up eventually. The machines did routine scans and discovered cancer in all of our bodies. Besides the cancer, we were all in greater danger than we realized. The lack of LVs caused us to become curious with each other, and our supervisor observed that we were taking too much notice of one another."

"We were exhausted from the events of the day, which may have led to rash actions. One of the others, a woman, tried to strike up a conversation with another women. The supervisor removed the two immediately and I never saw them again. I can only guess what might have happened to them."

"Our supervisor ordered more food brought to us, which of course meant LVs. I couldn't eat the food or the vitamins because I was too nauseous. The supervisor was busy talking on the phone, and the three of us had been put into beds in separate rooms. I dozed off, and when I awoke the tray was gone. I was rushed out of the hospital that morning, still too sick to eat."

"What happened to the other two? Are they here? And how did you figure out it was the vitamins?" I asked.

"I don't know where the other two went. And I

didn't know that it was the LVs at first, but the feelings were growing stronger. I was paying special attention to the person transporting me and the people at the rest stops. I was unsure why I was having these feelings, but probably like you, I was curious. I was dying to know more about them, and didn't want anything to make me stop being interested in other people. It was something new, something different. But I knew it was against the law, and was terrified because the two women had disappeared. I didn't want to end up with a similar fate."

"At first I thought I was going crazy. This new attraction was so foreign despite the warmth associated with it. I forced myself to act as if nothing was different, which of course was much easier said than done. I tried to make connections and think of something that could have caused these new feelings. My first thought was chemicals in the fire, and then the food, and then LVs. I wasn't sure of any of my theories, but I tested the only one I could test. By then I was starving, so I ate the food they gave me. I didn't take the LVs and the feelings continued. That night I did take the LVs with dinner, and noticed the feelings dampen almost immediately. That's when I knew it had to be the LVs."

"Wow . . ." I sat back, realizing I had been crouching on the edge of my seat to listen to Kim speak. "So now you're here."

She nodded. "Yes. I met Adam at a former job and he suspected that I wasn't taking the LVs. After his suspicions were confirmed, he introduced me to the rest of the group. That was a few months ago. You're the first new member since I joined. It's tough being sure that people aren't taking their LVs, and every search is risky. I've thought others were not taking the LVs and having feelings in the past, but I didn't have enough faith in my theory to bring them here. The tests never went quite as far as they did with you. I questioned you the minute I saw you."

"So what is it you guys do, if you don't mind me asking?"

Adam gave Kim a break and took over the explanation. "There isn't much we can do. I founded the group with my neighbor Griffin about a year ago. But taking action is dangerous. We are too small to change anything within The City. We try to research new things in The City and the LVs themselves. A few of our members work in the LV production center, so we have an inside advantage there."

"So you're not really a rebellion?" I uttered. "You're not really trying to allow people to be able to be interested in others?"

"Excuse me?" Adam growled. Kim touched his arm lightly and he seemed to calm a little. When he spoke again, his voice remained stiff but wasn't quite as harsh. "Of course we want everyone to be free to interact with other people. But how on Earth can a group of only sixteen take on The City? We don't even know exactly who to target, or where to start. And there's no way we could win. We're outnumbered."

"Seventeen," I replied.

"Huh?"

"You have seventeen members now," I responded.

I thought I saw a twinkle in his eyes, but he kept up his stiff front. "Regardless, you see how daunting a task it is. Not all of us can even make it to every meeting. What we focus on is gathering information. The more we know, the more prepared we will be if there ever is a time we can actually take on The City. And every Friday night we meet here for a few hours to unleash all the feelings we've been holding onto all week. We finally have the freedom to interact and discuss information."

"You're right," I admitted. "Taking on The City would be a huge task. And right now I'm just happy to be able to know why I'm feeling what I'm feeling. And a place where I'm actually able to express those feelings is more than I could ask for."

Kim let out a sigh and rested her head on the wall. She looked tired, probably from all of the talking she had been doing. I prodded one last time.

"Eventually the goal is for change right?"

"What?" Adam asked.

"Change," I repeated. "To be able to interact on a whole other level in public. That's what I want."

Adam shook his head and stood up. "You might want to lower your expectations, kid." He returned to the table where he'd been seated when I walked in and resumed conservation with another girl beside him.

Kim smiled at me. "Don't mind him. I like your spirit. Why not shoot for the stars?"

"My life needs change," I told her. "I've been stuck on the same repeat day for what seems like an eternity. And having relationships with people could be just what I need."

She leaned over and reached toward me, entwining her fingers with mine. She closed her hand and squeezed. "Don't give up. I'm not promising that one day we'll all be able to walk around with friends and significant others like they did in the past, but you never know."

She stood up, still holding onto my hand. She

helped pull me to my feet and stood beside me.

"One day," I told her. "One day."

Chapter 7

"This is crazy," I mumbled, eagerly flipping the page. My eyes flew over the words, trying to absorb as much information as possible. "Where did you get this stuff?"

It was the following Friday night and I was back at the abandoned warehouse. Kim was showing me the piles of books. They were from decades ago, the pages yellow and brittle.

"I stole them from work," a middle-aged man named Patrick replied.

"Where do you work?" I wondered in awe.

"Recycling department," he replied. "We get a ton of books that City Officials find in old buildings."

"Wow," I breathed. "You must be pretty high up for them to trust you with this kind of forbidden stuff." I hadn't seen a book since school. The only reading material circulating were pamphlets about the laws. According to The City, old books had fictional stories of relationships that delivered unrealistic ideas.

Patrick chuckled, pushing his glasses further up his

nose. "Not quite. I'm illiterate."

"What does that mean?" I asked him.

"It means I cannot read," he answered.

I ruffled my brow. "Huh? But everyone can read! They taught us during school!"

Patrick shook his head. "Not me. I didn't finish school."

I was shocked. I'd never heard of anyone not finishing school! It was simply what kids did. They went to school until they were seventeen, took the test, and were placed in jobs. "But if you didn't finish school, what did you do?"

Patrick gave a slight shrug of his shoulders. "I don't really remember honestly. But I do know that I didn't finish school because I just couldn't do it. It wasn't my choice. I remember having difficulties, and I think they thought me being there was a waste of time. I took the test early and got a job in the recycling department at around fifteen."

"Wow," I repeated. "That's . . ." My voice faded off. I didn't want to offend Patrick, and couldn't find the right word to finish my thought.

"It's the same with everyone in my department," he explained. "We are unable to read, so they don't worry about us looking through any of the old books."

"How did you know to bring these here?" I inquired. "If you couldn't read the titles, how did you know which books were what?"

"I didn't," he admitted. "I just brought what I could grab. I feel the books and bring the ones that feel most used. I figure those must be the oldest and most valuable."

"They don't notice you take them?" I wondered.

He laughed. "No. Our supervisor doesn't really pay

attention to us. Why would we steal books? We have no use for them."

"Wait!" I exclaimed, raising my voice in confusion.

"What?" Kim and Patrick asked in unison.

"I just realized something," I said excitedly. "We all have supervisors at work, right?"

"Right," Kim said slowly, exchanging a glance with Patrick. "So?"

"And what do the supervisors do?" I continued. "They are in charge of us, assign us jobs, and make sure we work."

"Yeah . . ."

"So," I went on. "Do they take LVs?"

"Everyone takes LVs," Patrick said simply.

"But they have to deal with people all the time," I protested. "Unlike us, they have to talk to a bunch of different people on a regular basis."

"Wouldn't that just create a stronger need for LVs?" Kim asked.

"Maybe," I replied. "But think about it! Have there ever been times when your supervisor has overstepped the boundaries? Like have you ever thought there was a hint of emotion in his voice towards you?"

Kim made a face. "I can't remember . . ."

"I hardly ever see my supervisor," Patrick answered.

"Have you ever been spoken to by your supervisor with emotion?" Kim inquired.

My face flushed. "Well, I'm not sure. I never really paid much attention to them before."

"I still don't pay any attention to them," Kim replied. "You can't, or they might get suspicious."

"But for them to get suspicious, they have to observe you," I pressed. "So they have to be interested in what you're doing."

"And by taking LVs, we have no interest in what other people are doing," Patrick put in, catching on to my thought.

"Exactly!" I said. "They *have* to watch us. It's their job!"

"So how can they be interested in us but uninterested in us at the same time..." Kim wondered. "Wow, I've never thought of that before."

"Right," I nodded. "So either they take some kind of special LVs or they don't take any. But I don't know how they could make LVs with such a fine line. You say LVs keep us uninterested in those around us, so we never have any emotions toward them. They keep any desires we have at bay."

"Adam!" Kim stood up from the small table beside the bookcase, motioning for Adam to come over.

I repeated my thoughts to Adam, but he was unresponsive.

"I don't know how we could have missed this," Kim said. "Vic you're so smart!"

I blushed and looked at my sneakers. "Anyone could have thought of it."

"Yea," Adam agreed. "Anyone could have thought of it. We don't even know what the truth is."

Kim glared at him. "Oh come on Adam. You didn't think of it. And what if supervisors don't take LVs? That would be a whole new thing to think about."

"It's ludicrous," Adam grumbled. "They have to take LVs. Everyone does." He turned on his heel and stormed into the adjoining room.

Kim looked at me. "Don't mind him," she replied. "I'll try to talk some sense into him." She followed Adam through the large wooden door.

"What's with those two?" I wondered.

Patrick smiled at me. "Ever since Kim joined the

group, Adam's been entranced by the girl."

"Huh?"

"They kind of have a thing, even a relationship if you will," he explained. "They've never officially declared it like a few of the other members, but they are almost always by each other's side."

"Oh," I replied. I felt a twinge deep inside my stomach, and from what I had recently been reading, I recognized it as jealousy. Was I really jealous of Kim and Adam? Did I really like Kim that much, or was it only because I was so overwhelmed by those unfamiliar feelings?

Reading some of the chapters of the novels that Patrick had stolen had given me a deeper understanding of interactions between people. There were words for every feeling such as love, hate, jealousy, revenge, desire. This was the first time I'd read a book since school and my brain was on overload. Yet from what I read, and the emotional and physical feelings swirling throughout my body, there was an indicator that I was jealous of Kim and Adam.

My emotions were running wild, but I was beginning to comprehend the difference between them. What I felt towards Kim was different than how I felt towards Amber and Adam and Patrick and so on. Each person that I spoke to was unique; I felt different things toward each of them. The feelings I had for Kim definitely were special. Ever since that night I had saved her she was the only person I had felt so strongly about.

Whenever I saw her, my heart beat faster in my chest. My blood flowed warmer and smoother, and everything negative in the background faded away. No matter how bad I felt or how tired I was, it was unimportant around her. The intensity of the feelings didn't die down or diminish. Even without physical contact the sight of her filled me with a feeling of ecstasy.

I wanted more than anything to have the type of relationship that Patrick described of Kim and Adam. I had noticed it before Patrick had even mentioned their connection. They were often around each other, and whenever they were they stayed within inches of one another. They frequently would brush up against the other and exchange secret glances, and sometimes even hold hands.

There were two couples in the group; people who openly stated that they had relationships with one another. They held hands and even kissed in front of the rest of the group. Adam and Kim never did that. If they had any "relationship", they didn't go around parading it in front of the rest of the group. I wasn't sure what exactly defined a relationship. The couples were what the books called "boyfriend and girlfriend". Adam and Kim didn't behave like these partners, but they definitely had more of a connection than friends.

The fact they didn't publicly announce they were a couple gave me a sense of hope. It seemed from reading parts of the books that to become a couple, a man or woman would simply ask the other one "out." The naturalness of the relationships blew my mind. Though some characters in the books had complications associated with their love, mainly the doubts they had in their relationships came from themselves or their partner. They didn't have any fear of breaking the law or getting punished; they merely expressed their feelings. I was a little jealous of the characters, even though they were fictional. I couldn't help it; the taste of feelings I had experienced was so wonderful that being able to show and share them anywhere would be incredible.

"So, have any girls around here caught your eye?" Patrick's question caught me off guard.

"What?" I asked, a hint of nervousness creeping into my voice. "Um, no. Well not that everyone here isn't great . . ." My voice trailed off and I scratched the back of my head awkwardly.

Patrick laughed at me. "It's okay, I get it. Everything is still overwhelming to you. I was just messing with you."

"Messing with me?" I raised an eyebrow.

"Kidding, joking," he explained. "Just something friends do."

"Oh . . . right." I gave him a smile as a feeling of warmth spread through my body. The word always made me feel different. "Friends."

"You want to read more?" Patrick inquired.

"Yes!" I said eagerly. I had already been reading for two hours but was still intrigued. I didn't want to miss an opportunity to explore more information about relationships, love, feelings, and whatever else the books held.

Patrick handed me a small book. I turned it over carefully in my hands, lifting the first yellowed page. As with many of the manuscripts, the cover was torn off. The page was coarse between my fingers and I was afraid that it would crumble from the pressure. I gently lifted the next few pages until I reached the first part of the actual story. The print was so tiny that I had to squint to read it. The first line confused me, and I had to reread it. I didn't understand the meaning after reading it a second time, or a third. My eyes flicked farther down the page, experiencing the same incomprehension with the rest of the lines.

"I don't get this," I told Patrick. "The language is odd."

Patrick put his hand out, waiting for me to give him the book. I placed it in his palm, carefully balancing it. His hand closed over the unraveling spine. He pulled the book in closer to him and examined it. He seemed to be studying it, but I wasn't sure how since he couldn't read.

"Ah." A chuckle escaped Patrick's lips as he laid the book back on the bookshelf. "Yes this language is not what we are used to. We had trouble understanding the story ourselves. Luckily, I took another book that happened to be the same story but was translated to language that is easier to understand. It's by William Shakespeare, and was actually written as a play."

"Can you tell me the story?" I begged him.

He nodded. "It's the story of two young lovers. Their families are sworn rivals, but the son of one and daughter of another fall in love. The daughter already has an arranged marriage that she does not wish to perform. At a party, she meets the boy of the rival family, though she doesn't know who he is at the time. They share a kiss and are immediately infatuated with one another. Upon learning that they have fallen in love with the spawn of their family's rivals, they are upset. Their love for one another is so strong that they decide to ignore the rivalry and choose to get married in secret. The man gets in a fight and kills another man, causing him to become banished from the kingdom. After the two are married, they say goodbye. The woman learns that she must marry her arranged husband the next day, so she drinks a potion to make her appear dead. Her real lover hears she has died and returns to her tomb, killing himself out of grief. When the woman awakes and sees her lover dead, she is devastated and kills herself as well."

"Wow," I exclaimed. "So love can be pretty complicated and cause problems."

"Of course," Patrick stated. He was smiling, as if amused by me. "The question is, is it worth it?"

I looked over at the couch where one of the couples lay together. Their bodies were stretched across the cushions, snuggled up against one another. They spoke quietly, smiles plastered across their faces. Every few minutes one would laugh or they would exchange a kiss. I looked back at Patrick, and he just shrugged at me, though he was still wearing a grin.

"How do you know so much? I thought you couldn't read."

"Well I can't," Patrick replied. "But everyone here has taken turns reading these books to me. I'm the only one here who has read . . . well, listened to . . . every book in our collection. They call me the bookkeeper."

"That's really cool," I told him sincerely.

"Thanks."

"I wish I could find half as interesting things in peoples' trash," I joked. "Not that I've ever looked."

"You'd be surprised," he replied.

"I have a question," I began. "If all these fictional and nonfictional books about people were banned decades ago, then why didn't they destroy them right then? Wouldn't they all be gone by now?"

"I like you."

Patrick's response startled me. "What?"

"Sorry," he chortled. "I like your questions I mean. You don't just accept something for what it is; you go a step further and try to analyze it as what it could be."

106

"I'm curious," I admitted. "I'm sick of sitting around, and I know that any change that might ever come to my life will begin with answers."

"Knowledge is an amazing thing," Patrick nodded.

"You didn't answer my question."

"I don't have an answer to your question, Vic. My guess is they just weren't found until later on."

"Do you think people were hiding them?" I asked eagerly, excitement building in my stomach. "People who are like us, and kept them to read for information and entertainment? They couldn't all be from abandoned buildings right?"

Patrick shrugged at me, pushing his glasses further up on his nose. "It's quite possible. I don't think we'll ever really know, but I think there are more important answers we need to find. I am confident that if there are as many of us here today to form a group, there must be others out there. Statistically, the odds of us finding one another would be higher the more of us there are in the city."

"You seem really smart," I told him. "Are you sure you can't read?"

Patrick shrugged. "I don't know. They told me in school that I couldn't."

"Have you tried since then?" I prodded. "Maybe illiteracy can change over time!"

He shook his head. "No I haven't tried again. And I don't think it works that way."

"But do you know?" I pressed. "Do you know for sure that you'll never be able to read? Is it some kind of disease?"

"I don't know," he responded. "I really don't know."

I sat back in my beanbag chair, allowing myself to slip further into the tiny beads. I had never sat in one of the chairs until I'd come to the warehouse. They were extremely entertaining and comfortable. "I think you should try again."

Patrick shook his head. "I'm okay thanks."

"Why?" I exclaimed. "Imagine limitless possibilities. You would never have to make anyone read these books to you again. You could read books, street signs, store windows, anything!"

"No. I'm fine recognizing things by sight." Patrick fidgeted in his chair, giving me the vibe that he was becoming uncomfortable.

I couldn't figure out why he wouldn't want to read. "But Patrick! It would open up a whole new world."

"Just drop it, okay?!" Patrick raised his voice, rising from his chair at the same time.

I didn't know what to say. I remained frozen in my chair, surprised and confused. Veins bulged from his neck and redness cloaked his face. His fists were clenched in tight balls at his sides.

"Sorry man," Patrick mumbled. He relaxed his shoulders and his hands, his entire body becoming less tense.

"It's okay . . ." My voice trailed off as I slowly rose to my feet. Standing in front of Patrick, I stuck my hands in my pockets. Still unsure of what to do, I attempted to change the subject. "Thanks for showing me your books."

He nodded. "Sure. Glad you liked them."

The sound of a door opening was a welcome distraction. I looked expectantly over at the entrance, watching as Kim and Adam emerged into the room. Their faces were expressionless; hiding any clue to what thoughts might be swirling inside their heads. They stood next to each other, but did not touch.

Adam's icy eyes burned holes through my body but

he remained silent as he passed by. He continued walking past, taking his usual seat at the head of the table. Kim stopped next to Patrick and I, staying silent for a few minutes as well.

"Did we miss anything?"

I exchanged a glance with Patrick, and we both shook our heads.

"Nope," Patrick replied. "Are you guys okay?"

Kim nodded, forcing a smile. "Yeah, we're fine." Her voice sounded tight but she didn't expand further.

The door flew open again, this time crashing into the wall. A girl named Noel dashed into the middle of the room, panting hard like a dog. We all looked at her in shock for a few minutes, Kim being the first to move.

"Noel!" she exclaimed, rushing to her side. "What happened?"

Noel leaned against Kim's shoulder, gasping in effort to catch her breath. Her wavy, platinum blonde hair was usually carefully intact, but today it looked as if she had run through a wind tunnel. Her normally pale face was flushed and her dark green eyes had a somewhat crazed look. The expression was fairly familiar but I couldn't place where I had seen it before.

Cautiously, I joined Kim by Noel's side. I turned around as someone bumped into me from behind. Adam shoved me out of the way to get in between Kim and I, holding a chair in his hand. Noel collapsed gratefully into the seat, burying her face in her hands.

"It's okay, Noel," Adam told her. His voice was soft and gentle, using a tone that he had never used with me.

"No," Noel answered, her voice weak and shaky.

"It's not okay."

"What's wrong?" he pressed, reaching out to place his hand on her shoulder. His hand rose up and down with the motion of her shoulders. In between her shallow breathing, sobs began to emerge.

Noel raised her head, wiping a droplet from her cheek. I had learned that these droplets were called tears, and appeared sometimes when one was happy or sad. "We need to get out of here." Her voice cracked as she broke down into another fit of tears.

"What? Why?" Adam demanded, the familiar edginess creeping back into his voice.

"It's not safe here. They know. They're coming." Noel's words were rushed and difficult to understand.

"Who?" Adam asked.

"The City."

Noel's words sent chills throughout my body. I looked over to see Kim and Adam's reactions. Kim stood frozen, one hand at her side and the other beside her mouth. Adam looked as if someone had slapped him, then his expression turned angry.

"How?" he cried, standing up. "How did this happen?"

"I don't know!" Noel wailed, her entire body shaking. "But I saw them. And I heard them."

"Where?" Adam growled, desperate for answers.

Noel stopped blubbering long enough to respond. "Down a few blocks. They had some special lights on their car."

"How do you know they're coming here?" I asked.

"I was eavesdropping," Noel admitted, trying to dry her face with her jacket. The coarse, gray material made her face even more red. "They were talking about signs of insurgence outside of the car. And they mentioned this address."

Everyone in the room shared the same terrified look, exchanging glances while we waited for someone to take initiative. The silence was eerie, as if no one had any idea what to do.

"We've got to get out of here," Noel repeated. "Now."

"Where are we gonna go?" Patrick started.

"Do they know our names?" Kim asked. "What if it's too risky to go home?"

"How could they know our names?" Patrick retorted. "If they knew we were part of this, wouldn't we have already gotten in trouble?"

Adam shook his head. "I don't know. But I agree with Kim. If they somehow do have our names, they probably are already scoping out our apartments. I'm not going home."

Patrick looked worried. "Maybe we're over-reacting, guys."

"Do you want to take that chance?" Kim asked him.

Adam glanced over at me. "I guess now you get the action you were hoping for."

"What?" I exclaimed, confused. I was hoping for change, but getting people in trouble and forcing them to abandon their homes was not in the plans.

Ignoring me, Adam tried to address the whole group. Everyone was talking in low whispers or anxious voices, oblivious to Adam's voice. Raising his fingers to his lips, Adam let out a loud, shrill whistle. The voices quieted, and scared eyes focused on him.

"Okay guys, look. I'm not gonna lie to you. I have no idea what to do."

The room erupted back into a buzzing chatter until Adam let out another whistle.

"I do know one thing though," Adam continued.

111

"I'm not sticking around to see if I get caught. I'm not sure where I'm going, but it's gonna be as far away from here as possible. Anyone who wishes to come with me is welcome."

A quiet voice rose from the group. "I can't leave here, it's all I know." I couldn't place the girl's name, but her piercing hazel eyes and the terrified look behind them became embedded in my brain. The girl had joined the group as an escape, but when it came time to try and change her life, fear held her back. The time to make a decision was so short and we were under pressure; I wondered if I'd choose the same.

Adam nodded. "All right. I'm not sure if they'll catch you, but if they do, you won't disclose our names."

The girl shook her head. "Not if they torture me."

Adam nodded again, but I heard him mutter "bullshit" beneath his breath.

"Anyone who does want to come with me, meet me around back of the Tenth Street Warehouse. We can't go together; we can't draw any more attention to ourselves."

"What are you going to do from there?" Patrick inquired.

"I'll figure it out," Adam growled, zipping up his sweatshirt. "In case they do know our names or faces, lay low." He turned to Kim, waiting for a reaction.

"Of course I'm coming," Kim told him. "There's nothing for me here."

Kim's words echoed in my brain. *There's nothing for me here.* She was right. This city was nothing more than an empty hole. As long as I stayed here, nothing was going to change.

"I'm coming too," I announced.

Patrick nodded. "Me too."

Adam's neighbor, Griffin spoke in agreement. "What choice to we have but to take a chance?" I hadn't spoken much with Griffin, but he seemed strong.

A few other voices chimed in, declaring they would be leaving as well. Others remained silent, exchanging worried glances with one another.

Noel stood up and headed for the door leading towards the back of the building. "Well either way we've got to get out of here now." Without waiting to see if anyone followed, she thrust open the door and disappeared.

Patrick rushed to the bookshelf, trying to stuff as many books into his backpack as he could. I could see the pages tear as he packed them hurriedly. He let out a cry when he noticed the rips.

"Hey!" I approached him from behind and put my hand on his shoulder. "Patrick, you don't need them. They'll only weigh you down."

"You don't understand," Patrick wept. "These are mine. They're all that I have."

"But you know them all by heart, right?" I reminded him.

"It's not the same," he declared.

Out of the corner of my eye, I noticed the number of people in the room had already dissipated. Adam slipped through the door that Noel had exited through, leaving just Kim, Patrick, and I.

Patrick tried to neaten the books in his pack, zipping it up and sliding it over his shoulder. "I guess we should go." He ran his fingers over the books in the bookcase, pulling out a few more and stuffing them in the outside pocket.

"I have to go home," I blurted.

"It could be dangerous," Patrick said.

"I need to get Amber."

"Are you crazy?" Kim demanded, slapping me on the shoulder.

"Hey!" I protested. "What was that for?"

"You can't bring a dog!" she told me. "No matter where we go, that'll raise suspicion."

"Well I can't leave her," I cried out. "I love her!"

Kim seemed taken aback by my declaration, but when she regained her composure it was my turn to be taken off guard.

"Then I'm coming with you."

"You guys are crazy," Patrick said.

Kim grabbed my arm and pulled me towards the door. "I'll keep watch while you go inside. But we've got to go now."

"Good luck," Patrick called, his hand cemented to the bookshelf.

"We'll meet you there," I promised. He nodded, though he made no indication of moving. All I could do was hope that both of us kept the promise.

CHAPTER 8

"You've just got to get in and get out."

We were crouched across the street from my apartment, sheltered by a cluster of garbage cans. The street was still, no signs of life anywhere. Kim's hand rested on my arm, paralyzing me.

"You ready?" she pressed, her skin glowing despite the gloomy sky.

I nodded, swallowing the lump in my throat. "Yup."

"I'll meet you at the bottom of the fire escape," she told me.

"If something goes wrong—" I started.

"Nothing will go wrong," she stated firmly. "There's no one here, and no one is coming. Just get Amber, then we'll split up and go meet Adam."

"Okay." I waited for her to pull her hand from my arm but she didn't move. Though I didn't want to, I forced myself to stand up. "I'll be fast."

She nodded, saying nothing. I could feel her eyes follow me as I looked around and strolled across the street. I tried to act as casually as I could. Struggling to keep relaxed, I inhaled a deep breath. I reached the door of my apartment and ducked inside. As I ascended the stairs, I exhaled the air I'd been holding in. Relief flooded my body with the rush of oxygen, allowing me to increase my speed.

The dismal gray walls and sprawling navy blue carpet seemed unwelcoming as I reached the top of the stairs. I shivered and hurried to my door, eager to get Amber and get out of the building. I could hear whining on the other side of the wall as I moved my hand against the scanner, trying to steady my shaking fingers.

The beep and shrill voice that followed seemed deafening, though it couldn't have been any louder than the beep I was used to. Denied.

Huh? I'd never been rejected before. The angry sounding beep repeated itself, along with the monotone voice. Denied.

"Shit!"

The hallway began to spin as I turned my head around, unsure what to do. My heart beat almost as loud as Amber's nails. Sweat trickled down the corner of my forehead. I bit my lip, fighting the urge to cry out in frustration. Desperate, I wiped my clammy hands across my pants, trying to dry them of the sweat.

Taking a deep breath, I slowly raised my right hand to the scanner. Pressing my thumb against the cold black surface. After what seemed like an eternity, the machine let out a more familiar beep. Welcome.

Fumbling for the doorknob, I pushed open the door and stumbled into my apartment. Amber danced around in excitement, leaping up with her paws on my chest. I closed the door behind me and shushed her with a finger to my lips.

"We don't have much time." Amber stopped jumping and her eyes locked onto me, watching so intently that I could have sworn she understood every word. I knew I couldn't bring much with me. Looking around my apartment, I realized there wasn't much to bring; only Amber.

"All right. Come on Amber." I rushed to the far side of the room, unlocking the door that led to the fire escape.

I stepped out onto the metal, making a loud clanging noise. The bang seemed to scare Amber. She shrunk away from the door with her ears pressed back against her head.

"It's okay," I whispered, holding onto the railing carefully. I reached my other hand towards Amber, beckoning for her to follow me. "Don't worry, I won't let you fall."

Amber sat down and looked at me, a low whimper rising from deep in her throat. She sat firmly with no intention of listening to me.

I glanced down towards the ground. Kim's head was visible below. She stood leaning against the side of the building, looking up. I couldn't see the expression on her face, but I knew that we had to move.

Losing patience, I raised my voice. "Amber, come on! You go to the bathroom here every day."

Amber stared, cemented to the floor.

A clink sounded from beneath my boots. Looking down, I saw that Kim was throwing rocks up to get my attention. She motioned for me to hurry, pointing nervously towards the street.

I couldn't tell if anyone was around but I didn't want to stay around long enough to find out. I hopped back into my apartment and wrapped my

117

arms around Amber, bending down and carefully lifting her off the ground.

"Oof." I staggered, caught off guard by how heavy she was. She fidgeted nervously in my arms as I moved back towards the door, stepping warily onto the fire escape. Perhaps all the weights and garbage bags I'd lifted were finally paying off.

Leaning against the railing, I paused, unsure of what to do. There was no way I could make it down the stairs carrying Amber. I would trip and hurt both of us. The steps were too narrow for me to lead her down side by side. One of us would have to go first and the other would have to follow.

"All right." I grunted, squatting down on the landing. I lowered myself down as carefully as I could until the backs of my hand brushed the top of the metal. Squeezing as tightly against the railing as I could, I set Amber on the landing. As soon as she was out of my hands I reached over and slammed the door closed.

She whined and pawed anxiously at the metal, looking up expectantly. Her tail quivered between her legs, tugging at my heart.

"Come on Amber," I told her, gently nudging her with my knee. "We've got to get out of here."

I thought she wouldn't move, but to my surprise she slowly placed one of her paws on the step below us.

"Good girl!" I exclaimed, relief surging through my body. I glanced down at Kim, who was pacing back and forth across the pavement. Every few seconds she'd look up at me and motion to hurry up.

Amber cautiously stepped down onto the next step, and the next. She was moving painfully slow, but it was better than nothing. I followed behind her quietly and slowly, cautious not to scare her and make her stop.

After many slow careful steps and urgent hand movements from Kim, we completed our descent. Amber stepped eagerly onto the pavement, her whole energy changing. Her tail began to wag as she greeted Kim, sniffing her excitedly.

Kim held her hand out for Amber but her gaze was set on me. She raised a finger to her lips and moved closer to me. Her breath felt hot against my neck as she whispered in my ear. "There are City Officials out front. What's the best way out of here?"

Her words cut through my body like a blade. Panic-stricken, I glanced around anxiously. She was asking me where we should go. It was my responsibility. Of course I knew the area and she didn't, but I was terrified. I had no idea if I could get us away undetected.

Not risking any attention, I didn't respond. I grabbed Kim's hand and pulled her towards me. She stayed closed, moving quietly. Amber followed at our heels, remaining silent as well. I don't think she understood the situation, but perhaps she was feeding off of our urgent energy.

I peeked around the corner, spotting a slick, black car out front. It was longer than The City's vehicles I'd seen in the past. The sight of the car made me shiver. The tinted windows made it impossible to tell if there was anyone inside or not. I wondered if the Officials had already gone into the apartment looking for me or if one was keeping watch in the car. I longed to ask Kim for more information, but was too terrified to make a noise.

The front of the building seemed too risky, but I knew the back only led to a dead end. There was no

119

safe way out. I could be leading Kim and Amber into horrible danger.

Signaling them to follow, I started moving forward. I didn't know what would be around the corner, but I figured if we stayed out back we would be discovered for sure. To my relief, the coast seemed clear. Except for the car parked beside the sidewalk, everything looked exactly how we had left it when we arrived.

Filled with a new sense of hope, I quickened my pace. Dashing out onto the sidewalk, I made a sharp turn to the right. I broke into a run, checking over my shoulder to make sure Kim and Amber were following. They caught up to me quickly and we fell into a rhythm of motion.

My breathing quickly became labored and pain tore through my legs. I glanced over to see if Kim was getting tired as well, but her face was too hard to read. Amber seemed thrilled, enjoying the run as if it was a game. Every so often she would run in front of us, dance around, and then hurry to catch up with us.

I decided to focus on the street signs to distract myself from the burning pain in my chest. I counted each one as we passed by, getting closer to our destination.

"Come on, it's this way." I gasped for air and turned down the sidewalk, almost tripping over Amber as I swerved. Kim followed without a word. I could see the wariness in her eyes and hear her heavy breathing. I wanted to tell her we could slow down, but was too scared to stop. We continued running until I felt like I was going to throw up.

"Slow down!" I cried out, my voice hoarse. "I feel like I'm going to die."

"Me too," Kim exclaimed, letting out an unnatural sound that I realized was an attempt at laughter.

120

Despite the situation, she still managed to lighten the mood. "I thought you were fine and was thinking you were in really good shape."

I shook my head as we slowed to a jog. "No! I think the only one enjoying this is Amber."

Loping alongside me, Amber looked up at the sound of her name. Her tongue hung from her mouth, flopping around as she jogged. She was panting, but didn't seem to be struggling as she ran.

Kim stole a glance over her shoulder.

"Are they following us?" I asked.

"I don't see anyone," she replied.

"Phew!" I sighed with relief but didn't stop moving. We continued at a steady pace until we were within a few blocks of Tenth Street Warehouse.

As the towers of the warehouse came into view, we began walking. The back of my throat burned and my stomach churned. I had to stop and lean against the side of the building for a few minutes, fearing I would throw up.

"It's okay," Kim told me, breathing hard. "We made it."

Amber licked my fingers as I leaned against the brick, praying for the pain to go away. When I finally felt like I could walk again, I eased my body away from the side of the building.

"Where is everybody?" I wondered, looking around expectantly.

Kim shook her head. "I don't know. They must be hiding somewhere."

"Probably," I agreed, still panting slightly.

"Are you ready?" Kim inquired, holding her hand against the side of her head as if to keep it from drooping.

"I think so. Are you?"

121

"Well my lungs are a little scorched but I think I can walk," she joked, forcing a smile.

I smiled back despite the exhaustion and nervousness tearing apart my stomach. "I would carry you but I might drop you."

We stood for a moment, awkwardly attempting to ignore our nerves.

She stopped smiling and started towards the warehouse. "Let's go then."

We walked slowly, looking around carefully as we moved to see if we could spot any sign of the others. The clouds looming overhead seemed to be getting darker, warning of a possible storm.

I stopped dead in my tracks as I spotted an all too familiar black car on the other side of the building. Amber stumbled into the back of my legs, startled. I reached out and grabbed Kim's arm, unable to find my voice.

"What?" Kim asked me, unhappy that we had stopped.

I raised my finger to my lips and motioned with my other hand towards the vehicle. There was no mistaking it; it was The City's car. I wasn't sure if it was the same one that had been in front of my apartment, but even if it wasn't, it only signaled bad news.

Kim's eyes widened and I could see her whole body tense up. She looked back at me, unsure of what to do. I just stared at her, equally troubled. If we kept going toward the car, we'd be in grave danger. If we ran away, we'd be leaving the others to fend for themselves. We didn't even know if everyone had arrived yet, or if they had run away upon the car's arrival.

Cautiously, I turned down the alleyway neighboring

the warehouse. Kim followed, quietly urging Amber along. We hurried down the alley and around the rear of the building, stopping at the end.

I peered around the corner, spotting the back of the car. It was parked crooked and half on the sidewalk as if the driver had been careless or in a rush. There was no one around the outside of the car or front of the building.

Kim took a step forward, exposing herself. She moved quietly and carefully, pressing her boots against the pavement as if she was avoiding wet asphalt. She looked back at me, waiting to see if I would follow. I stood frozen, my arm wrapped around Amber's chest to make sure she wouldn't follow Kim. I couldn't bring myself to move forward. My head was spinning and I was overcome by nausea.

A loud bang broke the silence, causing Kim to dash back behind the cover of the building. My heart pounded so loud I was afraid that whoever made the bang would be able to hear it. I could hear voices from the side of the building. The words were too jumbled to make out, but the tone sounded angry.

Amber fidgeted against my hand, but I desperately held onto her. Her warm body did not comfort me as it usually did; I was merely holding her to restrain her. I was afraid if I let go that she would bolt with curiosity towards the noise and the car.

The voices got slightly louder and I struggled to hear what they were saying. They were gruff and masculine, the words spoken quickly. They were still too far away for me to understand.

Without realizing what I was doing, I craned my neck around the side of the building. The sight of The City Officials paralyzed me, but as much as I wanted to run I couldn't tear my eyes away.

The men wore long black leather coats cascading over big black boots, and large leather gloves, leaving only the skin of their faces exposed. The outfits were intimidating enough, but their faces stole my breath and refused to let go.

Their skin glowed an odd silver color, shining in the shadows. Slick black sunglasses hid their eyes, concealing whatever secrets stirred behind them. Tight black beanies were pulled down to the top of their sunglasses, brushing the top of their silvery ears. Light pink lips stretched across beneath their glossy noses, set in a terse straight line. Their appearance was strange and haunting, like nothing I'd ever seen.

One of the men thrust open the car's backseat door. Another held open the door of the building, and a familiar looking man stumbled out, his wrists tied behind his back. Another Official shoved him forward. His face was stained with slices of red, as if he had been smacked with something hard. The scarred face and hanging head made him almost indistinguishable, but when he raised his head briefly, I recognized him in an instant. Adam!

I heard Kim gasp behind me, and felt the tremors although we weren't touching. I wanted to let out a sound, a scream of rage, and run forward to help Adam, but something stopped me. It could have been fear, surprise, uncertainty, or sickness. I was so overwhelmed with a plethora of emotions that I couldn't pinpoint exactly what I was feeling. All I could do was stand and watch in horror as the Official shoved Adam into the car. Adam fell onto his stomach, the top half of his body disappearing into the vehicle. His legs dangled out in the air until the man pushed them inside.

Behind him followed a few others from our group,

each one wearing the same dejected expression. The Officials were rough and blunt, forcing our friends into the back of the car one by one. Every time another was propelled into the vehicle, I felt as if I was kicked in the stomach. I was furious that my friends were being abused. Furious at the Officials. Furious at The City. Most of all I was furious at myself for not making a move to help them. I yearned to do something, but the logical part of my brain stopped me. I was clearly no match for the Officials and would only risk exposing Kim and Amber if I tried to do anything.

It appeared that they had cleared everyone out of the building, as the stream of people stopped. Two of the Officials climbed into the back of the car and slammed the door, while two remained outside. The duo's lips moved quickly, their hands flying equally as fast. One opened the front door of the vehicle and slipped inside, while the other went back into the building. The car revved to a start but stayed parked, probably waiting for the last Official to return.

I turned around to face Kim, shocked by what I saw. Her normally calm and collected face was puffy, her face streaked with tears. She was hunched over Amber, hugging her tightly against her chest. Crouched on the ground, she looked extremely small and vulnerable. Part of me wanted to reach out and wrap my arms around her. I wanted to tell her that everything would be okay and we could fix it, but I couldn't bring myself to give her a false sense of hope.

Kim looked up at me with sad eyes, parting her lips slowly. "We have to do something." Her murmur was so soft that it was barely audible. It was snatched away as quickly as it came by a rush of wind.

The wind would normally cause me to shiver, but my entire body felt numb. Even the icy breeze couldn't touch me inside. I avoided Kim's gaze, turning to the large gray clouds overhead. I didn't have an answer for Kim. I didn't have a solution. I had no idea what we were supposed to do, and wondered if she for some reason expected me to. My brain was frozen and I couldn't think straight. I could barely think at all.

Amber nuzzled Kim's face and ran her tongue up her cheek, slowly thumping her tail. Kim collapsed over Amber's furry body, her torso shuddering as she began to cry once more. I couldn't stand there and watch her.

The familiar wave of nausea broke through the numbness in my body, making me double over from the pain. Kim and Amber blurred before my eyes, the back of the building and the garbage pails spinning. Staggering over to one of the silver metal pails, I reached to open the lid. My fingers slipped as my stomach heaved, demanding me to release what was inside. I fell to my knees, my body forcing me to throw up. Again and again my stomach turned over until it was empty. Even when there was nothing else it still heaved, yearning for the relief of pouring out my insides. Sweat trickled down my face like raindrops on a building.

I felt a hand on my back as the space between the heaves became longer. Kim rubbed my shirt with one hand, leaning over and wrapping her free arm around the front of my torso. I allowed myself to weaken and fall into her arms, ignoring the twinge of embarrassment flickering in the back of my mind. It wasn't important. Nothing was important anymore.

The heaves gradually dissipated, the nauseous

126

feeling floating away from my body. Though I no longer felt sick, I still felt horrible. I wanted to scream, cry, kick and hit. I wanted to release all of the anger and sadness and hopelessness, sending it flying into the air to be taken away by the wind. Instead, I leaned against Kim's arm and allowed the numbness to return to my body. It swept through my blood like ice water, starting from the tips of my toes and flowing up through my skull. Masking all of my feelings would have to do for now. I couldn't handle them; I had no energy left.

"Let's go after them." Kim's warm breath tickled the edge of my ear, her voice serious.

Her words startled me, causing me to free myself from her grip so that I could turn around and face her. "What?"

"Let's go after them," Kim repeated, as if it was as casual a statement as asking where the next stop on the garbage route was. The tears had stopped pouring from her eyes, her face wearing a darker expression. A recognizable fire blazed behind her eyes, burning through me.

The flames spiraled through the air, dusting themselves across the top of my head. The coolness that had arrived with the numbness had dissipated and my face felt hot. There was an expectance in her eyes; one that I couldn't follow through on. She expected me to come with her, chasing the Officials.

"We don't have a choice," she hissed. I must have shown my thoughts on my face, because she seemed to spit the words at me. I still had difficulty hiding my emotions, no matter how hard I tried.

"What are we going to do?" I struggled for words, unsure what to say.

"We can figure it out when we get there," she

replied.

I shook my head at her. "We can't beat them."

Fire flashed at me, her eyes narrowing. "Weren't you the one desperate to take action? The one who wanted to actually do something? To rebel against The City?"

I hung my head, struggling to speak once more. "Adam was right. We're no match for them."

"We don't even know exactly who *they* are!" Her voice was exasperated, the corners of her lips tipping downwards into a frown. "How can you say we're beaten if we don't even know what we're up against?"

"We have no plan of action, Kim," I protested. "We know nothing of The City, except for the fact that it controls us. We don't question it, we don't mess with it. Or this happens!"

"So what do you want to do?" Kim's voice was louder now, making me fear the men inside the car would hear her.

"Shh!" I whispered, peering around the corner. The car was still, showing no signs of activity. Taking cover behind the building once more, I faced Kim. "I don't know."

"Exactly!" Kim told me, lowering her voice but not ridding it of the anger. "They were at your house! They know our names. We can't pretend this didn't happen and return to our lives, if you could even call what we were doing living."

I opened my mouth to counter Kim's words, but nothing came out. She was right. Life as we knew it was over.

"Either we stay here and wait to get caught, or we go with them and make an attempt to save the others." She crossed her arms across her chest, waiting for my response.

The words that came out of my mouth next surprised me. "So what are we going to do?"

A smile crossed her lips. "I've seen these cars operate before. I know that as long as they're unlocked you can open the trunk."

I gasped in shock. "You're suggesting that we stow away in the trunk?"

She nodded. "That's as far as I have planned, but how else can we expect to follow and keep up with them?"

"You're crazy!" I told her.

"Do you have a better idea?"

I shook my head, remaining silent.

"Okay." Kim looked around the edge of the building. "We don't have much time. The Official's been inside for a while. Let's get this over with."

"Wait! What about Amber?" I ran my hands through her fur. I couldn't leave her. I'd risked so much to be reunited, and would give almost anything to keep her safe.

Kim stared at me. "She could blow our cover."

"She won't."

"She's a dog; she isn't as smart as you think she is."

"She is."

Kim bit her lip, letting out a frustrated sigh. "You're not budging on this. I guess you two are a joint deal."

I nodded, patting Amber's head. I didn't possess as much confidence in her behavior as I appeared, but wasn't about to leave her. Hopefully she would rise up on the pedestal I had created and be no trouble.

"All right. Come on." Without waiting to see if I was following, Kim stepped out into the open behind the car. Taking a deep breath, I started after her, Amber sticking to the side of my leg like glue.

Kim hurried behind the vehicle and ducked down. I

followed her lead, crouching behind the large black tires. She raised herself slightly to get a better view at the trunk. I craned my neck to try and see what she was doing, in case I could use the knowledge to my advantage in the future.

She flicked her fingers over the screen, pressing down on a thin white button besides the sensor. The trunk produced a high-pitched hissing sound, causing me to cringe. It slowly rose a few inches, leaving enough space for Kim to move her fingers underneath. She raised the trunk slowly, motioning for me to get in.

I squeezed through the small opening despite the trepidation beating against my insides. I rolled over onto my back in a failed attempt to make myself more comfortable. The trunk was small, dark, and reeked of plastic. Amber leapt in after me, squeezing against my legs. Kim came last, pulling the trunk closed. The space was now pitch black. It felt smaller and the air tasted stale. I wanted to cry and jump back outside, but I forced my body to freeze. I told myself not to panic, but feared if I tried to calm myself with a deep breath that I would use up precious air.

The vehicle shook slightly as a door slammed, the engine growing louder. We began to roll forward. This was it. The car was moving. We'd made it inside just in time. A few seconds later and our friends would have been gone forever; a distant memory.

A million thoughts flew through my brain, but I tried to keep calm by focusing on Amber's warm body pressed against my legs. She remained quiet and still despite the hot, cramped space. Her presence comforted me as always, but it didn't take away all the fear. Terror dripped through every inch of my veins, a potent poison.

130

I fumbled in the darkness with my hand, feeling Kim's arm beside me. I slid my hand down her arm, stopping when I reached hers. Intertwining my fingers, she gave me a reassuring squeeze. I held onto her tightly, too afraid to let go. She strengthened her grip, slowly stroking my sweating skin.

The car accelerated faster and faster until it leveled out at a steady speed. The heat was becoming smothering; the tightness of the trunk unbearable, the darkness suffocating. I closed my eyes, trying to imagine myself in another place. I opened them once more, but saw no difference in my surroundings. I couldn't make out a thing.

I wasn't sure where we were going, or what we would encounter there. Maybe I was crazy for stowing away in the trunk of one of The City's cars. I was definitely mad. But thinking of Patrick and the others in the back of the car with the officials gave me the courage that I needed. We were going to help them. When we reached our destination, my life would be forever transformed. In fact, my life was already changed. Whether it was for better or worse, it was too soon to tell. All I could do now was hold onto Kim and wait.

CHAPTER 9

The warm sun kissed the corners of my cheeks, the emerald green grass tickling my palms. Humidity hung in the breezeless air. The land around me lay barren and still, but it was peaceful. There were no loud noises, no blustery winds. It was just me, watching the puffy white clouds meld into one another in the pastel blue sky. It wasn't perfect, but I was happy. I could close my eyes and dream. The quiet was so deafening, so wonderful, so welcome.

The silence was broken, but I refused to open my eyes despite the sound. The voice called my name, louder this time, a hint of agitation rising in its edges.

"Vic."

I buried my face in the grass, the pleasant aroma of the blades drifting through my nostrils. Pressing against the earth, I felt as if we were one. The dirt was gritty against my lips, but as long as I held them tightly together it did not bother me. I wanted to sink into the ground, drift below the surface and disappear for a while. No matter how close I became to the earth, there was a barrier. There was always an obstruction. Something standing between me and the things that made me

132

happy. I was a puppet on a string, being pulled back whenever I got too close to bliss.

"Vic!"

The voice rang in my ears, shattering the blissful experience for good. As hard as I tried, the earth refused to become penetrable. My body was a separate entity now and forever. Despite the angry voice, I couldn't bring myself to move. I needed to savor every second I had left. If I pressed hard enough, perhaps I could ingrain the sensations into my head. The warm, the sticky, the tickly, the grainy, the smelly. This was perfectly imperfect. If I could catch it, store it away, save it for a rainy day, this moment would not be wasted like all the others.

"Hey!" A hand tugged at my shoulder, forcing me to roll over onto my back. Fresh air flooded my lungs. Despite being easier to breath, it was not wonderful. My eyes remained closed, my arms tucked tightly at my sides. I didn't open my eyes; I couldn't. I knew what was waiting for me. I knew who would be standing above. If I moved, I knew what would follow.

I tried to keep still, tried not to whimper. There was no chance of disappearing into the grass. I had nowhere to hide, but a tiny part of my brain had convinced me that if I kept my eyes closed, I would be harder to see. Harder to pierce.

The hand clamped over my shoulder again. I could feel the hot breath inches away from my face. "Why don't you listen to me huh?"

"Please," I stammered.

A laugh erupted from above, the cackling sound resounding through my bones. The noise was loud and strange. I knew it was a laugh, but it wasn't human. There was only one thing that could make a noise so horrible, so haunting. It was far from a human. It was a monster.

"Vic!"

The soft voice shattered the images flashing through my brain, shaking me out of the nightmare.

My eyelids fluttered open, pupils flicking back and forth. I couldn't see a thing.

"I can't see! I'm blind!" I cried. The darkness seemed to swallow me, clasping me in its clutches so I could not break free.

"Shh! We're in the trunk, remember?" I recognized Kim's voice in the blackness, holding onto the ounce of reassurance that accompanied it.

"Oh." The events of the day came flashing back to me, brief and terrifying patches of proceedings. Noel told us we were discovered. The City's men stormed my apartment. The Officials took our friends. Kim, Amber, and I stowed away.

"You fell asleep," Kim told me. "But the car stopped a while ago."

"I did?" That would explain the grogginess in my head. Or perhaps it was from the intense heat of the tiny space. Either way, it was an unpleasant sensation. My body was cramped, uncomfortable, and lightheaded. I could feel Amber shift her position against my leg, her tail thumping lightly across my calf.

"What did I miss?"

"Not much. I heard them leave. It's quiet here, but it's still impossible to tell where we are or if we're alone."

"How much longer do we have to stay in here?" I wondered aloud.

"That's entirely up to us," she replied. "Any time we choose to open the trunk, it'll be a risk."

"So I suppose now's as good a time as any?" The temperature was taking a toll on me. My brain was foggy, and I feared drifting off once more. I couldn't resume the nightmare. It was more than a terrifying dream; it was a memory. Something I had tried to push out of my head. Something I'd successfully forgotten until now.

"Right. But I need a light. Do you have one on your watch?"

I wasn't sure how Kim remembered I was wearing a watch when I hadn't even recalled myself. I moved my arm that housed the watch, discovering with surprise that my hand was still intertwined with hers. Her delicate fingers were as clammy and sweaty as mine. Her thumb rested against the edge of my wrist and the watch.

"Yes," I said. I was reluctant to let go of her hand, hesitant to illuminate the space and shine reality on the situation. She made the decision for me.

Slipping her hand out of mine, she slid her fingers to my watch. Fumbling for a few seconds, she unhooked the band. The skin on my wrist took in a breath of the stale air, sticky with sweat from the rubbery material.

"Which button is it?" she inquired.

"Top right."

The flash of blue light was momentarily blinding, though any other time the glow would have been insufficiently dim. I had to close my eyes, slowly opening them and allowing them to adjust to the brightness. I wasn't sure how long we'd been in shadows, but it seemed like an eternity. Though I didn't enjoy the inky blackness, I had become used to to it.

Kim shined the light on the far side of the trunk, the area we had entered. Even when I squinted, it was too difficult to see what she was looking at. It must have been hard for her as well since she moved away from me and closer to the edge. She fumbled around, running her fingers against the metal.

135

"Do you know how to open it?" I demanded, unable to contain my impatience.

"No," she admitted.

The words struck like a blow to my chest, forcing me to close my eyes again. I longed for a breath of new, clean air, but didn't know if it would be possible. Counting backwards in my head, I tried to keep myself from panicking.

Were we going to be stuck in here forever?

"I found it!" she exclaimed triumphantly.

"What? I thought you didn't know how to open it?" I cried out.

She snickered slightly. "I was just testing how strong your heart was."

"Hey!" I retorted angrily, not in the mood for jokes.

"You're gonna need to be strong now," she said seriously. "So am I. Are you ready?"

"Ready as I'll ever be."

"Right," she nodded, her voice cracking slightly. I could tell that she was just as terrified as I was, no matter how confident she tried to appear.

I watched her fingers twist a small red rod in the corner of the trunk. She turned it as far as it could go, pressing it with her thumb. The trunk let out the same hissing noise as when we had opened it the first time. I flinched, knowing that if anyone was nearby they would hear the noise and investigate. Clutching Amber tightly, I held her against my leg. She didn't try to bolt as the trunk opened, but I didn't want to take any chances.

I could feel Kim's already tense body freeze beside me. We waited for what seemed like years for the trunk to stop hissing. When it ceased, a crack of light lit up the trunk. The opening couldn't have been more than two inches wide, but it still managed to

136

banish the shadows of the space.

I exchanged a glance with Kim in the dim light. Her eyes were fiery, but I could still sense the fear. When I had first met her, she seemed invincible. She was a hard rock that nothing could move and nothing could touch. Now I realized she had imperfections. Knowledge of her flaws only made me more attracted to her. No longer did she stand atop a pedestal; now she seemed within my reach. I wasn't sure if she had deliberately tried hiding her emotions from those around her, or if that she was so used to hiding in public that it had become her normal. My mind returned to the night in the dump when I had saved her life. The feeling of gratitude she had directed at me, letting me know she appreciated me. That she had needed me, and she wasn't above me. The way she had wrapped her arms around me, filling my body and soul with pleasure. I longed to repeat that moment.

Fingers flicking against my wrist snapped me out of my head. Kim was staring at me, waiting for me to give her some kind of sign. I shrugged at her, not sure what she wanted me to do. She nodded at the gap. She wanted to open the trunk more.

My heart pounded in my chest. We had no idea what was outside; it could be nothing or it could be everything. It must have been a few minutes since she had made the small opening. No one had come running to the car to investigate. There were no noises audible to my ears. The only thing we could do was open it further. I nodded back at her, gritting my teeth in anticipation.

Her arms moved towards the opening, shaking slightly. She slipped her fingers into the light and with one fluid motion pushed the trunk up.

137

Momentarily blinded by the overflow of light, I blinked rapidly. The brightness was stunning after what seemed like hours of darkness. I moved my free hand to my face and rubbed my eyes, trying to help them adjust faster. After a few more seconds of blinking and rubbing, shapes began to materialize.

We were in some kind of large room with bright white walls and a towering pearl ceiling. A black vehicle identical to ours was parked behind us, flanked by two other matching cars. The back wall was lined with shelves and cabinets overflowing with various kinds of tools. A large, closed wooden door stood in the corner, partially blocked by a wheeled cart covered in more tools.

Seeing no signs of life in the room, I dared to move. My legs and arms felt stiff and uncomfortable. I struggled to sit up, Kim following my lead.

I swiveled my head around the room, seeing no one. A large white door stretched the opposite side of the room. The door was big enough to allow three cars through; it must have been where we had entered. The room had to be some kind of garage. There were two matching black cars on each side of the car we were in as well, making six in total. The floor was covered in dirt and mud.

Amber stretched beside me and hopped out of the car without warning, dropping to the floor like a sack of potatoes.

"Amber!" I yelped, cringing at her lack of grace. No one came rushing from one of the corners or doors, allowing me to exhale with relief. For the moment, the three of us were alone. Hopefully it would stay that way.

Kim followed Amber, hitting the floor much more softly. I climbed out next, closing the trunk delicately behind us.

"Don't touch any of the cars in case they have alarms," Kim advised, slipping past the car to our right and leaning against the far wall.

I squeezed between the cars and stood beside Kim. Amber bounded along after us, rubbing her fluffy body against my leg. I ruffled the fur on top of her head, looking to Kim for guidance regarding what to do next.

"What?" she asked, her arm resting on her hip.

"Nothing," I murmured.

Kim's hard expression softened. "I don't know where to go from here," she admitted.

"Well . . ." I glanced around the room, doing a one-eighty to make sure I had scanned every corner. "There doesn't seem to be anything in here. So we can either hide in here for a while and try to think of a plan, or go through one of those two doors."

Kim laughed softly. "I don't think I'm going to come up with any better plan than that."

I shook my head, shoving my hands in my pockets. "Me neither."

"I have no idea where we are . . ." Kim continued, pacing back and forth. Her boots crunched softly on the dirt-covered floor, leaving marks where her shoes had been.

"Somewhere in The City," I answered lamely.

"Perhaps their headquarters, or some kind of meeting place for Officials," Kim mused, her eyes continually moving across the room.

"Do you think the others are here too?" I inquired, wondering if she had heard information I had missed while I was asleep.

She nodded. "I heard them take them out of the car. There were a lot of doors slamming, and a lot of orders to obey. I'm guessing they went through that door, since the big door would have made louder noise."

She started towards the door, checking over her shoulder to see if I was following. I hesitated, shifting my feet slightly.

"What if they're on the other side of the door?"

"Who?" she asked, her voice sounding nervous.

"The Officials . . . Adam . . . Patrick . . . anyone!" I blurted, throwing my hands up in the air. "What are we supposed to do if we run into anyone? We have no idea where we are or who is here or what we're doing! So what if we find the others? How are we supposed to get them out of here? We don't even know where *here* is. This place is probably crawling with City Officials. There's no way we can get the others and get out of here without anyone noticing. And we don't even know how to get home. We can't even go home!" My face felt hot as the words rolled off my tongue.

Kim stared at me, looking hurt. She looked at her feet, then to Amber, and back at me. "So are you saying we came here for nothing? You would have rather stayed back behind that building hiding for the rest of your life?" Her words were soft and gentle. There was no anger backing them up. She sounded tired, her expression matching her unusually quiet voice.

"No," I murmured, rubbing my face with my hands. "I would have never been able to live with myself. I think The Officials followed us. It was our fault that the others got caught."

She shook her head, walking slowly towards me. She lifted her hand and rested it on my shoulder. "No, you can't think like that. We'll never know if

140

that's true or not, but thinking about it is a waste of time."

"I'm just scared," I blurted. Embarrassed, I avoided her eyes and focused on the floor.

"So am I," she admitted, her hand slipping from my shoulder. "But it doesn't matter. We're here now and we can't change what happened."

I buried my face in my hands again, trying to escape the hopeless feeling that was smothering me. I was not prepared for this. I was just a lowly garbage man who should have stuck to garbage collecting. The dreams for change and a world where relationships were welcome were all nice and fluffy, but virtually unrealistic. I was in over my head, and now Kim was expecting me to live up to what I had said. Change was what I wanted, but when it came down to it, I was just a coward.

"We're here now," Kim whispered. "What have we got to lose? There's nothing to go back to. There's only one direction to go."

Despite the overwhelming sickness building in the pit of my stomach, I nodded. "All right. Let's go."

Kim forced a smile, sliding her shaky hand into mine. A shock of electricity shot up my arm, awakening my entire being. Squeezing her hand tightly, we started towards the door. Amber trailed behind us, her nails clicking on the tile floor.

Upon reaching the door, Kim stopped. "We can't bring her. She'll blow any chance we have of cover."

"We can't just leave her here," I protested.

"It was stupid to bring her here," Kim pressed. "I know that she's important to you, but it's risking both her life and ours. It's not fair to anyone."

"Fine, so let's split up," I retorted, angry at her suggestion. I let go of her hand and instead placed it on Amber's head, her tail wagging swiftly in response. "There could be a hundred people behind this door, or there could be no one. Either way I'm not leaving her."

"There comes a point when being stubborn turns into stupidity," she snapped shortly, the soft look gone from her eyes. "You have to be realistic."

"Realistic?" I cried out, perhaps a little too loudly. "What is reality anymore? My life has done a complete one-eighty in the past two weeks. Everything I thought I knew has changed. And if I learned anything, it's that I really don't know anything."

"I can't go by myself," Kim objected, her voice breaking.

"Then I guess it's the three of us." My decision may have been rash, but no matter what happened on the other side of the door I couldn't abandon Amber.

Pressing my ear to the wood, I heard nothing. The shining gold doorknob felt cool to touch as I wrapped my hand around it. Turning it slowly, I glanced at Kim and Amber and cracked open the door.

Peering through the small opening, I frowned. All I could see was the color white; it was too narrow to make out any objects. I pushed the door open another inch, then another, until I could begin to make out my surroundings. The door led to a long hallway with intense white walls and a sprawling silver carpet. Bright fluorescent lights illuminated the corridor, covering the closed doors lining the hallway in an eerie glow. From my line of vision it appeared deserted.

Though my limbs felt like putty, I pushed the door open the rest of the way and revealed the passageway.

Kim tensed beside me as the door flew open. The hallway was empty. It was long, with doors spaced several feet apart on each side and another door at the opposing end.

I forced myself to step out of the garage. My boots sunk into the soft plush carpet and the intense light made me squint. Amber followed, squishing against my left hip. Kim hesitated before moving beside us. She closed the door quietly, leaving us exposed in the hall.

We started down the hallway silently, unsure of where to go. The doors were labeled with large silver roman numerals across the front. The symbols may have meant something to someone who lived or worked here, but they were useless to us. Reaching the end of the hallway, we stopped at the door labeled five.

I turned around, looking to see if there was something I missed. The hallway hadn't changed; the only things behind me were five doors and the sparkling carpet. Looking to Kim for help, I received a shrug.

"Pick a door?" she murmured, her voice barely audible. The weakness I'd recognized earlier had returned. She was scared, and rightfully so.

Biting my lip, I surveyed the five doors. Aside from the numbers, they were all exactly the same. There was no telling where they led; we had no choice but to leave our fate up to luck.

I leaned against door number five, straining my ears to hear what was on the other side. The door was either too thick for sound to penetrate or wherever it led to was silent. Closing my eyes and taking a breath to regain composure, I gripped the handle. I opened my eyes and in turn opened the door.

The wood was heavy, swinging suddenly open and destroying my attempt to be discrete. Flying to the side, it exposed the contents of the space along with our pathetic trio. I cringed at the sight, wishing I had picked another door.

The room was large and circular with a lofty ceiling and large square windows. An elaborate silver chandelier dangled from the ceiling, shimmering in the sunlight. Tall white bookcases lined the walls, overflowing with piles of different colored books. The silver carpeting matched the chandelier. It was beautiful and spectacular, but what stood in the center made my heart stop.

A large white desk was placed in the middle of the room, covered in papers, a large computer, and a small silver desk lamp. The ticking of a clock exacerbated my nerves. The woman seated behind the desk in a large silver swivel chair looked up from the papers.

Her fiery red curls dangled past her shoulders, framing her porcelain-like face. Her skin was smooth and pale, her dark emerald eyes brimming with a wild look that could only be described as hunger. At first her bright red lips were set in a frown, but the corners twitched up into a smile. Her mouth opened, revealing two rows of perfectly straight, shining white teeth. A bright red tongue slipped out between them, sliding slowly over her deep red lips. She paused for a moment and leaned back in her chair, her eyes scanning us as if we were specimens under a microscope.

Her voice startled me, its tone deep and chilly. It was dark and uninviting, sending shivers scraping up and down my spine.

"Why hello there." She snapped her fingers and the

door slammed shut behind us, making me jump.

Instinctively, I turned to flee. Pulling at the door handle, I realized my efforts were futile. Somehow she had locked the door with a mere snap. I twisted slowly back to face her, noticing that Kim and Amber were frozen in place.

"Don't be afraid," she murmured, her words sliding out of her mouth like a snake. "Stay a while! I'm interested to learn how you made it past security."

Amber whined and looked at me, her tail lowered between her legs.

The woman laughed shrilly, making me shudder once more.

"Besides. It's always fun to play with your prey before you eat it, don't you agree?"

Chapter 10

"Please, have a seat." She motioned to two large silver chairs in front of her desk, extending her pale arm towards us. Her fingers stretched long and thin with bright red nails that matched her lips.

Kim turned to me, remaining rooted to her spot, her expression emotionless despite the situation.

I opened my mouth to speak but no words came out. My tongue felt like sandpaper in my dry jaws. Paralyzed next to the door, I stared at Kim. After seeing no change in her face, I looked back at the woman. Her gaze flitted back between the two of us, a smirk spreading across her mouth.

"Any day now." A hint of impatience rose in the woman's voice. The voice sounded eerily familiar, but I didn't remember meeting the woman before. She placed her fingers on the desk, tapping her claws to the rhythm of the clock.

To my surprise, Kim turned away from me and started toward the desk. She moved one of the chairs over and sunk slowly into it. Sitting with her back to me in the enormous seat, Kim looked tiny for the second time that day. I felt an instinctive need to protect her. Summoning ever ounce of courage in my body, I padded over to the open chair and sat down.

The cushion was soft and welcoming. Unlike my chair at home with the springs poking at my bottom, it felt like I was sitting on a cloud. Flecks of sparkles twinkled on the velvety material, mesmerizing me for a few seconds.

"What is that?" the woman demanded, narrowing her fierce eyes.

I followed her gaze, my eyes landing on Amber. She was sticking to me like a shadow, sitting down beside my feet. I attempted to speak, but terror had stolen my voice.

"No matter." The woman let out a sigh and stopped drumming her fingers. She placed her hands together and rested her chin on them. "We'll deal with it later."

A wave of anger rushed through me as she said the word "it." Amber had a gender, and a name. I longed to speak up in defense, but my voice refused to cooperate. All I could do was stare across the desk at the woman. She was even more intimidating up close.

"Now." The sinister smile crept back across the woman's lips. "I suppose we should get to know each other a bit. My name is Angel. And you are . . ."

After a few seconds hesitation, Kim spoke. Her voice sounded even and strong, as if part of the fire had returned to her being. "I'm Kim. And this is Vic."

Angel nodded, her smile widening. "Pleasure. Now, what brings you to my humble abode?"

Kim glanced at me, as if she was unsure of what to say. I wanted to help her but I was just as lost as she was, if not more. If we told Angel about our friends, it could endanger all of us. They were probably captive here somewhere, but if we told her of our connection to them it could further complicate things.

Tired of waiting for an answer, Angel spoke up once more, her voice oozing with fake sweetness. "Come on, I don't bite."

"Where are we?" Kim demanded, skirting the question.

Taken aback by her spunk, Angel remained quiet for a moment. A low laugh rose up from her throat, spilling out of her lips. The more I stared at them, the redder they seemed. The color was identical to fresh blood pouring from an open wound. After she finished her cackle, Angel cleared her throat.

"Well, I suppose I can tell you since you won't be leaving. You're in The City's Center; The Ring." Her eyes lit up as she spoke, her voice laced with an inhuman excitement.

"What is that?" Kim wondered, avoiding Angel's wild eyes.

Angel laughed once more. "You mean you don't know what it is? You've gotten all the way here without knowing your destination? And the fact that you are together is beyond suspicious. I would think such rebels as yourselves would have a little more knowledge under your belt, no?" She focused on me, the sneer returning. "And what's wrong with this one, is he a mute?"

Her condescending tone made my building anger bubble over, releasing my voice from its prison chamber.

"I'm not mute," I hissed.

"Oh, so he can speak. Goody!" Angel brushed a curl out of her face, tucking it behind her ear. A flash

148

of silver caught my eye. Her ear was covered in glittery silver objects, a hoop and a line of circles and stars creeping up the side of it. She noticed me staring and snickered. "You really don't know anything, do you?" She pushed her hair back to give me a better view at her ear. "It's called jewelry. Earrings to be specific. Of course they're banned. Something so shiny and beautiful might attract another person."

I fidgeted in my seat, the cushions feeling suddenly uncomfortable. Angel's voice had given my body a permanent chill. Goosebumps spread across my arms and the hair on my neck stood up. Without looking, I felt Amber lie down and rest her head on my feet. Regret jabbed at the corners of my mind. It might have been safer to leave Amber on the streets to fend for herself.

"The Ring is where everything important happens. All of The City's decisions are made here. Well, my decisions." Angel waited for a reaction, but noting our silence, she continued speaking. "My Officials report back to me on how everything is going out there in my kingdom. Normally things run smoothly, but of course there are always those select few who can't seem to follow the rules." She stared at me and giggled, as if she got some kind of sick pleasure out of making me squirm.

"You mean people who figure out that it is possible to form real relationships?" Kim growled, trying to sound brave.

Angel stopped laughing and glared at Kim. "Something like that."

"Did you create the LVs?" I asked curiously, surprised at the sound of my own voice.

Angel shook her head, causing her jewelry to shimmer in the light. "If only I could take credit for

149

such a wondrous creation. Of course it was my idea, but I would be lying if I said I discovered how to make them. That was carried out by my scientists in the lab. The plan was nearly flawless, except when little slugs like you decide to stop taking the vitamins."

"Plan?" My voice sounded shaky and soft, threatening to fail me once more.

She clapped her hands together, her eyes lighting up. "Oh my favorite thing to do; tell others of my genius experiment. Sit back and relax. This will take a few minutes. Hmm, let's see ... it all started when my parents were killed in a car crash. Parents are the people who create you and bring you into this world. I was devastated, and furious at the same time. They had no right to just leave me on my own at fourteen years old. I lived in a few foster homes after that, all of them wretched. Of course you don't know what a foster home is, but it's a place where another family took in a kid for a period of time. After finding a boyfriend, or a companion, at eighteen, my faith in relationships became somewhat restored. After two years he broke up with me." Her expression turned to angry, and her voice sinister. "The pain was unbearable, unending, and ultimately unnecessary. This was the second time in my life that I had been abandoned and left alone. That's when I decided relationships were useless. After getting rid of my ex, I got to work plotting out my idea; a world with no relationships. Everything would be simple; people would work, eat, sleep, and there would be no complications. Paradise."

"You built this whole world?" I breathed, unable to hide the awe in my voice.

She nodded. "Yes, with some help from my

laboratory of course. I pitched the idea to some special, powerful people, and they agreed. Of course you wouldn't know, but there used to be a different kind of government. Something called a democracy. I knew the government would never support such a radical change; they were too comfortable. So I got some inside access, and proceeded to carry out my government takedown. It wasn't that difficult, the world was crumbling anyway. Disease, starvation, overpopulation, destruction, and war were raging. My plan wasn't as broad as I liked, and I only was able to canvas something previously called a state for my experiment. But nonetheless, it was something to work with. The people were left confused and terrified. They needed a leader, someone to step up to the plate and tell them what to do. How to live their lives. They needed me."

"First order of business was to cut off all contact with the outside states. Easily done; I was gaining more and more intrigued scientists to execute my plan. They constructed an impenetrable barrier that I placed around my empire: The City. The invisible fence they made would cause anyone who came within a hundred feet of it to be electrocuted and inevitably killed. The voltage is higher than that of a lightning bolt; it's impossible to survive. After shutting off my area from the rest of society, I decided the best way to get the full result of my experiment would be to not tell the lab rats of my plans. Devising "life vitamins" that would extend the lifespan and increase health was my idea. People are so gullible. Of course the vitamins have no affect on an individual's health. Instead, they prevent one from having any inclination to associate with another living creature on an emotional level. People ate up the

151

vitamins like candy, literally. It took months before everyone took them, but after enacting the laws against relationships, everything really began to fall into place. Finally, they had structure once more. People need structure to survive. The laws did not seem far-fetched with the diminished desire for any type of relationship."

"Of course, there was the matter of destroying the relationships that already were in place. The pills did a decent job of that, making parents and children, brothers and sisters, husband and wives feel numbness towards each other. But it wasn't enough for me. I couldn't risk sabotaging my experiment; I wanted a clean state. Recruiting an army of obedient, power hungry individuals, I executed the massacre. It was all for science of course; but I must say it was quite fun." Angel winked at us, taking a deep breath and a pause before resuming talking again.

"I got rid of the elderly; they knew too much. Sending my workers to observe all of the adults, I eliminated those who could potentially threaten the success of my research. I decided it was still too risky, and The City was purged of anyone over the age of eighteen. With a new generation of dulled minds to carry out the experiment, I created schools. Scientists created electronic teachers that brainwashed the children into believing this was how things are meant to be. After finishing the school, the older children were sent to jobs to set the wheels in motion. Since The City stands on its own, all production and natural resource collection must be done inside our walls. They were put into fields that would keep The City up and running. Professions with too much interaction between people were replaced by technology. The children were kept in homes with other children and one of my workers until they were old enough to live on their own. In addition to the life vitamins, weekly injections to prevent feelings associated with living creatures were administered due to the proximity of the children with others."

"Once all relationships and chances of ties forming were abolished, there arose the question of how to repopulate The City. I decided to use the test tube method, requiring all males to donate their sperm. We randomly select the mothers. I will admit, the mother and child relationship is the hardest to break. Along with the vitamins, and injections, the mothers are pumped with IVs full of drugs. Even with the combination of the three emotion stoppers, some mothers still feel something towards the child when it is born. As soon as the child is born, it is taken to the baby ward in the hospital and taken care of by robots. After they are in good enough shape to leave the hospital, they are placed in homes where they are taken care of by appointed workers. A highly difficult and risky job, my workers take care of dozens of children in the same house until they can live on their own. The worker only teaches the children until they can clean and cook on their own. Then they have minimal interactions with the child."

"That's insane!" The words slipped out of my mouth like water before I could control myself.

Instead of getting angry, Angel flashed me a shining smile. "Thank you!"

"How did you pull all of that off?" Kim inquired.

"I have thousands of workers, loyal followers, and scientists. They do as I say; they get rewarded, simple as that. It took many years and a lot of hard work, but I'm pleased to say this is year forty of the experiment."

"How long do you plan on forcing people to live like this?" Kim growled, leaning forward in her chair.

"I'd say the testing is going quite swimmingly. I someday wish to expand this to the rest of the country, and maybe one day the world. Of course that could take centuries," Angel replied.

"You've already been doing the experiment for forty years . . ." I started, unsure of how to ask the question that was tapping on the tip of my tongue.

As if reading my mind, Angel stated, "You're wondering how I appear so youthful and beautiful? I have some of the smartest scientists of all time working for me. If they can discover how to stop humans from forming relationships with each other when humans are naturally social beings, they surely can discover the fountain of youth. And they did. At least, for me. The procedure is too expensive and time consuming to be administered to anyone outside of its creators and myself. I have the body of a thirty year old, and as long as I keep getting the procedure, I will for many years to come."

"Are you saying you can live forever?" I gasped.

She shrugged. "We'll see." Sitting back in her chair, she tapped her fingers together in front of her face. "Now is there anything else you'd like to know before you're taken below?"

"Below?" I asked meekly, shifting again in my seat.

"You can't expect me to let you live after learning such confidential information," she scoffed.

I looked at Kim, then around the room nervously. We had to keep her talking until we could think of a plan.

Panicking, the first words that popped into my head flew out of my mouth. "You're crazy!"

Kim's eyes widened, but Angel didn't seem phased

by my comment. She winked at me and licked her lips before speaking. "All geniuses are a little mad."

"Why would you take away everyone's free will just because of an experience that you had?" I demanded, anger building inside my chest. "It should be someone's choice how they live."

"Like I said, people like to be told what to do," Angel replied. "Without structure, society would crumble. The more structure the better. Society was going to hell, and people looked up to me."

"It's not structure! You're just obsessed with control!"

"While the power is a nice touch, it's not the reasoning behind The City I created. This is why it's better for people not to know; you don't understand."

"No I really don't," I answered. "I believe if people want to have relationships, they should be allowed to. Just because things didn't work out exactly how you wanted to with the people around you doesn't mean you have the right to destroy things for everyone else."

"Oh, but I do. And that is why you're here." Angel smiled at me. "To be disposed of." Her fingers flew to a red button on the edge of her desk, pressing it firmly.

"You evil witch," Kim spat. "You're not going to get away with this."

Angel stood up from her desk, causing me to shrink back into my chair. Standing up, she was even more intimidating. She towered over us, leaning over her desk and placing her face inches from Kim's. "Hate to break it to you hun, but I already have."

I heard the door behind us open and swiveled around in my chair. Two Officials entered, striding swiftly to Angel. Unlike the Officials who had taken our friends, these men appeared to be normal human beings.

She straightened her posture and smoothed out her flowing white dress. "Take them away," she ordered, flashing a shimmering white smile. "And take extra special care of that one." She nodded at Kim and slowly lowered herself back into her chair. "Pleasure meeting you."

"Get up," one of the Officials demanded gruffly.

I hesitated, looking up at him. Sunglasses covered his eyes and his face was expressionless, making him impossible to read.

I must not have moved fast enough for him. He grabbed my arm with his hand and lifted me up as if I was the weight of a pillow. Pulling my arms behind my back, he clicked handcuffs over my wrists. I winced in pain as the cold, hard material dug into my flesh, cutting off the circulation.

"The more you move, the tighter they'll get," he snarled.

Speechless, I looked at Kim. The other Official held her hands as he cuffed them, keeping her body facing away from me. Even though I couldn't see her face, I could tell she felt defeated. Her posture was slumped slightly, her head tilted down towards the floor. The tall man loomed over her, making her look like a defenseless child.

Amber pressed against my legs, a low rumble emitting from her throat. The noise startled me. She had never made such a threatening sound before, and it seemed unfit coming from such a sweet dog.

"Ugh," my Official grunted, his body tensing at the sound. "What are we supposed to do with that thing?"

Angel tapped her fingers against the side of her

face, staring off into space. "Hmm . . . leave it here. I'll take care of it." Her eerie, toothy grin crept over her mouth as she hissed the words.

"What? No!" I lunged towards Angel, stopping short as the Official grabbed my arm. A burst of pain surged through my wrists as the cuffs tightened. I gritted my teeth, giving Angel an icy glare.

"Ooo, scary!" Angel spat, chuckling slightly. "Trust me. I'll take special care of her." She winked at me before bursting into a fit of laughter.

Still gripping my arm, the Official jolted me backwards. Veering off towards the left, he dragged me to a glass door that I hadn't noticed before. The other Official and Kim followed close behind, stopping inches away.

Amber bounded after us, my Official grunting angrily again. "Get that thing away from me!" he ordered.

Giant shoved Kim towards us and grabbed Amber by the scruff of her neck. She let out a cry, sending chills throughout my body. Instinctively, I sprung forward in attempt to stop Giant.

Grunt effortlessly stopped me short once more, holding onto my arm with one hand and Kim's with the other. I looked at Kim, trying to read her. Why wasn't she helping me? Why wasn't she doing anything? Her face was blank, her eyes aimed at the floor as if she wasn't even aware I was beside her. Her inferno was gone, all that remained a blown out candle.

I cried out in pain as my wriggling caused the metal around my wrists to tighten even more. The sting I felt digging into my skin was nothing compared to the look of fear in Amber's eyes. I felt defeated. I had tried so hard to keep her safe, but none of my efforts

157

mattered now. I was a failure. We were both finished.

I heard a sliding noise behind me and Grunt pulled us backward into the now open door. Giant shoved Amber to the side, causing her to whimper once more. He ambled through the door, closing it behind him.

Anger gushed through my veins as he stood beside me. All I wanted to do was attack him. How dare he hurt Amber like that and take her away! Realizing any attempt to tackle him would be useless, I slumped slightly against the wall. I didn't know anything about fighting anyway except what I'd read from the books. The pain in my wrists was spreading up my arms, causing them to throb.

The room we were in wasn't a room at all, but an elevator. It wasn't like any elevator I was used to; it was compact enough that the four of us could not stand without touching one another. The walls, floor, and ceiling were all a shiny silver color. A small screen and some buttons were mounted on the wall next to Giant.

He pressed a button and the elevator dropped with alarming speed. My head slammed against the wall, making a sickening cracking noise. Wincing in pain, I tried to shift position off the wall. Grunt shoved me, slamming me into the side of the elevator again. Black spots clouded my vision.

My mind raced as we flew downwards. My head and wrists throbbed in pain, my surroundings spinning. Nausea was building within my stomach and my brain was cloudy. I wanted to scream and run away, but I felt too sick to put up any fight. I was stuck in a tiny cubicle with two angry, over-sized men and one girl who had checked out of this world.

Though things were still spinning, the elevator must

have stopped because the door slid open. Grunt propelled me forward, laughing as I stumbled. Taking a few seconds to regain my footing, I closed my eyes and inhaled. Opening them once more, I was relieved to see that the room had nearly stopped spinning.

The area was large with a towering ceiling. It was dimly lit by some sort of wall lights, allowing me to see what was inside. Black iron tables lined the walls, snaking through the center of the room. There were small spaces in between I assumed were used for walking. The tables were covered in books, computers, papers, flasks, beakers, and bottles. A row of chairs stood adjacent to one set of tables, each one filled with a man or women furiously typing away on a computer.

I could hear Kim's shallow breathing beside me. I looked over at her, concerned with the labored noises. Her eyes were still glazed over, glued to the concrete floor. Giant didn't seem to notice she was having trouble; he pushed her forward as forcefully as Grunt was moving me.

"Code 4," Giant called out, startling the busy workers.

One man swiveled around in his chair, gave us a frightened look, and swirled back around to face the computer. He pressed his head closer to the screen, his fingertips flying over the keys a mile a minute.

Grunt made a disgusted noise and shook his head, shoving me against one of the tables. "Where is she?" he demanded.

"I'm over here." The voice came from a small woman with short dark hair. She stood crouching over one of the tables to our left, punching something into what looked like a calculator and scribbling notes on a large pad of paper. Like the others, she didn't

159

make any move towards us.

"Code 4," Giant repeated, shoving Kim into my side.

I wobbled, my balance compromised by the pain inside my head. My fingers gripped onto the cold table to steady myself. Kim slumped against the table, not even acknowledging the fact that she had almost barreled into me. I wanted to shake her to try and get some sort of reaction, but I was in too much pain to move. I turned my attention to the conversation between Giant and the woman.

"I heard you the first time," the woman responded, flipping onto the back of the paper to continue whatever she was writing.

Grunt shook his head and stomped over to her, tearing the pad of paper out of her hands. The woman raised her head finally, glaring at Grunt.

He slammed the paper back down onto the table in front of her. "If you heard us, then take care of it!"

The woman looked at us for the first time, a sad look filling her eyes. She sighed and put her pen down on the table. "All right. I'll do it."

Grunt stomped back over to us, shoving us in the direction of the woman. "Just tell us where you need them so we can get out of here."

"Follow me," the woman said softly, motioning her hand as she started off towards the side of the room.

I wasn't sure what Code 4 meant, but I was confident it wasn't good. From these people's reactions, you would think that something bad was going to happen to them.

Grunt shoved me forward, catching me off guard. My feet slipped and I stumbled sideways, grasping blindly onto what must have been another table in attempt to avoid hitting the ground. The papers crinkled beneath my fingertips, rough and gritty against my skin. The handcuffs dug into my wrists as my back pressed them against the metal table, causing me to gasp in pain.

"Watch it!" He squeezed my arm and pulled me back up, giving me half a second to regain my footing. I grudgingly followed the woman, his hand jammed into my lower back to ensure that I kept moving. I felt a tickle on the palm of my hand but was too tired to turn and try to see what it was.

I closed my eyes for a moment, wishing that I could be anywhere else in the world. When my eyelids fluttered open, I was still in the enormous dismal room. The woman was stopped in front of a large red door, waiting for us. I could hear Kim dragging her feet behind me, Giant snapping and swearing at her under his breath.

I stopped beside the door and dared a glance over my shoulder, twisting my shoulder forward and my palms up so I could see my hand. Thin trickles of blood streaked my already scarred hands, twisting down from my wrists. Now that I could see it, the throbbing pain became harder to ignore.

The woman looked nervous, her eyes darting from side to side. Her hand was shaking as she raised her finger to the shiny silver sensor. She looked up, her pink lips parting to speak.

"I can take it from here." Her voice sounded hoarse. Her eyes flashed, momentarily making contact with mine before moving back to Grunt.

My muscles relaxed as I felt Grunt pull away from me.

"Come on." I didn't look at him, my eyes still focused on the woman. Footsteps faded away as Grunt and Giant left, leaving Kim and I alone with the woman.

"Follow me," the woman told us, pushing the door open. She stepped through the opening and flipped on a switch to illuminate a hallway on the other side.

For some reason, my body chose to do exactly as she said. My feet slid across the floor, stepping delicately through the door. My eyes refused to leave the woman's face, captivated by her. She was beautiful, there was no doubt. Her skin was smooth and light, freckles splashed across her nose. Her eyes were dark and soft, despite her somewhat hard voice. She sported a boyish haircut, her hair sticking up on the top in spiky strands. The feeling I felt for her was warm, but different than that I felt for Kim. Even though she was ordered to lead us to our doom, I couldn't help but want to be closer to her. She seemed so safe.

Kim followed as well, bumping into me as the woman closed the door behind us. I was still waiting for Kim to say something, to scream, to try to break free. It scared me to see her spirit wilted and defeated. If she couldn't be strong, then what chance did I have?

CHAPTER 11

We followed the woman down the tunnel, the corridor winding as we walked. The walls shone a bright silver color, dim lights stretching across the ceiling. The hall seemed to extend on forever. The three of us were quiet; the only sound was the clicking of our boots along smooth gray floor.

The woman startled me by stopping in the middle of the hallway. She turned to face us, her eyes glossy. As she spoke, her voice was quiet and cracking.

"Hey," she murmured. "Why are you guys here?"

I glanced at Kim, who appeared just as surprised as I was. Why would this woman be interested in us? She could probably get into trouble by talking.

Kim startled me next by speaking. "It was a mistake."

The woman nodded, gently touching the corner of her nose with her finger. She averted our gazes for a moment. "You're right, it was a mistake. A terrible mistake that cost you your lives."

"This Angel lady, is she your boss?" Kim inquired,

ignoring what the woman had just said.

The woman turned around and began walking again. Kim and I hurried to catch up with her as she strode quickly down the corridor.

"I guess you could call her that."

"Don't you think she's a little bit . . . out there?" Kim ventured, struggling to keep up with the woman. "This whole idea that she has . . . do you support it?"

The woman let out a noise that I interpreted as a laugh. "I wouldn't say that."

"But you're with her?" Kim pressed.

"Sadly, yes."

"Are you saying this wasn't your choice?" I inquired.

The woman stopped again, causing us to almost run into her back. She spun around once more, narrowing her eyes and crinkling the freckles on her nose. "Why all the questions?"

"Well you're taking us to our death aren't you?" Kim spoke. "I think that it would be the least you could do to entertain us for our final hour, don't you?"

Freckles' eyes widened and a droplet of water slid down her cheek. She started walking again, her legs moving slower this time.

"Why do you keep doing that?" Kim mumbled, stumbling after her. My eyes drifted to her wrists as she stepped in front of me. Her hands were red and bloody as well, even worse than mine. Had she been struggling despite her silence?

"Why are you here?" I asked.

"I don't have to answer you," Freckles responded. Her voice softened as she continued a few minutes later. "I'm sorry . . . it's just, not easy."

She came to a stop, this time halting because the

164

hallway ended. She leaned against the bright red rectangle, sounding tired. "I was young, I made my own mistakes at the time, and things spiraled out of control." She let out another laugh, shaking her head. "I never thought it would last this long, honestly. Something so crazy, it would never work. But she's smart. And powerful. Once you're in, you can't get out."

"Does that mean you don't support this?" Kim jumped in, seizing the opportunity.

Instead of answering, Freckles unlocked the door and pushed it open. "Let's get this over with."

Kim and I gaped at each other in desperation. I wasn't sure what to do. One minute it seemed like Freckles was on our side and the next it was as if she was a robot.

"Are you taking the pills?" The words rolled off my tongue like marbles before my brain could process them.

Freckle's eyes burned holes through my skull. Her lips parted slightly as if she was about to speak, then closed again. Her face flushed before she whipped around and stepped purposefully through the doorway.

I trailed after her, sensing that I had hit on something important.

"We stopped," I said.

"Incredible," Kim said as she slipped through after us.

Freckles yanked the door shut. She narrowed her eyes, still glaring at me as if she hadn't heard Kim. Tiny beads of sweat collected on her forehead beneath her hair. Her gaze dropped to the floor, something like a raspy cough sounding from her throat. When she looked up once more, her eyes were

165

painted with a glossy finish.

"We don't take them."

The moment the words escaped her lips, my heartbeat accelerated like slamming the gas pedal in the truck. The way she was treating us made me suspicious, but confirmation that she had feelings meant hope. If we could get through to her somehow, we might have a chance.

"Why not?" I pressed, working up the nerve to step closer to her.

She shrugged at me, her shoulders slumping. Now averting my gaze entirely, she seemed smaller.

"Why does it matter?" She turned so quickly that if she had longer hair it would have slapped me in the face. Her boots squeaked against the metal tiled floor as she stomped towards the center of the room, opening my eyes to my surroundings.

The room was small, about the size of my bedroom. The walls wore a metallic silver paint and were lined with weak circular lights. A large tank full of a bubbling white liquid stood against the opposite wall beside a large control panel. The multicolored buttons flashed rapidly and a loud whirring noise blew from the machine. Stone silver steps stretched up to a tiny metal platform above the tank.

"What the hell is this?" Kim breathed. She yanked on the doorknob with her cuffed hands but it refused to budge.

Freckles ignored her and strode over to the machine. She spread her fingers over a small touch screen. The machine beeped and emitted a loud robotic "Approved."

Kim reached down and grabbed my hand, intertwining her warm fingers through mine. She pressed her hip against my legs with such force it was as if she was trying to melt into me. My heart thumped into a deafening crescendo.

She pushed away from me before moving in front. She stepped closer and whispered in my ear.

"What do we do?"

She backed off just enough for me to see the uncertainty in her dark eyes. She flicked her gaze across my face, waiting anxiously for some kind of response.

I glanced over at Freckles, who was busy pushing buttons and tapping keys on the machine. Her back was to us, and she seemed to have forgotten we were there. Or perhaps she was confident in the fact that her job was about to be completed, and knew that we were trapped and helpless.

Kim wrapped her fingers around my arm, catching me off guard and pulling me back towards her. The motion was awkward, as we were still handcuffed, but all I could concentrate on was her. Though I could tell she was scared, the blaze inside her pupils still burned dimly. The flames captured my attention, mesmerizing me. The rest of the world seemed to melt away as numbness swept gently over my body.

Her breath blew warmth across my cheek. I felt her pull closer to me, my limbs mimicking hers as if I was merely a puppet. Her lips pressed against mine, an electric shock awakening the feelings throughout my body. I stiffened in shock, overwhelmed with a wave of emotions. Before I could figure out what was happening, Freckle's voice snapped me back to reality.

"STOP!" Her bellow echoed throughout the small room, sounding strained and strange. The screech was terrifying, like nothing I had ever heard before.

I broke away from Kim, shaking. Her body

167

separated from mine as we turned to face Freckles.

Freckles' eyes were wide and distraught, unblinking. The only thing more terrifying than her scream was her unwavering stare slicing through my skin. It tore at my heart, slowing down its electric rhythm.

One second she was glaring her animal-like stare, the next she collapsed into a fit of trembles. Her shoulders quivered as she buried her face in her hands, wailing muffled noises into her palms. Tears slid from her eyes and over her fingertips, dropping to the floor like an avalanche. Knees buckling, she fell forward and reached out to catch herself.

Instinctively, I darted forward. Kim frowned and stood rooted to the ground as I attempted to grab hold of Freckles with my bound hands. She jolted at the touch of my fingers, ripping forcefully from my weak, backwards grasp. Streaks of moisture ran down her face. She stood up to her full height, stepping back.

"What are you doing?" she demanded, her voice cracking.

Speechless, I looked at Kim, then back to Freckles. "I . . . I don't know."

"What are *you* doing?" Kim retorted, not moving from her stance. She seemed angry and confused, unsure of what to do.

"I can't do this!" Freckles cried, throwing her hands up into the air. "I can't do this again."

"Can't do what?" Kim inquired, shifting her weight to stand up straighter. She leaned forward, waiting for Freckles to answer.

Freckles wiped her cheek with the back of her hand, sniffing. "I can't kill you."

Kim's eyes burned brighter. Still in shock from my contact with Freckles, what she had just said, and the

168

whole situation, I didn't know what to say.

Freckles walked back to the control panel, flicking a switch and pressing the touch screen again.

"Why?" Kim asked.

My head whipped back in her direction, shooting her a pained glance. What was she doing? Why would she question something that worked in our favor?

Freckles just shook her head. "I can't. I can't."

"Why are you letting us live?" Kim pressed.

Freckles let out a sort of snicker, continuing to shake her head. "I didn't say I was letting you live. But I'm not going to kill you."

"What?" I managed.

She didn't answer; instead she strode quickly to the entrance. She pressed her hand over a small screen on the door. Thrusting it open, she nodded. "Go. They'll find you and kill you, but I can't do it. Not this time."

"But . . ." Kim started, her voice trailing off. "Why?"

"I don't have to answer your questions," Freckles snapped. "I'm already going to be executed for letting you both go and failing to terminate you."

"I don't understand," Kim said. "Why would you let us go if we're all going to be killed anyway?"

"Because."

"Because why?"

"BECAUSE!" Freckles shouted, her face red. Her voice softened and she leaned against the door for support, as if she was very tired. She deflated like a popped balloon. A tear slipped down her cheek, making me afraid she was going to burst into another fit.

Regaining control of my body, I stepped over to the door and closed it. This startled Freckles, but she didn't object.

Kim jumped. "What the hell, Vic?"

"I know how it feels," Freckles whispered, looking at the ground. "I know how it feels to love someone. And I know how much it hurts to have them taken from you."

"Love?" There was that word again. It was so forbidden, but yet so attractive.

"Yes, you two have it." A smile broke through the tears. "Even though it goes against everything you were taught, you can't control it. It's a feeling ... probably the strongest, most powerful, and most passionate thing that we have. Caring about someone so much, and feeling closeness to them that you can't compare to anything else in the world. Someone that you would do anything for."

Was this true? Did Kim and I have love? I cared about her of course and would do anything to help her. I had thought I loved her, but I was so naive with these feelings it was sometimes hard to distinguish them. Half the time I didn't even try to label them, just let them carry me off on a wave.

"I wish we had more time," Kim murmured.

Freckles nodded. "Me too."

"Well we have some time, don't we?" I said. "This procedure, doesn't it take some time? Will they be looking for you soon after?"

Freckles shrugged, her brow ruffling. "It depends."

"What happened to this person you loved?" Kim inquired, persistent with her intense questioning. The anger she had directed towards me for locking us inside was replaced with curiosity.

"It's a long story," Freckles said, not sounding eager to go into it.

I pressed against the door. "What have we got to lose?"

Freckles looked at both of us and let out a sigh. She dropped gently to the floor, crossing her legs. "Sit."

We obeyed, sitting facing her with our backs to the door.

"I grew up in this society, like you guys. I'm thirty-six years old, and Angel's plan has been in place for forty years now. When I was seventeen, I left the Safe House and went to live on my own like everyone else. I was assigned an apartment, but there were problems with it. I was on the top floor. During a snowstorm the first week I was living there, the roof caved in. I wanted to go report it, but I was not feeling well for some reason that day. Losing consciousness, I woke up in an alley freezing and hungry. I wasn't sure how long I had been out for, and I was so numb I thought I was going to die. My limbs were unmovable and all I could think about was how I was going to die in a disgusting alley beside some smelly dumpsters. I must have passed out again, and the next time I woke up, I was inside on the floor next to a heating vent. Blankets covered my body and I was able to wiggle my toes and fingers.

"A man emerged from the doorway, scaring me half to death. That's when I knew something was wrong. Why would he take me in off the streets? I was no concern of his. He gave me some food and something warm to drink. All I could do was drink it because I was so famished. Falling asleep once more, I awoke to find him dozing on the couch. The light from the electric fireplace illuminated his face, and I found myself drawn to him. This strange, beautiful man had saved me. Ignoring everything I had learned in school, the two of us became very close. He was the one who explained to me about the LVs controlling feelings.

171

"I didn't leave the apartment, afraid that someone would be looking for me. I stayed there for months. One day while he was out at work, there was a knock on the door. I didn't answer, but they were persistent. Finally the insistent knocking was beginning to get to me. I trudged to the door and opened it. I didn't have time to see who was outside before I was on the ground, my hands pressed behind my back. I remember a lot of yelling before something was placed over my head and I lost consciousness. I woke up in a room with Angel, who told me that anyone else in my situation would have been killed. She gave me a choice to join her or die. My scores on my test had been off the charts, and she knew my scientific knowledge could be used to her advantage."

She stopped to take a breath. She looked tired, as if she had just aged years in a matter of minutes. Her features drooped and she closed her eyes, swaying slowly back and forth.

"What happened to your friend?" I asked gently.

Her eyes slid open at my question. Tears began to gather again and her eyes grew red. "I don't know. I'm assuming they killed him, but have never had the nerve to check for sure."

Kim scooted closer to Freckles. "Can you fix our hands?"

Freckles seemed startled, but she nodded. We slid forward so she could squeeze between the door and us. The pressure intensified on my wrists, then with a soft click it was gone. Freckles returned to stand before us, tossing the blood-stained handcuffs aside. They skirted across the floor, skipping like a stone in a stream. The sight of them made me shudder.

Kim reached out and grabbed Freckle's hand with her crimson fingers. Slowly, Kim leaned forward and

172

wrapped her arms around her. Freckles collapsed in her embrace, resting her head on Kim's shoulder.

I looked away and fingered my wrists with the opposite hands. I began to rub the circulation back into them and pick away the flecks of dried blood that had accumulated on my skin.

"There's more," Freckles whispered. She backed away from Kim and wiped the water off her cheek with the back of her sleeve. "We had a child."

"What?" My mouth dropped open. All I could do was stare at her.

She nodded. "I . . . at first I didn't know what was happening. I didn't know that you could make a child with two people. Without test tubes. But it happened to me. And at the time I was taken, the child was only a month old." A faraway look spread across her face

"He was the most beautiful thing I ever saw. I loved him. A different kind of love, but equally overwhelming. The biggest, most inquisitive eyes. The cutest little nose. And the best part was that we, two people, had created him together."

Kim and I exchanged a glance, and she asked the question I couldn't work up the nerve to present.

"What happened to him?"

"I don't know. I have always had a tiny glimmer of hope that he would be out there somewhere. Both of them. But I wouldn't even recognize the child if I saw him again. He'd be nineteen by now."

I felt dizzy suddenly, the room spinning before my eyes.

"Vic? You okay?"

The monster was on top of me, running its nails down my arms. Pain rushed through my body, claws digging into my spine and tearing it in two. I curled up into a ball, my eyes still

173

pressed shut.

"Please stop!" I wailed. "Leave me alone."

I felt the weight lift, and it cackled again. "Pathetic."

"I wanna go back to the house!" I cried, my small body quivering in pain and fear. "Please let me go."

"Why are you doing this to me?" it screeched.

"Ow!" I yelled as something rough struck my forehead. My hands flew to my face, trying to protect myself.

I was struck again, and again. I could hear myself screaming, but I couldn't move. The bone-chilling laughter filled the air as it pounded me repeatedly.

Suddenly, the blows stopped. I heard a loud thump, as if it had thrown away whatever object it had been using. Footsteps crunched on the grass around me and it tapped my foot.

"Hey!"

My head was on fire and I could feel the blood trickling over my fingertips. I didn't have the strength to answer it, or even to cry out in pain. I lay there trembling until I felt a harder force on my bare feet.

"Listen to me! Do you hear me?"

I summoned my strength, but I didn't know what to say. Instead, I used the energy to coil into an even tighter ball. I tried to touch my forehead to my knees as if the connection would somehow free my body of the agony.

"Do you know what I've done for you? Stupid! Ahhh!"

I writhed, gritting my teeth as it rammed its boot into the arch of my foot. Somehow I found my voice again and managed to answer it. "Please! I just want to go back. It hurts."

"Useless!" it growled. "I should have gotten rid of you when I had the chance. You have two minutes to get the hell out of my sight or you're dead."

Shaking, I removed my hands from my face and rolled over onto my knees. My fingers pressed into the grass as I attempted to push myself up. I strained to open my eyes but my vision was clouded with blood.

174

Slowly I rose to a kneeling position, struggling to my feet. My head throbbed and my whole body felt weak. Fear propelled me forward as I forced my eyes open. Refusing to look at it, I started to walk as fast as my little legs could take me.

"Move it!" it yelled.

I struggled to speed into a run, tripping and falling onto my knees again. Its laughter was at my back, driving me forwards. My feet pounded against the grass, twigs and rocks scraping along the bottom. I was on fire, but I was flying. I had to get away. I knew it would be back.

"Vic! Are you okay?"

I opened my eyes, Kim's concerned face coming into view. She was holding my shoulders a few inches off the ground. When I moved, she dropped me back on the floor.

"Ow!" My face was hot and sweating. I shook my head and used my elbows to sit up. "I'm sorry. I don't know what happened."

"You were screaming again," Kim said. "Like when we were in the trunk."

"It was horrible," Freckles murmured. "Haunting."

"I . . . I . . ." I shook my head and shrugged. I couldn't explain what I had just experienced. I couldn't remember when it had occurred; it had seemed unreal. Yet I knew it had happened. Why had I just remembered it now?

"Well, you were out for a few minutes and we're losing time," Kim decided.

"Time for what?" I wondered.

"Amber is gonna try to help us find the others," Kim breathed excitedly.

"Amber? But Amber's with Angel . . ." I whimpered sadly.

"No," Freckles told me. "My name is Amber.

175

Pleased to meet you, though I wish it were under different circumstances." She forced a weak smile and opened the door.

"You? Well . . . okay." I didn't have time to think. Kim grabbed my arm and pulled me to her feet.

"Let's get out of here." She shoved the door further and dragged me into the hallway. I turned around and saw Amber at the control panel again. After pressing a few more buttons, she followed us out of the room. She closed the door quietly behind us.

"Even if we reach your friends, I'm not sure what we'll do," Amber admitted as we hurried down the hallway. "They may be coming to look for me already."

"Is there any way out of here?" I asked.

"We got in here," Kim pointed out. "We could go out the same way."

Amber shook her head, making a sharp left down another hallway. "Angel will be monitoring the exits."

"But what if we could get away?" Kim demanded.

"What if?" Amber said sadly. "She'll still be after you."

"So we could hide out somewhere! Haven't you ever dreamed about escaping before?" Kim exclaimed.

Amber nodded as we broke into a run. "Of course I have. But the keyword is dream. I was never stupid enough to actually try it."

"What about everyone else?" I asked. "Are they still going to be okay? Has she done something to them?"

"I'm not making any promises" Amber said, gasping for breath. "Angel is . . . unpredictable."

"So what are we doing if this is all as useless as you say it is?" I breathed as we slowed and stopped in front of another door. Amber unlocked it without answering and we started down a spiral metal staircase. The stairwell was dark and I couldn't see how far down it led.

"Kim asked me to take you to your friends, so that's what I'm doing. I'm not sure how much more help I can be," Amber replied.

"But you know Angel! You know how things work here! There has to be a way we could all escape," Kim pressed.

It took Amber a few minutes to answer, and when she spoke her voice was sad. "I do know her. And that's why I know that it's futile to think that we can run away. And naïve to think that anything would ever change."

We descended in silence, even Kim uncertain of what to say. The minutes ticked by in my head. It seemed like we were trudging along forever. Our boots clanked on the steps and echoed throughout the stairwell.

Amber stopped suddenly, causing Kim and I to bump into her in the darkness. "We're here." I heard her fumbling around with a touch pad before slamming against the door, revealing a long tunnel. It was dark, lit only by dim candles lining the walls.

"Why would you sacrifice your life if there's no escape?" I blurted out. The thought had been lingering in the corners of my mind and I couldn't hold it in any longer. I glared suspiciously at Amber, though the darkness prevented her from seeing my face clearly.

Hearing the tension in my voice, Amber sighed. "I've . . . eliminated too many people. I can't bring myself to do it this time. Especially two people who share something as special as you do. The others, they were close. But you're different."

"But why us?" I demanded. "How do we know you're not leading us into a trap?"

"Vic!" Kim yelped. She had thrown all her trust into Amber awfully quickly. I couldn't blame her, but I had an uneasy feeling about all this.

"Why would I do that?" Amber murmured. "I could have gotten rid of you back there if I wanted to."

"Well . . ." My voice trailed off. She had a valid point.

"Look, this is where we keep the prisoners while they're waiting to be questioned. After this, they normally come to me and well . . . you know what I have to do."

"Prisoners? How many people do you get down here exactly? I thought the pills kept everything in control in Angel's perfect society? How many others are like us?" Kim demanded, catching onto my interrogation train and fueling it further.

"Not many," Amber replied. "Not enough for some kind of rebellion, if that's what you're hoping for." I suspected she had spent more time thinking about these things than she let on.

She stepped through the door, motioning for us to follow. "If you want to see your friends, you've got to do it fast."

Kim went after her, but I hesitated. I shifted my weight uncertainly from one foot to another and glanced over my shoulder.

"We've got to try," Kim said gently. "We've got to try to save them. They'd do it for us. We didn't come all the way here for nothing."

I knew she was right. Images of Patrick, Adam, and the others flashed through my minds. Even if somehow Kim and I managed to escape, I would never be able to live with myself knowing that I'd abandoned them. Besides, Amber made sense. Leading us somewhere else to kill us when she had us right where we were supposed to be would be foolish.

"Okay." I forced my feet to move, following them through the doorway and into the darkness.

"Shut the door please," Amber told me, turning and starting down the hallway without waiting to see if I obeyed.

I closed it as softly as I could and hurried after her, Kim walking swiftly beside me. As our pace accelerated to a slow jog, I couldn't shake the uneasy feeling about Amber. She made me nervous. The fact that she had the same name as my dog was strange. Did she know about Amber? Was she taking her name to mess with my head? If so, she was on the right track.

A pang tugged at my stomach at the thought of Amber the dog. What was Angel doing to her? Was she okay? My feet quickened, propelled by my motivation to find her as well. The hallway took a sharp turn to the right, causing me to bump into Kim. She didn't seem to notice, focused on the ground.

"All right," Amber breathed, slowing as we reached a series of doors. "This is it."

"Are they in there?" I asked, sliding over to one of the doors.

"Stop!" Amber whispered. She grabbed my arm and pulled me away from the door. "You can't get too close without me opening it or an alarm will go off. I'm authorized to open them, which will turn off the sensors."

She stepped in front of me and pressed her thumb against a touch pad beside the door. The pad emitted a beeping noise and Amber used her other hand to open the door. "Come on."

We followed her inside, finding ourselves in another poorly lit room. It was empty except for the figure slumped in the far corner. His head hung limply against his chest, his arms linked behind his back. The cuffs were attached to large metal chains on the stone walls. A massive white spider scampered across the links and up the rock, retreating to an extensive web near the ceiling.

"Hello?" I whispered.

The figure twitched and slowly raised his head to look at us. A spark leapt from his eyes as he recognized us.

I gasped. "Patrick!" I dashed over, kneeling down beside him. The floor felt dirty and uneven. "Patrick, are you okay?"

He opened his mouth but no words came out. His eyes looked foreign without his glasses; the bright blue circles normally hid behind heavy frames. They darted back and forth between Kim, Amber, and me. The expression behind them was hard to read.

"What's wrong with him?" I asked softly.

"It's a speech disabler," Amber said as if it was an everyday item. "They keep it in them until they're questioned so that they don't cause any ruckus." She reached gently behind Patrick's ear, pulling out a small, circular, metal object.

As soon as her fingertips emerged with the item, the words flew from Patrick's lips.

"Kim! Vic! What are you guys doing here?" Patrick asked, his voice sounding strained but excited. "Who is this?"

"We followed you guys," Kim admitted.

"What? Why? That was so stupid!" He squirmed, causing the chain links to clink together.

180

"Yeah, we know."

"It's not important now," Amber whispered urgently. "Come on." She stood up and brushed the dirt off her pants.

"Who are you?" Patrick asked, speaking directly to Amber since we had failed to answer his question.

"This is Amber," I said.

"Amber?" A confused look spread over his face. "But Amber is a dog . . ."

"A different Amber," I told him. "She worked for The City, but now she's helping us get away."

"A sad attempt at an escape," Amber murmured.

Kim ignored her and wrapped her arms around Patrick's torso. "We're gonna get out of here, don't worry." She turned to me. "Can you help me get him up?"

Together, we helped Patrick to his feet and Amber unlocked his handcuffs. They swung in the air before clashing back against the wall with the chains. Red lines stretched around Patrick's wrists, fresh blood trickling down his hands and dried red liquid sticking to the cuts. The back of his shirt looked as if cherries had bombed it.

I grabbed Patrick's hand and lifted it for a closer look. He yelped in pain and I immediately let go. "Are you okay?"

Patrick nodded. "I'll be fine." His voice was unconvincing, but I didn't have time to question him further. Amber was already at the door, motioning urgently for us to hurry.

"Are you sure she can be trusted?" Patrick whispered, eyeing her suspiciously.

"No," Kim admitted at the same time I said yes. We exchanged glances and I narrowed my eyes slightly. We seemed to have suddenly switch roles, as if I had been feeding my original suspicions to Kim as she passed me her trust.

"She risked everything for us," I hissed. "Besides, I have a good feeling about her."

"That's what I thought—" Kim began.

"Guys!" Amber called softly. "Come on!"

We broke away from each other and rushed after her. I stopped after a few seconds, realizing that Patrick wasn't with us. Turning around, I saw his body hunched over as he moved forward with a slow limp. Every time he took a step, his face contorted in pain.

"Patrick!" Kim was already at his side, draping his arm across her shoulder. "What did they do to you?"

"I'm fine," he repeated, gritting teeth. Despite his declaration, his eyelids drooped and he made no attempt to walk further.

I slipped under Patrick's other arm, helping him into the hallway. Amber opened the next room, and the next, until eight of us stood outside. The others looked scared and shaken, but none of them were in worse shape than Patrick.

"This is the only one we haven't checked," Kim grunted under Patrick's weight. We had opened all of the doors in the hall, some of them empty. According to the others, these were all the members of our group that had met at the warehouse. The only person we were missing was Adam. "He has to be in here."

Amber pressed her hand against the screen and pushed open the door.

Kim slipped out from under Patrick, Terry taking her place to support him. Kim hurried past Amber and into the room. I glanced to the left and nudged Griffin.

182

"Can you take over for a minute?" I asked.

Griffin had his arms wrapped around Noel, who was buried in his chest and whimpering softly. Griffin nodded, stroking her hair and pulling her with him towards Patrick.

The second Patrick was slumped against Griffin, I darted after Kim. Amber and the others lingered in the doorway.

Inside, I found another dark room. Kim knelt in the center, her body shaking, face buried in hands. The room was empty except for the bugs crawling across the walls and the rusty chains hanging in the corner.

"Kim . . ." My voice trailed off. I dropped to the floor silently beside her. Sensing my presence, she lifted her face. Lines of tears streaked down her cheeks, blood from her hands staining her beautiful skin. She burst into a fit of tremors, falling into my arms. We sat there for what seemed like hours, Kim's face pressed against my shirt and my chin resting atop her head. I felt a wave of negative emotions as I closed my eyes and hugged her closer.

"We need to go." A gentle voice broke me from the trance. I looked up to see Amber standing above us.

I nudged Kim and pulled her up with me. "We're missing someone," I explained to Amber.

Amber frowned. "They must have taken him to interrogation already."

"What does that mean?" Kim demanded. She sniffed wiped her cheeks with her sleeve.

"It means . . ." Amber stared at Kim, glanced at me, and then focused on Kim again. A sigh escaped her lips as she murmured, "It means it's too late."

Kim locked her gaze on Amber as if she was the enemy. "WHAT?" Her voice was shaky but loud.

"Shhh!" Amber pressed her finger to her lips and

183

stepped closer to us. "We need to go now if you want any chance of getting out of here."

"I'm not leaving without Adam," Kim whispered.

"You've got to trust me," Amber replied, moving towards the door. "We've already wasted too much time."

I led Kim to the door, feeling moisture gathering in my own eyes. "Amber . . . we came here to rescue our friends. Leaving without Adam and the other Amber would be—"

"Impossible?" A familiar voice boomed, turning my blood to ice.

Our entire group turned around slowly to face Angel. Kim shoved through past the others so that she stood about a foot away from her.

"What have you done to him?" Kim cried out, her face flushing red. Her fingers tightened into fists at her sides.

"Why don't you ask him that yourself?" Angel smirked, stepping to the side to reveal Adam.

"Adam!" Kim gasped, rushing towards him. She opened her arms as if about to hug him, but Adam held out one arm and stopped her.

"Enough," he growled.

"Adam?" Kim said.

"It's time to stop this insanity," Adam said in a static tone. "It's over." His eyes were blank and emotionless; his gaze aimed nowhere in particular.

"Adam! It's me, Kim!" She didn't attempt to get closer to him again, just looked at him with crinkled eyebrows. "Aren't you happy to see me?"

"Happiness is a waste of energy," Adam replied. "Emotions are useless and must be destroyed."

Kim lunged at Angel, firing a fist at her face and catching Angel by surprise. Adam reached over and yanked Kim away before she could deliver another blow. He held her effortlessly, pulling both of her arms behind her back.

Angel held her nose and narrowed her eyes. She moved her arms to her hips, revealing a line of blood dripping from her nostril. She stepped closer to Kim, looking like she was about to explode. Just when I thought she was going to charge Kim, she dropped her head back and let out a crazed howl. It took a few moments to recognize the noise as laughing.

"What did you do to him?" Kim screamed, struggling to break free from Adam's grasp. Her efforts proved futile, and after a few moments she grew still.

"It's just a little pill," Angel giggled. She draped her long fingers over the top of Adam's ear and slid her nails gently down his jaw line. Her nails left two trails of red scratches on his cheek. "Besides, I like him better this way, don't you?"

"Can't you give it up?"

I turned around in the direction of the voice, my eyes falling on Amber. She looked ruffled, but the second time she spoke her voice was stronger.

"These guys haven't done anything to deserve this," she continued. "Why don't you let everyone go and leave them alone?"

"You!" Angel exclaimed, clapping her hands together. "Why I couldn't have planned this more perfectly!"

"I'm serious Angel. It's about time to realize that you can't control everyone," Amber hissed.

Angel threw her head back and giggled. "This is just splendid." She sauntered over, her boots clicking on the stone floor. Her eyes flicked up and down as she circled me, stopping next to Amber. "Have you

185

two had the chance to introduce yourselves?"

"What are you talking about?" Amber demanded. She sidestepped as Angel tried to touch her shoulder, avoiding Angel as if she was a bucket of bubbling toxic waste.

"You are crazy!" I snarled, clenching my fist. "What have you done with Amber?"

Angel cocked her head and smiled at me innocently. "Why, Amber's right here, my dear."

"You know who I'm talking about," I said through gritted teeth. Heat flushed my face and I coursed through my veins.

"No, I'm afraid I don't," Angel replied, returning to my side and draping her arm around my back. "I have a funny story though."

"Get off of me!" I cried, shoving her arm off. "What have you done with her?"

"The story goes like this," Angel began, ignoring me completely. She continued circling me. "Once upon the time there was a man and woman. They were not very good people, for they did not listen to the rules. In fact, they were so bad they actually conceived a child. Of course, this child was undocumented and illegal. One day one of my workers discovered this child, and the parents. We decided to give the child a chance, why kill an innocent baby? The parents were initially sentenced to death for disobeying the law, but the woman had a talent. She was too smart to waste. I gave her a choice to work for me." She paused and looked at Amber.

Amber's eyes watered, a frown plastered across her lips. "Why are you doing this?" The color drained from her cheeks; even in the murky light I could tell her face was the color of bleach.

Angel continued, "So this woman came to work for

186

me. The man, let's just say we disposed of. Now that those two were taken care of, the question arose: what to do with the child? We sent him into society like the rest of the children, to be brought up in a Safe House. And do you know that, since I am such a curious individual, I decided to look up what had happened to him. I hadn't seen him in years. Somehow, things worked out that he's standing in this very room."

A cry escaped Amber's lips. "What?"

"That's right. Your son is right here."

I looked around, from Patrick to Adam to Griffin. What were the odds that Amber's son would end up back here?

"I wonder if it is some kind of defect; if the rebellion runs through the genes like a cheetah." A faraway look crossed Angel's face for a few moments before she snapped back to the present. "But! No matter. You'll get to face the end together."

"Who is it?" Amber whispered, her voice shaky. "Tell me you're not lying."

Angel tossed her hair over her shoulder and flashed her dazzling smile. "Have I ever lied to you?"

"Tell me," Amber repeated. She wiped her puffy, overflowing eyes and glared at Angel.

"Why? You wouldn't like to guess? Make a game out of it? Why not wait until you're on your deathbed?" Angel let out another piercing laugh before snapping her fingers.

Instantly, the room broke into chaos. A surge of Angel's men crashed into the room, seizing us from behind. Shrieks filled the air as we desperately attempted to fend off our attackers.

I whipped around, trying to put up a fight with the man coming after me. I swung clumsily, hoping that

187

instinct would kick in. His face was angry, his muscles tense beneath his black leather uniform. I was strong, but he was stronger. He clamped his iron grip onto my arm, his nails digging into my bare skin. I yelped in agony, wriggling in his grasp and kneeing him in the stomach. The blow stunned him momentarily. I turned to try and help Kim, wasting precious seconds. I caught a glimpse of her pained expression before a heavy weight crumpled over my head, plunging my world into blackness.

Chapter 12

"I knew you would be trouble. Pain in the ass."

My fingers tingled as she pressed the needle into my arm, yanking it out and tearing my skin. I winced but remained quiet, my eyes glued to the tan leather table I sat on.

"What is that?" Another voice asked, softer and kinder.

"It's a stronger type of liquid emotion suppressor."

"Those have only been in the lab for a few months, we haven't had the chance to learn the full effects yet!"

The angry voice replied. "Well we'll call this an experiment. For some reason the LVs and regular injections aren't strong enough for this one."

The softer voice asked, "Do you think it was how he was conceived?"

The sharp sound of flesh on flesh echoed through the room, followed by a cry of pain.

"You are never to speak of that! If anyone knew how this boy was created, it could cause mass insurgence. Shut your mouth unless you want me to do it for you, permanently."

"I'm sorry," the softer voice whimpered.

"He's just a boy. After this injection, I will never have to

worry about what goes on in his head again. He can be a normal citizen. Besides, the only side effects we've observed were mild depression and suicidal tendencies. That was barely four percent."

"Why does it matter so much?" This was a different voice, male.

I was afraid of what she would do. I closed my eyes tightly, trying to cut myself off from the world. Images of trees, grass, and wildflowers danced behind my eyelids. She couldn't touch me here. No one could.

"I don't care, but it's his . . ." Her voice trailed off, and she spoke so softly that I could barely catch it. I wasn't supposed to hear it. "It's his mother. She's a valuable asset to my empire. I think that one day he could be as well."

"Isn't it too much of a nuisance?" The man coughed, hacking up phlegm.

"Shut up," she snapped.

"So you go through all the trouble to keep him safe, but you must remember he's older now. He's going to know what you did to him," the male answered.

"Memory is one of the easiest things to manipulate," she replied. "Thoughts can be distorted, emotions repressed, but memories, memories vanish all on their own. Unpleasant recollections are pushed down in the back of ones mind by their host. No one wants to remember the bad times. The bad times twist us; make us old, bitter, and insane."

I heard footsteps move away and then the man gasped. The steps clicked softly back in my direction. The room was silent. I wasn't sure if the woman was talking to someone or to herself.

"Just in case he is weak enough to allow his memories to resurface, this will keep them at bay."

A needle jabbed into my forehead, pain obliterating the false reality I had created inside my mind. Splotches of color exploded across the backs of my eyes. I wanted to scream. I wanted to cry. I didn't.

"It's me!" I rolled over and opened my eyes, struggling into a taller seated position. "It's me," I repeated as I blinked, trying to shake the dizziness that was hindering my vision.

"You're awake!" I recognized Kim's voice, my head snapping in the direction of the sound. The room was spinning, but the blurry images slowly began to materialize until I could see Kim beside me.

"It's me!"

"What are you talking about?" she asked.

Before answering, I surveyed the room to see where we were. It was small, too small to be called a room. It was half the size of my bathroom. There wasn't enough room to move. The only thing in the tiny cubicle was a thin silver bench that propped us against the wall. I was squished into Amber, who lay slumped on my shoulder. My other arm pressed against the cold metal wall. Kim and Griffin sat facing me on an identical bench. We were so close together that the toes of our boots touched. They appeared groggy but conscious, unlike Amber who was completely still.

I grabbed Amber's shoulders and shook her gently, maneuvering as best I could in the small area. Her head bumped into the wall as I shook her. "Amber wake up!"

"Vic, take it easy," Kim advised. "These walls are hard."

I paused, realizing she was right. My back thumped against the metal as I slumped into my seat.

"You're not helping the situation," Griffin murmured, who seemed to be performing some sort of deep breathing exercises.

"Where are we?" I inquired.

191

Kim shrugged. "We were both unconscious. We just came to a few minutes ago." Inflated red splotches circled her tired eyes. Her ponytail hung messy and limp, her clothes ruffled. She looked as if she had been stripped of her courage and dignity, as if her character had been stolen and thrown away.

"You were dreaming again, weren't you?"

Dreaming wasn't exactly what I would call it, but I nodded. I didn't know why I was having all of these flashbacks, but I guessed it had something to do with the fact Angel was the monster in my nightmares. And the realization that Amber was my mother.

"What do you dream about?" Kim asked gently. "Why do they make you so upset?"

I shifted uncomfortably in my seat. "I think there were some pretty dark times in my childhood. But I also think that I am Amber's son."

"You?" Kim said in disbelief.

"You believe that psychopath?" Griffin asked.

"I filled him in briefly on what Angel told us," Kim put in, glancing at him. She turned her attention back to me and leaned forward, placing her hand on my leg. "Why do you think this?"

"I . . . I have memories. When I was younger, I remember a woman came to visit me in my Safe House. She was cruel, wicked, and hurtful. I think she was Angel. And I think she was monitoring me to see if the fact that I wasn't a test tube baby was affecting me."

"Wow," Kim breathed, leaning back. She tilted her head and stared at the ceiling. Silence overcame her as she tried to take in what I'd said, genuinely considering my theory.

"I don't remember everything, but I've been getting bits and pieces since I stopped taking the vitamins.

192

Perhaps the memory suppressant she gave me expired. Or maybe it only worked with a certain chemical in the vitamins."

"Isn't your dog named Amber?" Griffin asked, brushing a lock of dark hair out of his face.

"Yes," I answered.

"But you didn't know about Amber when you named her?" he asked, wrinkling his brow in confusion.

"No . . . well, yes. I think my subconscious somehow did. I never met anyone with that name before. But when I met Amber, the dog, she made me feel safe. She gave me a purpose. The name just seemed fitting."

"That's freaky," Griffin commented.

"It's incredible," Kim breathed, a smile creeping across her face and crinkling the corners of her weary eyes.

"It doesn't matter now," I mumbled. "Amber's probably dead. And we're not far from it."

Amber's head twitched on my shoulder, slowly lifting. "We're in a gas cube."

"Amber!" I exclaimed. "I'm—"

She wrapped her arms around me before I could finish the sentence. "I know, Angel told me."

"I don't believe it," I whispered. "Never in a million years would I imagine I would meet my mother."

Amber let go and backed away, her eyes watering. "And me, my son."

We sat for a few minutes in silence, gripping one another's hands as if our lives depended on the contact.

"I know this reunion was short lived . . ." Griffin began.

"But do you know how we can get out of here?"

193

Kim asked Amber, cutting to the chase.

I had to smile at Kim, relieved to know that she still had a stroke of spirit left. I let go of Amber's hand, though our sides still touched in the tiny space.

Amber shook her head sadly, her happy face gone. "No. I don't know anything about these. That's why she put us here."

"Shit," Griffin growled, slamming his boots down on the metal floor. The cube shook under his weight.

"Take it easy," I said.

"Wait a minute! Why are we shaking?" Kim asked. "Griffin's not that strong."

"Hey!" Griffin shot back.

"The cubes are suspended in the air for easy disposal. And no escape. Once the gas is released, the wires release the cubes and they fall into the earth," Amber answered.

"So you do know something about them!" Kim's voice was excited.

"That's the extent," Amber replied.

"Come on, can't you think of anything else?" Kim asked. "There has to be a way out. There's always a way out!"

"I'm sorry, Kim," Amber said. "I told you from the start that we couldn't get out of here."

"How can you just be okay with that?" Kim's voice rose in volume until it cracked.

"We have no choice," Amber responded.

I closed my eyes, visualizing my happy place. I remembered where it was now; in the backyard of my Safe House. There were wide meadows abundant with a rainbow of flowers and tall oak trees. I remembered going there every morning to lie in the grass and breathe in the smell of the outdoors. It was hard to believe that places like that existed. They were so far away from where we were now. So far away from where we were before. But why? Why couldn't we live in a place where we were happy? A place with beauty, bliss and, most importantly, company. It didn't make sense.

The impossible had happened. We had broken into The City's inner walls. We had found Adam, Griffin, Noel, Patrick, and the others in our group. I had found my mother. Someone who had given birth to me. Someone who had created me as a product of love and compassion, not merely a product of The City. I had accessed the area of my memory supposed to be erased by Angel's drugs. If all of these things had happened in only a few hours, why couldn't we have one last miracle? Kim was right. There had to be something we could do. Some way out.

I opened my eyes, surveying the unhappy faces of my friends. "Please, Amber. Try to think, Mom."

The words sounded strange coming from my mouth. In some of the books I'd read the characters had moms. They used the word "Mom" as if it had no meaning, and I hadn't given it a second thought. But the word applied to a real life person was incredible. Magical, even.

The word must have been enchanted because a spark erupted in Amber's eyes. "I have an idea, but it's risky."

"Well, we don't really have a choice," Kim said dryly.

Amber looked up at the ceiling a few feet above our heads. "If we open the top of this, there may be some kind of control panel on up there. Angel usually has control panels everywhere."

"Brilliant!" Griffin mused. "But how do you suggest we open the ceiling? Is that even possible?"

"I have no idea," Amber admitted. "And that's the easy part." She struggled to her feet, placing one foot in front of the other and shifting sideways so she had enough room to stand. She craned her neck and stretched her arms up, running her fingers around the edges of the ceiling. Her arms dropped back down and her head shortly after.

"Anything?" I asked.

She shook her head. "I don't see any mistakes in the construction. Like everything in The City, it's flawless."

"You know that's not true," I replied. "The City is far from flawless."

"Nothing's flawless," Kim agreed, shrinking up against the wall to try and give Amber more space. "Can you look again?"

Amber let out a long sigh and stood on her toes. She ran her fingers across the middle of the ceiling and around the sides again, repeating the motions for a few more minutes.

Realizing I was holding my breath in anticipation, I exhaled as she dropped to her seat.

"I don't know."

The words smashed me like a train. "Thanks for trying," I managed, my tongue turned to pebbles.

Griffin stomped his feet again in frustration, shaking the cube violently. He was tall and wide with a stocky build. The City never let anyone grow overweight anymore, but his frame was large and heavy enough to easily unbalance the cube.

"Careful!" Kim exclaimed. "We don't know how strong these cables are."

Amber glanced at me, her eyes sad. "I'm sorry."

"What if we all pushed on it at the same time?" Griffin tried. "Couldn't we pop the screws or something?"

"By the look and feel of it," Amber responded, "it's solid titanium. Unless you're a lot stronger than you look, we can't break through it."

Griffin rose to his feet, causing the cube to shrink even more. I pressed myself along the wall. I couldn't tell if we were running out of air, or if it was just my imagination. Part of me wanted to ask Amber how much longer we had, but the other part was too terrified of the answer.

Griffin pressed his knuckles against the ceiling, grunting with irritation. Beads of sweat gathered on his forehead as he increased the pressure he was inflicting on the metal. His arms flopped to his sides, his hands clenched in fists. "Nothing."

"Can we plug up the vents?" Kim reasoned. "Where the gas comes out?"

"It's a good thought," Amber said, "but Angel would never construct something that could be so easily stopped. She's sneaky and slithery. She thinks of everything."

Kim narrowed her eyes. "If she's so smart, why does she need you?"

"You really think someone could pull off something like this all on her own?" Amber retorted. "She's brilliant, but you can't run The City alone."

"I still don't understand how she did it in the first place," I put in.

"She got enough powerful people on her side. She's very persuasive," Amber told me. She was studying the walls of the cube intently.

"How could you work for her for so long?" I asked. "Do you really support this way of life?"

"Of course not," Amber sighed. "We went over this already. But everyone is afraid of death. And I had

197

unfinished business here. Like finding you."

Fire began to build in my stomach. "I'm happy to find you too." My breathing grew rapid, my face growing hotter. "Happy doesn't even begin to describe it. But you've done so much that I couldn't even imagine doing to other human beings."

"I'm not proud of the life I've led," Amber said, her voice hoarse. "But I didn't want to do it forever. I had dreams of somehow going out into the world. Looking for you and your father. I hoped you both were still alive. I thought somehow I could find a loophole in Angel's messed up world and we could live together like they did in the past. Three people who care about each other. I wanted to believe this didn't have to last forever . . . but like I said she's a genius. I wouldn't be any help to anyone if I was dead."

"I thought you had no hope for change," I retorted.

"The logical part of me doesn't," Amber replied.

"Give her a break, man." Griffin now had his torso twisted halfway and his palms pressed against the wall, pushing with all of his weight.

I couldn't find words to describe the way I was feeling. I was getting better at labeling emotions, but this wasn't just anger. I wasn't just happy, relieved, or sad. A giant knot was writhing in my stomach as if it was full of snakes. The mixture of emotions and the small, hot space was making me nauseous. My head ached. I felt an undeniable love for this woman, I was sure of that. I wanted to be reasonable and try to understand where she was coming from. Something inside of me was furious with her for not coming after me sooner. If Angel had access to records that allowed her to discover my identity, couldn't Amber have used them somehow? Amber was also right;

Angel was a genius. Evil, but a genius no doubt. We had seen what she was capable of, and if I was in Amber's shoes would I have taken the risk?

Amber's faced was tear stained and flushed. "It doesn't matter now. Can't we just appreciate each other for a few minutes? While we still can?"

I looked at her, then across the way at Kim. Kim also had her eyes set on me, waiting expectantly for her to answer. She reached out and took my hand, squeezing it reassuringly.

"I . . . I . . ." I struggled for words.

A loud squeak interrupted my muddled thoughts. We all focused Griffin, his eyes widening. He appeared just as surprised as we were.

"What was that?" Kim asked.

Griffin straightened up, moving away from the wall. "I think I moved something."

We exchanged excited glances.

"How?" Amber asked in disbelief, jumping to her feet so fast she almost fell over.

I wanted to stand up, but there wasn't enough floor space. Amber and Griffin were already squished against one another. I pulled my knees into my chest and rolled into a kneeling position. Kim did the same, craning her neck to see the spot Griffin was staring at.

"The wall," Griffin continued. "It moved."

"That's impossible," Amber stated in awe.

"Help me push," Griffin told her, placing his hands back on the wall.

Amber looked skeptical, but flattened her palms out underneath Griffin's. She gritted her teeth and closed her eyes, scrunching her face up with concentration. After a few seconds she let go, releasing a whoosh of air.

"It's not budging," she declared.

"Something moved," Griffin insisted, kicking the wall as forcefully as he could in the cramped space. "You all heard it."

"Maybe the noise was from outside," Amber murmured.

"No way," Kim asserted.

"She's right," I agreed. "We all heard that."

Amber looked thoughtful for a few seconds before her face lit up. "Wait!"

"What?" Kim and I cried in unison. Griffin stopped pushing on the wall to hear what Amber had to say.

"I remember something about these walls!" Amber cried excitedly. "I was going to get my lunch one day, and while I was waiting I spotted blue prints on a table. I think they might have been for these cubes! They had to be. The walls are made up of several layers. It's a safety measure, just in case one of the workers got locked inside while building it. If you press certain spaces of the wall in a specific order, it will open!"

"Do you remember anything about the combination?" I asked eagerly.

Amber shook her head. "I didn't have time to study the prints."

"Well you'd have the best chance of figuring it out of all of us," I pointed out.

"I have some ideas," Amber confessed.

Griffin plopped back down in his seat, wiping his brow with the back of his hand. "Be my guest."

"We don't have much time." Amber leaned against the wall, flicking her fingers across the metal. "There could be thousands of different combinations. We're just going to have to get lucky."

"And you thought you were so strong," Kim teased Griffin. She tried to keep her tone heavy, but I recognized the nerves in her shaky voice. Tension was tight in the small space. We stayed quiet, avoiding each other's eyes.

My heart was a beating drum. I begged it to silence itself; worried the others could hear it. Inside my body it was deafening, and it didn't slow or quiet. The temperature inside the cube rose with each passing second. I was breaking a sweat sitting motionless. Stiffness settled into my limbs; I yearned to move but ordered my body to remain still. Fidgeting wasn't going to help, and space was limited. My mind began to wander, images of Amber, Patrick, and Adam running through my brain. I wondered if Patrick was in a similar cube with Noel and the others. Was Amber still alive, her tail thumping against the floor somewhere? How had the pills had such a fast effect on Adam? It was like he was another human being, a stranger. Perhaps it was due to the fact that he hadn't taken the vitamins for so long. The sudden exposure may have put his body into shock and caused a quick, heavy reaction. Or maybe Angel had given him different pills. Or maybe the pills always had such a strong effect. How would I know? I'd been taking them for too long to remember how I'd started. Where was Adam now, and what was Angel's plan with him? He was a rebel too. Why would he be given a second chance and not the rest of us? Or had she planned to kill him too? Did she only use him to demonstrate how powerful the vitamins could be? To instill the image of a non-responsive Adam as the last living memory of our friend? There were so many unanswered questions.

A second squeak disturbed my thoughts, causing me to jump a few inches off the bench. I looked eagerly towards Amber, who was still staring at the wall with fierce concentration. Her fingers slid delicately but purposely across the metal, seemingly un-phased when the wall emitted another squeak.

"What—" Kim began, but Amber silenced her.

"Please," Amber answered, tapping the wall above her head with her index finger. She let out a triumphant noise as she continued working on the puzzle.

This time I reached over and grabbed Kim's hand. It was hot and clammy, but the touch granted me the calmness I needed to sit and wait. I squeezed her fingers and looked at my feet, feeding off her composed energy.

Griffin sat like a statue, his eyes glued to Amber. I was close enough to clearly see the sweat dripping down his tanned brow. He made no attempt to brush it away as it slid down his cheek, into his chestnut goatee, and off his face. I watched the droplet fall to his jeans. I wanted to reach out to him with reassurance, but was afraid I would startle him.

A series of shrill, consistent squeaks filled my ears, making me cover one of them with my free hand. The squeaks escalated into a loud ripping sound. The fluorescent light inside the cube flickered before the wall gave way with a huge creak.

"Guys!" Amber cried out, reaching to grab onto the side of the opening to gain her balance. The toes of her boots tipped over the edge into the air before she managed to steady herself.

"Oh my gosh!" Kim breathed. She released my hand and craned her neck to look out the doorway.

I leaned over, careful not to bump into Amber, and peered outside. My head began to spin, my stomach muscles clenching. The ground wasn't visible, the only thing below us a chasm of inky blackness. I struggled to breathe as I raised my head. Identical silver cubes stretched out from a thick black cable across the ceiling, each one a few feet apart.

"Holy shit," Griffin commented, staring over Kim's shoulder.

"Of course, when these were being constructed, they weren't raised up on the cables yet," Amber said weakly. "They could just crawl out."

"I think I'm gonna be sick," I groaned, rolling back away from the opening.

"We just have to think logically," Amber reasoned. "They had to get us in here. They must have lowered it down somehow. There has to be a way to do it without destroying the cube."

"What?" I shrieked. "We have no idea how far up we are. How can we know if we'd survive the drop?"

"There has to be a slower option," Amber persisted. She observed the top of the cube. "There's only a foot or so of space between the ceiling and the top of our box."

"I highly doubt Angel climbed all the way up here to lower this thing down," Griffin said dryly. "She must have some kind of remote or control from somewhere else."

"This is true," Amber answered. "But that doesn't mean we can't check the top of this for an emergency button or control panel like I said."

"What?" Kim gasped. "You want one of us to climb up there? If we fall . . ." Her voice trailed off, unable to finish the sentence.

"We don't exactly have any other option," Amber pointed out. "Now who's the best climber?"

I could feel shivers spiking my blood. It was insane. It was the craziest thing I've ever heard. The hairs on the back of my neck stood up as if a supercharged magnet was yanking them from my skin. It took a few moments to realize that everyone was staring at me.

"What?" I asked.

"You're the strongest one here," Kim said.

"What?" I yelped. "No way. Griffin's arms are way bigger than mine!"

Griffin shook his head. "It's not about size man. You're way more agile than me. Plus I work in a factory. I lift weights, but you're out there conditioning yourself every day."

"I hardly see how lifting garbage applies to climbing up onto a very small piece of metal and dangling who knows how many stories high, waiting to fall to my doom."

"You saved me once before," Kim reminded me softly. "I can try to do it, but I don't have very good balance."

"I'm too big," Griffin added. "You're smaller so you could be a more nimble climber."

Amber spoke up, "I haven't worked out in years. I have the upper body strength of a child."

"You guys can't be serious." The stone cold expressions plastered across their faces told me that they were indeed very serious.

"We don't have much time," Amber pressed. "Angel will be notified of the opening."

"But, won't she come up here and have to fix it or something?" I mused desperately. "Then we can try to get away."

Amber shook her head gravely. "No way. She'll send this thing flying into the ground when she notices it's been opened. We've caused too much trouble already."

"I really have to do this?" I squirmed in my seat, trying to avoid looking out at the darkness below.

"You don't have to do anything," Kim said. "I can try it."

The memory of her falling into the hole at the dump replayed before my eyes. She had done it on purpose, but it didn't matter. This fall would be much farther. It was deep, almost never-ending, and it was something she couldn't come back from.

"No," I told her as she started to stand up. "I'll do it."

"You're sure?" Amber asked, turning sideways so she could rest a hand on my cheek as she sat back down.

"You heard him," Griffin muttered.

I pulled Amber's hand away from my cheek. I didn't need any distractions. "I'm sure."

I mustered every ounce of strength in my body and straightened my knees to stand up. My legs felt like rusty door hinges; they hadn't been used and were difficult to move. Sandpaper scratched my throat as I tried to swallow, my tongue thick as a bowling ball.

Kim opened her mouth to say something, but I held up my hand and shook my head. I couldn't take it right now. She nodded and forced a smile. Her hands drifted up to her hair, pulling her long ponytail over her shoulder and running her fingers through the strands.

I forced myself to look away, stepping carefully across their feet to the edge of the cube. My sweaty hands gripped the outside of the doorway as a rush of air rose up from below, rustling my hair. The darkness beckoned me, eager to swallow me up forever. Its arms outstretching and wrapping themselves around my back. It whispered sweetly in my ear, inviting me to enter. So comforting, so calm, so quiet. It promised a land of peace, free of pain. So close I could almost taste it. Temptation got the better of me. My fingers began to loosen, my body swaying in the air like a piece of laundry on a clothesline.

"Vic!" Kim grabbed my leg, pulling me back. The darkness let out a cry of anger, releasing me from its grasp and darting away.

I tightened my grip again and considered Kim. Her dark eyes were as fiery as ever, but I could sense the fear flowing in her fingertips. She pulled me back into reality; seeing her awakened me.

Words were out of reach, but I sent her a small smile and a nod. I was strong now. Angel was wrong. Feelings didn't make you weak; they made you strong. Emotions and attachments to other living creatures gave far more satisfaction than eternal darkness could ever hope to. A few weeks ago, I would have fallen into the abyss without looking back, but things were different now. I'd met so many people who I had connected with, who had touched me. I was no longer alone. I had people now who cared about me, who gave meaning to my actions. That feeling of being loved was indescribable, irreplaceable, and something I had to hold onto.

I couldn't let everything I had gained just slip away. I had a purpose now. I had a reason to get up in the morning. I had a reason to get the hell out of here and show Angel who she was messing with.

The jelly-like sensation seemed to melt from my arms. I reached up and grabbed onto the top of the opening with one hand, twisting my body around so I faced the inside of the cube. The breeze kissed at my back but I ignored it, focusing on the top of the container. Balancing to the best of my ability, I took a deep breathe and let go of the side of the doorway. In one fluid motion, my hand found its way to the top of the door so both of my hands held onto the top of the opening.

My arms felt like they were being ripped apart. I rose up onto my toes, reducing the pain slightly. Sweat was gathering rapidly on my skin. I knew I was wasting valuable time, and it would only get harder. My grip was already beginning to loosen. Forcing my eyes to ignore the darkness beneath me, I shifted my focus to holding onto the metal. Gathering all my strength, I pulled myself up as if I was doing a pull-up in one of my workouts. I caught a brief glimpse of the top of the cube before one of my hands slipped off. The other followed, not strong enough to support my weight alone.

The world spun as I fell, landing hard on my back. I felt hands on my legs, holding onto me tightly. My torso tilted back, the blood rushing to my head as I gazed down into the abyss. My arms flopped underneath me, flailing around in the air. I wanted to scream but the wind had been knocked out of me. I couldn't muster the strength to breathe.

"Hang on Vic!" Kim called. Her voice sounded far away.

Pressure increased on my ankles. I felt a strong tug and shooting pain. Within seconds, my back was sliding along cold metal. My shoulders rolled over the edge, my head banging against the floor as I lay on my back. I was tilted slightly; there was not enough room to lay flat.

"Are you okay?" Amber asked, reaching her hand down to rest on my head.

I blinked and tried to gather my breath, unsuccessful. I lay there for a few minutes in shock, closing my eyes to rid myself of the dizziness that was wrapped around my head. My stomach felt as if I had been hit by a truck and my lips refused to move. I focused on my nose, trying to take in air through my nostrils. After a few more moments, I could feel the oxygen drifting into my head. The corners of my lips twitched and the muscles obeyed my brain, parting to allow exhalation.

Mustering my strength, I opened my eyes once more. Amber, Kim, and Griffin were all leaning over me, staring intently. Kim jumped in surprise when she saw me breathing again.

"You're okay!" she cried, her hair falling over her shoulder and brushing the top of my chest.

"Oh my gosh," Amber sighed.

"You scared the shit out of us," Griffin commented.

I tried to sit up but my arms were weak. I flopped back onto the ground, my head thumping against the floor.

"Stay where you are," Amber advised. "Your body is still in shock. It wouldn't be wise to move right away."

"I'm fine," I mumbled, gritting my teeth and ignoring the throbbing pain in my head and back. My arms and legs felt light as air, the numbness a welcome change from the stabbing pain.

"That was way too dangerous," Amber murmured.

"We don't really have another choice," Kim pointed out.

"I'll try it," Griffin offered.

"We don't have much time," Amber admitted.

Griffin turned his attention back to me. "What did you see on the top?"

I winced as I tried to move again. "There was a vent that was shallower than the rest of the metal. If you can get a hold on that, it would be the best way to pull yourself up. I only had a quick look, but I'm pretty sure there was a control panel or some kind of buttons."

"I'm gonna need to move you so I can stand up," Griffin told me. "It's gonna hurt."

I let out a laugh. I think it was inappropriate, but I didn't have the energy to do much else. The pain and fear were overwhelming. "Okay."

Griffin leaned toward me and wrapped his arms around my shoulders, pulling me up. He grunted as he dropped me next to Amber. My head thumped against the wall with a loud crack. I let out a soft cry.

"Sorry man," Griffin told me. He reached behind my head, touching the bruise I suspected was forming across my entire skull. When he took his hand away, it was covered in dark, scarlet blood.

Amber slipped her jacket off and slid it in between my head and the wall, providing a cushion and a material to absorb some of the blood.

"You better hurry," she told Griffin grimly.

He stood up and nodded, his features stiff and serious.

"Maybe I should do it," Kim suggested, eyeing me nervously.

Griffin shook his head. "I got this."

"Wait!" Amber ordered as Griffin moved to the opening.

"What?" he demanded, gripping onto the side of the wall with his hand.

"I have a better idea! Why don't you lift one of us up there?"

I turned my head to look at her, surprised that we hadn't thought of that before. Ignoring the pain that came from the movement, I summoned my voice.

"That's genius!"

"Let me go," Kim said.

Amber nodded. "Okay. We've used too much time already."

Griffin planted his feet firmly, his boots a few inches from the opening. Kim rose to a squat on the bench and crawled over so she was beside him.

"I'll hold onto your legs so you don't fall forwards," Amber said. She wrapped her hands around Griffin's thighs.

Kim took a deep breath. "I'm ready."

Griffin reached for her hand and pulled her so that she stood in front of him. If he hadn't been holding onto her, she would have fallen through the air. Only her toes rested on the floor. Her face was unreadable, using the skills that she had practiced for so many years. I wasn't sure if it was for my sake or hers.

Griffin pulled her in closer to him, their bodies pressing against each other. His voice was muffled against her skin. "One, two, three!"

As soon as the last word escaped his mouth, Griffin was bending over and grabbing Kim's calves. He hoisted her up past his shoulders, the muscles bulging through his shirt. His body jerked forward, but Amber held tightly onto his legs.

"I got it!" Kim's voice was barely audible. "Let go!"

Griffin obeyed, his arms dropping down to his sides. Kim's feet disappeared from view as she swung them up onto the top of the cube. I heard her boots clang above my head.

Griffin grabbed the edges of the opening and craned his neck to try and see what she was doing. "Do you see the buttons Vic mentioned?"

"Yeah!" Kim replied. "But which one do I push?"

Griffin looked back at Amber. She let go of his legs

210

and stroked her chin thoughtfully. "There should be a button that will send the cable into motion. I'm not sure if it will send us down below or over into some sort of loading area like a conveyor belt."

"But what would it look like?" Kim called.

"Tell me what you see," Amber instructed.

"There's a big red button that doesn't look like the rest of them."

"No!" Amber cried out urgently. "Don't press that one. That has to be the one to drop us down at high speed." She rubbed her eyes with her palm, her face tight.

"The rest are black circles! Three by three, they all look the same."

"I'm going to give you a combination," Amber said firmly. "I can't promise it'll be right but I need to try. It's a long shot, but so far Angel uses a similar code for most of her operations."

"Hurry!" Kim's voice sounded strained.

"Two, four, four, six. You got that? Two, four, four, six!" She looked at Griffin and I and explained. "It's the year she started her civilization."

"The numbers go across right?" Kim called.

"Yes!" Amber answered.

Four beeps filled the cube as Kim pressed each of the buttons. The cube began to vibrate, the lights flickering. Without warning, it jolted to the side as it started to move.

"Yes!" Amber let out a cheer.

"Hold on Kim!" Griffin called,

"Flatten yourself against the metal!" Amber yelled, but her voice was lost beneath the noise of the cube sliding along the cable. The other cube to the side of us was moving in the same direction, along with the ones beyond it.

The pain was still devouring me, but I was able to ignore it long enough to wrap Amber up in a stiff hug. "We did it!" I whispered excitedly, resting my chin on her shoulder.

She hugged me back, not saying anything. I felt an indescribable safeness in her arms, reluctant to pull away. The sparks in my spine were calming and my limbs had lost their numbness.

The cube screeched to a sudden halt. Amber let go of me and backed away. "Can you walk?"

I managed a crooked smile. "I'll walk."

She helped me to my feet, peering into the darkness outside the opening. The only light came from the dimly illuminated cubes adjacent to us. A musty smell drifted through my nostrils, like an old building with stagnant water.

"How do you know there's somewhere to walk?" Griffin inquired, crouching on the bench impatiently.

"I don't," Amber replied. She closed her tiny fingers around the side of the door and knelt down. She stuck one foot out into the murky air, smiling as it made a thump against something hard. Straightening up into a standing position, she stepped out into the blackness.

Griffin moved in front of me and grabbed my hand, leading me out of the cube. My boots crunched on what felt like dirt. Walking caused the pain in my back to amplify, but I gritted my teeth and tried my best to ignore it. It was a relief to be out of the suffocating space.

"Kim?" Griffin called. His voice was strong and steady, as hard to read as Kim's trademark expression.

"I'm okay." Kim peered over the top of the cube, lying flat on her stomach. She turned around and dropped her feet over the side. Sliding the rest of her body down the wall, she fell to the dirt with a loud thump. "Ow."

She wasted no time, darting over towards the light of the next cube. "Is there a way to open this from the outside?"

Amber looked around, biting her bottom lip. "We really don't have time."

"Amber, please," Kim begged.

"Give me a boost," Amber told Griffin, following Kim.

Griffin hoisted Amber up on his shoulders. Amber rolled onto the top of the cube, carefully punching in a few numbers. The cube beeped as she pressed each button, but nothing happened. She muttered under her breath, smacking the metal with her palm in frustration.

I hobbled over so I stood between Griffin and Kim, our eyes glued to Amber. Her head hung down in concentration, tapping her fingers against the metal thoughtfully before returning to the buttons.

A familiar squeak emitted from the cube, then the sound of tearing metal. Amber leaned over the side opposite us where the door must have opened. Griffin and Kim hurried around, leaving me staggering after them.

"Patrick!" I heard Kim shriek as I rounded the corner.

Patrick tumbled out of the cube, his hand pressing his jacket tightly across his nose. The tunnel was dark, but the light from the cube allowed me to see how awful he looked. His eyes were swollen and red, his skin pale, his fingers a dull gray. Sweat dripped profusely down his skin and he was shaking violently.

"We need to get away from here!" Amber ordered, dropping to the ground and shoving Kim and I in the direction we had came from. "The gas won't be as strong in a bigger space, but that doesn't mean it won't be strong enough."

Griffin stood like a statue in front of the doorway, staring at the others inside. I paused for a moment to take in the sight that had stunned him. Noel's head hung over the side of the opening, a frosty finish painted over her eyes. Her mouth stretched open, her tongue sickening black. Her hands were gray and her skin glistened, shiny with sweat. Another girl, Tina, was slumped over her, her body still and her face stuffed against Noel's shoulder. A twisted figure I suspected was Terry was crunched upside down in the small floor space between the benches.

Amber didn't give me any more time to observe the horrifying scene. "We need to go *now!*" She ordered fiercely, shoving us forwards and sending a set of fireworks down my spine. "Unless you want to be exposed to Angel's deadly gas, then *move!*"

Kim grabbed Griffin in one arm and pulled him away from the doorway. "Help me with Patrick." Griffin remained in a daze until Amber gave him a good shove. He grabbed Patrick and threw him over his shoulder. Patrick was still shaking and coughing, sounding like he was having a difficult time breathing. Every few seconds his entire body would tense up in a spasm. I couldn't look at his face without getting the chills.

Amber led us down the dark hallway and back past our lit up cube. She was walking quickly, despite the darkness in between cubes. If she walked any faster she would be running. I struggled to keep up, bringing up the rear behind Griffin. I think he was struggling a bit under Patrick's weight, but he didn't have time to say anything. Kim kept at Amber's heels,

214

the gap slowly widening between her and Griffin.

I glanced over my shoulder, unable to shake the image of Noel and the others from my mind. This was not the first time I had seen the dead, but it was the first time I felt anything from it. It was horrifying. Sickening. Painful. Those were my friends. And they were gone forever. It was more excruciating than the feeling in my spine.

"Wait!" I yelled. "What about the other cubes? Are there any more people in them?" Amber had said that there were other rebels, but she said they were infrequent.

I didn't expect Amber to hear me, but miraculously she did. "They're empty," she screamed back, gasping for breath.

"How do you know?"

"The lights are tinted blue. That means unoccupied. Angel uses that code for everything in the facility."

Now that she pointed it out, I could see a blue tint to the cubes as we flew past them. Ours had emitted a pale white light. No one was in these. Anyone else who had stumbled across this place was already dead. As dead as Noel, Tina, and Terry. Patrick, Adam, and Amber Dog could be close behind. And so could we if we didn't get out of here. I tried not to think about the twisted, stomach-turning bodies that had been in the cube. My eyes kept rolling around in my head, unsure of where to settle. If I looked straight ahead, I would see Patrick. If I looked down at the dirt I would bump into them.

Suddenly, the air in front of me seemed to waver, sparks appearing out of nowhere. The sparks grew denser, the space flickering like a firecracker. The flashes disappeared as sudden as they had come. In their place stood something much more terrifying.

Angel.

Chapter 13

My heart froze in my chest, the walls around me tightening and swallowing me up. Cement poured down my throat, replacing the air in my lungs. The dirt below glued itself to my boots. Everything was still; time had stopped. Then she spoke.

"I'm coming for you."

Cocking her head to the side, Angel flashed me her fake innocent smile. A shrill, high-pitched noise filled my ears as sparks began to gather along her skin. Her smirk remained plastered to her face as the sparks spread over her flesh like a plague of bugs. The noise intensified, the sparks grew brighter, and then she was gone.

I gasped, filling my lungs with the stale oxygen in the tunnel. The sudden blast of air sent my body into a coughing fit. Blood rushed to my face and water gathered in the corners of my eyes.

A hand grazed my back. I looked up to see Kim extending her hand. Realizing I had fallen, I took hold of her and allowed her to help me to my feet.

"It was just a hologram," Amber called. She had stopped running, but stood a few feet ahead.

"How did she know exactly where we were?" I panted. Wiping the dirt off my pants, I followed Griffin and Kim over to where Amber waited impatiently.

"Tracking devices," Amber snarled angrily. "She wasn't taking any chances."

"Can we take them off?" Kim asked.

Amber shook her head. "No. They're injected beneath one's shoulder blade. Once we're off the premises they'll lose signal. We can be scanned and identified if brought back to the machine, but she can't monitor our location."

"So we're screwed?" Griffin asked, breathing heavily. He lifted Patrick off his shoulder and placed him gently on the ground. Patrick didn't look any better. I wasn't ready to admit it, but he looked even worse.

Amber shrugged helplessly. "I . . . I don't know." She seemed defeated.

"Why isn't Patrick dead?" Kim demanded bluntly.

Amber sighed. "He's pretty close to it. But the gas affects everyone differently. His body is just putting up stronger resistance."

"Can you help him?" I asked.

"Maybe," Amber replied. "But we need to keep moving."

Griffin knelt down and picked up Patrick once more. I hadn't been extremely close to him when we'd met before, but I had developed a large amount of respect and admiration for him in the last few hours.

Amber turned around and resumed her long, quick strides. Griffin fell into step behind her. Kim walked beside me this time, slipping in front when we passed a cube and there wasn't enough room to stand side by side.

The encounter had shaken me up, even if the figure was merely a hologram. It had looked so realistic that she could have reached out and hit me. The fact it wasn't real wasn't much consolation. The hologram was just another demonstration of how smart Angel and her team were. Angel had shown us what she was capable of. We only had one of her own on our side. Was it really possible to defeat a whole army of Angels? And Angel herself? I wasn't ready to give up, but the negative voices were buzzing in my ears.

The hallway took a sharp turn to the right. We plunged into total darkness as the last cube disappeared behind us. Part of me was scared of the blackness. It would be easy to go back towards the cubes, to be able to see something. Not knowing what was around you was unnerving. Who knew what could be lurking in the dimness, waiting to strike.

I shuffled along, slowing down to avoid tripping. Kim stuck close by, our shoulders brushing every few minutes. As reassuring as her presence was, I still felt extremely uneasy. I had no idea where we were. Angel had built this entire facility. We were like lab rats running through a maze; at any moment we could be plucked up by the mad scientist behind the experiment.

I heard a thump and stopped walking, holding my hand out to the side to prevent Kim from continuing.

"It's okay guys," Amber spoke up. "I found a door."

I heard a beep as a piercing white light flooded my eyes. The rectangular shape of the open door sent flutters of relief through my chest.

Amber stepped through the entrance, her silhouette dark against the blinding glow. She peered through the other side and motioned for us to follow. Griffin trudged through the door, hunched over under Patrick's weight. Kim tapped my thigh and hurried after them. I trailed onwards, eager to be able to see again but still trying to adjust to the brightness.

As I stepped through the doorway, the dirt beneath my feet was replaced with hard tile. I rubbed my eyes as the room slowly fused into focus. The space was large, the walls covered in dozens of blinking screens. Huge control panels full of flashing lights and buttons sprawled beneath the displays. Empty black swivel chairs were scattered around the floor as if the occupants had left in a hurry.

A closer look at the screens made me cringe. Most of them showed empty little rooms, but my attention locked on the one showing the girls I recognized. The screens presented the inside of the gas cubes, fixing the image of Noel and the others sharp in my mind.

No one else seemed focused on the screens. Griffin had dumped Patrick in one of the chairs and was rubbing his shoulders. Kim had her hand on Patrick's head, staring quietly at him as he burst into a fit of tremors. The grayness on his hands was spreading up his forearms. His skin looked deathly pale and his lips had turned purple. The red mask around his eyes was growing sharper, sweat drenching his face and hair. He was beginning to emit an odor similar to something I picked up on my route. I didn't need the brightly lit room to realize that he was almost gone.

Amber had plopped into one of the chairs and was tapping furiously away at the buttons, changing some of the images on the screens to show different hallways and rooms. She concentrated intently on her work, melting away from us into a different world.

"Can you help Patrick?" I interrupted.

She continued tapping away, rising up from her seat to observe one of the screens more closely. Her head turned to look at me as if she had just noticed I was there.

"There is a vitamin that will stop the deterioration process," Amber answered. "I think."

"That's not very reassuring," Kim grumbled.

"Like I said, this wasn't my department," Amber retorted. "She needed a little safety net in case I ever got out of hand again. My rebellious tendencies weren't easily disposed of, as you can see."

"Where is this vitamin?" Griffin asked.

"Haven't we learned that the vitamins that come out of this place aren't ideal for consumption?" Kim pressed.

"That's why I'm not sure," Amber responded. "But there's not enough time for me to perform an operation, so this is the only hope."

"Where is it?" Griffin repeated.

"In Angel's study," Amber replied. "She keeps a ton of vitamins there. Life Vitamins may be her claim to fame, but she's never satisfied. She always wants to know more, do more, control more. She created the poisonous gas in the cubes out of synthetic materials. If I know her, she wouldn't create a killer without a cure."

"You want us to go to her study?" I gasped.

"No," Amber sighed. "I want us to try and get out of here." Her voice softened. "But I know what it's like to lose someone you care about. And I know if we don't try to get the vitamin, you'll always regret it. Frankly, I'm getting tired of trying to argue with you."

"Thank you," I mumbled.

221

"What's the fastest way to get there?" Kim asked.

"Follow me," Amber told us. She finished tapping away at the control panel, sending all of the monitors into darkness. Satisfied, she hurried over to the big metal door at the far side of the room.

"Do you need help?" I asked Griffin as he bent to grab Patrick.

He hesitated and shook his head. He hoisted Patrick over his back and headed after Amber.

Kim and I closed the door behind us.

"Where do you think Angel is?" she asked as we jogged after them.

"I thought she would be on us already," I admitted. "But I think this is a game to her. She might enjoy the chase." I hobbled along unevenly, trying to ignore the stabbing pain in my back.

"She's so fucked up!" Kim snapped. "How did this spiral so out of control?"

"I can't believe that I didn't recognize her the first time I saw her. She visited me all the time as a child. And I didn't even remember it."

"I don't remember much of my childhood either," Kim offered. "Remember she mentioned weekly injections besides the LVs?"

"It's not important," I told her. "It's in the past and we can't change anything."

"Do you think we can change the future?" Kim asked the question that had been poking around in the back of my head all day.

I shook my head, taking in a gasp of air. "I don't think we have that kind of power."

"What if we could?" Kim asked. "What if we could learn the real history of what happened? Gather a hundred times the books Patrick stole and educate others on them?"

My lips couldn't help but turn up in a smile. "That's what I love about you." I was referring to her sparkle and fiery energy, but the words that came out of my mouth stunned me. I had said love.

I couldn't tell if Kim had noticed. There was no time to assess her reaction, as Amber was opening another door.

"She wouldn't expect us to come here," Amber was saying to Griffin as Kim and I stopped beside them. "I think she's got men on all the exits. That being said, she is still tracking us and will figure out our location shortly."

"What does this vitamin look like?" Griffin asked. "The one we are looking for?"

"Good question."

Griffin frowned at the answer none of us wanted to hear.

"You'll know it when you see it, right?" I tried, stepping into the room.

Amber didn't reply; she went straight to digging through the piles and stacks of paper. The room was indeed a mess. Towering piles of paper, books, and other miscellaneous objects covered the floor. Some swayed as I walked by, threatening to tumble over with the slightest touch.

"This is her study?" Kim blurted out. "What does she study in here? And where?"

Amber ignored her, vanishing behind a turret of books.

I couldn't stop looking at Kim. Despite all the fear, worry, and emotions fencing in my mind, there was something else. There was another feeling battling for its place in my heart. I was becoming more skilled at identifying things like fear and sadness and anger. They were overwhelming and becoming hauntingly familiar. But this feeling was not like the others. It made me lighter, not weighing me down like negative emotions. Amber's words were stuck in my head. Love . . . was that what this was? I had just spoken the word as if it was nothing, though I'd never used it aloud before in my life. I had thought I loved Kim and both of the Ambers, but never officially declared it. It made my stomach twirl, but not in a sickening way; more like a feather tickling my insides. It gave me a sense of hope, a sense of something more. And every time I looked at Kim, it took control of me.

Kim noticed me staring. "What?"

"Nothing." My face flushed and I stepped to the side. My foot hit the bottom of a large stack of papers, causing the top to tip over. The pages drifted to the ground like leaves, twisting and dancing in the air as I tried to catch them. One of the pieces fell between my fingers. It felt rough and foreign against my skin.

This paper was large and an off white color. Big black words stretched across the top of the page. "Kidnapped Girl Found After Two Years." Underneath the letters was a faded picture surrounded by smaller sentences. The image showed a woman holding a teenage girl. Beneath the picture read, "Anna Coleman reunited with daughter Amelia Coleman (15)."

"Trouble, trouble." Two long, black fingers snatched the paper from my hands. "I try to give you a nice, quiet way to go. But you insist on being difficult."

I rotated to face Angel, my knees shaking.

"It's a little impressive, actually. Though most of your success stemmed from help from Mommy." She chuckled, standing before me with her hands on her hips. She had changed her clothes, now wearing silver leather pants, knee-high black leather boots, and a fitted dark leather jacket. Tight, black leather gloves masked her hands, her flaming curls pulled back into a tight bun. She must have noticed me staring at her clothes. "You like? They were more appropriate for a chase."

"Look, can't you just let us go?" I asked. "What harm could it do?"

"Hah!" Angel laughed, licking her dark red lips. "I don't need to take any chances of you jeopardizing anything. You can't compete with my power, but you've shown to be annoyingly persistent."

"Are you going to just let this go on forever?" Kim demanded. "This demented society you've created out of resentment for those who wronged you? What happens when you die?"

"Sweetie," Angel purred, stepping over so her face was only inches away from Kim's. "I'm invincible."

"Oh yeah?" Kim growled. She swung her arm to punch Angel, but wasn't quick enough. This time Angel was prepared. Angel grabbed her hand and cocked her head to the side as Kim struggled to free herself from Angel's grip.

"What's wrong dear?" Angel asked. She thrust her body forward and let go of Kim, sending her hurtling into a stack of papers. The movement appeared effortless, demonstrating her immensely terrifying strength.

I hurried to her side, digging in the mess of paper to free Kim.

"Stop wasting your energy," Angel sighed. "It would have been so much easier to just do what you were supposed to. This all would have been over by now."

225

"You're sick," Griffin spat, Patrick still slung over his shoulder.

"What's that you got there?" Angel giggled. "It's quite remarkable actually. That man has lasted an unusual amount of time. Though no one has ever escaped mid-gas before, so I can't say I have much to compare it to. Never mind, he'll be dead soon enough."

"Shut up," Griffin growled.

"Where are your manners, boy? Don't you know who you're talking to?" Angel fingered a silver bracelet on her wrist.

I uncovered Kim in the mess and helped her to her feet. I was furious. This woman who stood in front of me had killed my friends. She had destroyed Adam and taken away my dog. She had killed my father, humiliated my mother, and had just hurt the girl I was pretty sure I was in love with.

"Your face is a little red, Vic," Angel commented. "Anything you'd like to say?"

"Where is my dog?" I demanded. "And where is Adam?"

"Oh that raggedy thing? I have my men fattening it up. Then I think it would look lovely above my mantel. And Adam? I must admit I quite like having him around. I'm testing out some new drugs on him. I think I will make him part of my team when he comes around completely."

I couldn't take it anymore. My rage bubbled up inside of me, spilling from ever orifice in my body. I lowered my head and charged Angel, ramming into her stomach. We tumbled through a batch of books. I pinned her against the wall, glaring angrily at her face. For a moment, I thought I caught a glimpse of fear in her eyes. The flicker was gone before I could be sure.

226

I felt a blow to my stomach as Angel's knee connected with my ribs.

I released her as I staggered backwards, bending over in pain.

"I think I have underestimated you," Angel snickered. "I thought you were just a little bitch. Like your mother."

The words stung harder than her bone cracking into mine. I bellowed an angry cry and charged at Angel again, but she was too quick for me this time. She stepped effortlessly to the side and caught my arm, flipping me onto my back with superhuman strength.

"What are you?" Kim screamed at her.

Angel sighed. "Haven't I done enough explaining today? You guys are really tiring me out. I'm going to need to turn in early tonight."

Out of the corner of my eye, I saw Griffin place Patrick on the ground. He tightened his hands into fists, bouncing lightly from foot to foot. Without warning he grabbed a big book from the stack behind him and flung it across the room, smacking Angel in the jaw with a deafening crack.

She let out a startled cry, her palms flying to her face. She swore under her breath, blood dripping from the corner of her mouth. Picking up the book from where it had landed a few feet away, she hurled it back across the room. It hit a large stack of books behind Griffin. The pile swayed and collapsed, burying Griffin and Patrick beneath the hardcover pages.

I reached over and grabbed her ankle, the leather icy cold to my touch. I almost yanked my hand back in surprise, but managed to hold on long enough to pull her foot out from under her.

She caught herself before she fell, her boot

stomping down on my fingers. I cried out in pain. She smiled as she swished the heel back and forth, moving her head from side to side as the cacophony of cracks erupted from my bones.

Kim rushed over to help me but Angel easily shoved her aside. Angel lifted her foot off of my fingers, releasing another shot of pain.

"You guys need to give it a rest!" Angel sighed. "You can't beat me."

Kim narrowed her eyes. Her mouth moved but no words came out.

"See," Angel pointed out. "There's nothing to say. You know I'm right."

Amber appeared out of nowhere, fiddling with a large silver watch on her wrist.

"Where did you get that?" Angel snarled.

Amber didn't answer. She raised the watch and aimed it at Angel. Her fingers clamped over a button, sending a white laser flying across the room. The laser pierced Angel's eyes, causing her to scream. Angel's limbs went limp and she crumpled to the floor, colliding with a pile of books. The stack crumbled, her body disappearing in the mess.

"Amber!" Kim cried.

"Come on," Amber said. "It won't last for long."

"What is that?" I asked, rising to my feet.

Griffin popped his head out from under the books, shoving them aside and digging for Patrick. He pulled them both from the pile and dragged Patrick to us.

"It's a watch that also acts as a tranquilizer," Amber explained briefly. "But Angel has modified her body. It won't have as heavy an affect on her as it would a normal person. We need to go."

She didn't wait for us to follow, dashing out of the room.

The endless running and rushing was killing me, but I followed her anyway. The pain in my legs was a nice distraction from the agony in my back. My boots felt heavy, like I was dragging tires. I was glad that Griffin was carrying Patrick. He was bigger than me, but he had to be exhausted by now. He must have been running on pure adrenaline.

I pumped my legs furiously, keeping pace beside Amber. "Do you know an exit that might not be guarded?" The words came out in strained gasps.

Amber didn't answer. She was breathing hard, and I wasn't sure if she could. She shook her head. I interpreted it as a "No", though she could have been just moving as she ran.

I let out a cry as I tripped over something, landing flat on my stomach. My hands slid along the tile floor, my palms burning. "What the?"

A familiar furry face filled my vision, dousing me in kisses.

"Amber! How the—"

"Get back here you stupid thing!"

I looked up to see two of Angel's men running frantically towards us.

My mother Amber swung her watch and fired the laser. The men fell to the ground with a bang.

"I don't believe it!" Kim cried, ruffling the fur on top of Amber Dog's head.

"She found me!" I said, wrapping the wriggling ball of fur up in my arms. Her tail thumped excitedly, beating against the tile like a drum.

"Vic," Amber warned me, tapping her watch.

"Right," I mumbled. The reunion was short lived, but I couldn't complain. I never thought that I would see Amber Dog again.

I rose to my feet, Amber Dog jumping up with me

and placing her front paws on my chest. She looked happy and unharmed. Her tongue hung out the side of her mouth and she tilted her head.

"Come on, Amber," I told her. I took a few steps down the hallway. Amber Dog lowered the front half of her body, her butt sticking up in the air like she wanted to play. "Come on," I repeated, walking a few more feet.

Amber Dog bounded after me happily, leaping over the men who lay on the ground. I stroked her head and gave her a scratch behind the ears. "Good girl."

Amber, Griffin, and Kim were already far ahead. Kim looked over her shoulder and motioned for me to hurry. I ran after them, looking over every few seconds to make sure that Amber Dog was at my side.

Amber ran through a swinging door marked "Kitchen." The door flapped closed in my face after Kim. I pushed it open, holding it for Amber Dog before entering. Amber stood in the middle of the kitchen. I was surprised she had actually stopped running.

"I have an idea, but you may not like it."

"Shoot," Griffin replied.

"Angel definitely has guards on all of the exits. There's one way out that she forgot to block though." She motioned behind her to a small opening.

"What is it?" I asked.

"The garbage chute."

Angry shouts rose up from the hallway, getting louder every second. I could hear the boots slamming on the tile floor. I didn't want to come in contact with the men wearing the boots.

"Lead the way," I answered. Amber was already squeezing into the opening before the words left my mouth.

"I'll see you guys on the other side. Wait a few seconds in between each person if you can." She slipped through and was gone.

Griffin pushed Patrick through the hole and stuffed himself after him, squirming. "Guys I'm stuck."

Kim and I ran over and pushed on his shoulders, but he wouldn't budge.

"Come on," Kim grunted, shoving all her weight against him. The footsteps outside were getting closer.

I spotted a bottle on the counter beside the chute and stopped pushing Griffin to grab it.

"What is that?" Kim asked, her face scrunching up in confusion as she continued pushing with all her might.

"It's oil." I unscrewed the top and poured it on both sides of the opening, spreading it over Griffin's arms. He made a face as it dripped down his clothes, but remained silent.

He continued wriggling and I helped Kim push again. After a few seconds, Griffin slid down through the opening. Kim and I fell forward, landing on our hands and knees. I shot her a grin but she was already on her feet and hopping into the chute.

"Hurry," she whispered, disappearing from view.

I picked up Amber Dog. She wriggled frantically in my arms but I held on firmly and slid her through the shaft. I heard the door open as I squeezed into the tight space. Looking over my shoulder, I caught a glimpse of legs crashing into the room. I used my arms to push myself off, sliding into the darkness.

Chapter 14

"Amber!" I landed hard into the pile of garbage, sinking in below my shoulders. I reached over and pulled Amber Dog up before she could disappear below the surface. Wrapping my arm as far around her broad stomach as I could, my other arm propelled us to the edge of the enormous dumpster. My fingertips tore at the plastic bags, flecks of food getting caught beneath my nails and burning my cut up palms. The metal rim was shockingly cold to the touch. One look at the blanket of stars across the dark sky explained the chill in the air and the icy gusts of wind. It was the middle of the night. Inside of Angel's Ring, I had lost all sense of time. The seconds blurred into minutes, minutes to hours. I was completely disorientated. A stabbing pain in my back caused me to cringe, reminded me of my fall. I threw my leg over the side of the dumpster, straddling it like a horse. Amber Dog still in my grip, I mustered all my strength to descend down the twenty-foot ladder.

My boots dropped to the dirt with a jolting thump.

Loosening my hold on Amber Dog, I collapsed on my back. All of the pain, terror, and stress of the past events could no longer be outrun. The suppressed exhaustion and emotions attacked like a hurricane. I buried my face in my filthy, smelly palms and let out a muffled wail. I reeked of sweat, garbage, and blood. A cold nose poked through my hands, trying to separate them from my cheeks. I opened my eyes and stared at Amber Dog. She sat in front of me, waiting expectantly for me to return her affection.

Unable to hold myself together any longer, I threw my arms around her. Her fur was rough against my skin, but the warmth and undeniable love radiating from her body was healing. My breathing was labored and shallow. I closed my eyes and tried to focus on steadying each inhalation and exhalation. Amber Dog's stench-soaked body only exasperated the wrenching in the pit of my stomach. I held my breath instead, closing my eyes and trying to push back down whatever small amount of food and water remained in my stomach. My efforts were pointless. I released Amber Dog from my arms and fell down onto hands and knees. My stomach heaved and twisted, bile rising up in the back of my throat. I puked repeatedly, sweat pouring down my forehead and heat rushing through my nerves. I could feel my abdomen contracting and releasing. The nausea remained strong, dry heaves plaguing relentlessly. My arms and legs wobbled beneath me, threatening to give way. I tried to sit up but my muscles were useless. I fell forward into the pile of muck. The horrible odor enabled my body to throw up one final time.

Puking had not relieved my unsettled stomach. I could hear it growling and screaming. My back throbbed from landing on it earlier, feeling like it was soaked with gasoline and lit on fire. Sharp stabs of pain attacked the back of my head, sending flickers of light behind my closed eyelids. Thousands of needles prodded my legs. My arms felt as if they had been pumped with gallons of Novocain. Every time I inhaled I felt sicker. I tried to focus on breathing again, inhaling through my nose and exhaling through my lips. Coughs erupted from my lungs. My head jerked with each cough, slamming my already aching skull into the hard earth.

I couldn't think straight with so much pain. I tried to picture Amber Dog, Kim, Griffin, Patrick, and my mom. I needed to find them. I had to know they were okay. Part of me wanted to get up and look for them, but my brain dismissed the idea. All I could focus on was the agony. My head spun from exhaustion even though my eyes were closed. I lay still. The world began to melt away like snow on a warm winter day. I couldn't hear anything. My body was screeching at me, assaulting me. In between stabs of piercing pain there were flashes of red. Red, red, red. Everything melted to black.

*   *   *

My brain was fuzzy. I must have fainted. This was becoming a habit. My head weighed a hundred pounds; it didn't move an inch when I told it to lift. The pain had subsided slightly but soreness still slid up and down my spine. With much effort I began to wiggle my toes in my boots. Movement returned slowly to my fingertips as I shook the pins and needles away finger by finger.

Voices materialized around my head, the words

unrecognizable. My tongue twitched, a thick metallic taste suffocating my gums. Air moved through my nostrils. It wasn't a full breath, but something stirred inside. My eyelids fluttered before sliding open to reveal blurred images. A damp sensation crept over my cheeks as the world slowly slid into focus.

"Oh my gosh," Kim breathed, lowering her head and letting out a long sigh. "You had us so scared."

Amber Dog lay against my side, standing up when she felt me move. I twisted my head to the side, seeing Griffin sitting against the dumpster. His knees were bent towards his chest, his arms sloped over them. At the sound of Kim's voice, he raised his head and looked in my direction. A figure lay on the ground next to him, quiet and unmoving.

A gust of frosty wind swept over me, causing me to shiver. I noticed Kim trembling in the cold, her jacket gone. Her arms were bare under her black tank top. Goosebumps covered her skin, illuminated only by the light of the moon. She lifted her head to focus on me again, a smile creeping across her face. The air of vulnerability had returned to her. Her eyes were swollen and drained, but still as beautiful as always. I couldn't tear myself from her irises.

She spoke again, her fingers brushing my cheek. "I'm really glad you're okay, Vic."

I managed to move my sandpaper lips and tongue. "Is everyone else all right?"

Kim didn't answer at first, her teeth tugging at her lips.

"What?" My heart stopped at her hesitation.

"We don't know yet," Kim answered softly, nodding at the figure on the ground. "Patrick . . ."

"Did Amber get the pill?" I asked. As soon as the words were out of my mouth, the queasiness returned. Amber. "Where is she?"

"She's okay," Kim replied.

"Where is she?"

"She ran off without telling us. She said not to move and that she'd be back soon."

"She went off alone?" My voice came out as a screech, my throat scratchy.

"I think she's proved she's quite capable of handling herself," Griffin spoke up.

I bent my elbows and struggled to prop myself up. Kim moved her hand against my back, helping me into a seated position. A wave of dizziness brushed through me, but it was fleeting. My hand landed on a piece of fabric that had been under my head. It was Kim's jacket.

"Don't touch the other side," Kim advised. "I used it to wipe the blood and throw-up off your face."

"You must be freezing." I started to take off my jacket but she stopped me.

"I'm fine." Her voice was firm. I wanted to ignore her and give her my jacket anyway, but I knew she was too stubborn.

"I'm freezing," I muttered.

"Exactly. That's why you need the jacket. You must have puked up half your organs."

I shuddered. "What about Patrick?"

"Amber gave him something before she left," Griffin said. "He hasn't moved since I pulled him out of the trash."

"Was it the right vitamin?" I pressed. Patrick looked like a corpse already,

"She didn't say," Kim said. "She ran off in a hurry."

"Are we safe here?" I asked.

"I don't think so," Kim answered. "That's why she was hurrying."

"You have no idea where she went?"

"No," Griffin told me. "But it's nice to have a few seconds of rest. I don't think I could have kept running."

"Thank you for bringing Patrick," I said sincerely.

He glanced down at Patrick's body. "Let's hope it wasn't for nothing."

Kim slid across the ground on her butt, her boots digging into the dirt as she pushed herself back next to Griffin. She leaned against the dumpster for support. "Nothing is for nothing."

I shuffled over next to them in a similar fashion, relieved that my muscles were working once more. Amber Dog followed, plopping her head into my lap as I squeezed next to Kim. My hand wandered into hers, trying to share any heat in my body with her icy skin. She didn't move at my touch, staring off with a faraway look in her eyes.

Griffin glanced at me. "Did you ever think that Angel was right?"

"What?"

"You know . . . about emotions? I've never seen a dead person before. I can't stop picturing them . . . you know."

"I . . . I never thought about it like that." His question scared me, making my brain delve into an unfamiliar and uncharted area. Ever since I'd stopped taking the life vitamins, I'd assumed that feelings were wonderful. I had experienced some awful things, but never stopped to question my convictions that the vitamins were detrimental.

"I'm not saying that I like the girl, believe me. She's fucked up. But so was what I saw back there. I don't know if I'll ever be normal again." Griffin's voice was deep and serious.

237

"Normal?" Kim scoffed. "What normal are you referring to? An unfeeling robot?"

"I don't know," Griffin mumbled.

"Take it easy," I told her. "He's got a point."

"So you agree with him? And that freak?" Kim scowled.

"No, I'm not agreeing with anyone," I stated. "I'm just acknowledging the fact that emotions also have a dark side. I always assumed that they were positive, or that the positive at least outweighed the negatives. But it's scary because our friends died back there!" My voice broke and I had to swallow hard, pausing before continuing. "They died, Kim. No one ever taught me how to deal with this!"

Kim stared at her boots, clicking them together uncomfortably. "Me neither."

"So how are you dealing with it?" Griffin asked.

"I'm not," Kim muttered.

"You can't just block it out forever," he reasoned.

"Well I don't know what else to do!" Kim raised her voice, her eyes flashing at him.

"None of us do," I realized.

"How do we figure it out?" Griffin asked. "I've never felt so horrible in my life."

"It's complex," Kim put in. "Like some kind of puzzle."

"We can't let it control us," I decided.

Griffin wrinkled his brow. "How do you suppose we go about that?"

"I have no idea." I sighed. A spark ignited somewhere in the back of my brain. "Or maybe I do."

"What?" Kim pressed.

"Well . . ." I could feel myself blush and hoped it was dark enough that she wouldn't notice.

"Everything we've lost today makes me sick to my stomach. But there is something that eases that sickness." I paused. "You."

Kim raised an eyebrow at me and remained silent, waiting for me to continue.

"And you," I told Griffin. "And Amber." My free hand drifted to Amber Dog's head, ruffling the fur behind her ear. "Both Ambers. When I think about you guys, how we helped each other, how we supported each other. You're all so important to me. And I think you care about me, too. And that makes the pain a little easier to deal with."

Kim's face was unreadable, but Griffin slowly nodded. "I see where you're going. But . . . the pain is still there."

"I'm not saying that it's gone," I started. "But maybe, with other things . . ."

"You're saying we have to just push through it?" Kim suggested.

"Well yeah, but we're not alone," I pointed out. I wanted to tell her how much I really cared about her, but I couldn't muster the courage. I thought back to when I had blurted I loved her. Had she heard me?

"You're oddly optimistic," Griffin commented.

"We don't really have a choice," I remarked. "We're all we have. The only hope for each other's survival."

"Well, when you put it that way," Griffin joked dryly.

"I hope Amber gets here soon," Kim commented, shaking at a gust of wind. She looked up past the dumpster and at the long tube we had come through. The cylinder attached to a looming silver building with spiraling towers.

I looked out across the grass to observe the scenery for the first time. Trees lined the horizon, big tall

239

trees with strong branches. Scattered leaves danced along the ground in the breeze. The sight was incredible, breathtaking, even in the darkness. I couldn't remember the last time I'd seen so many trees. It made me sad momentarily, but the beauty cancelled out the gloom. I was here now, and that's what was important.

"Are you sure you don't want my jacket?" I tried.

Kim shook her head.

"How about my blanket?" I smiled, gesturing at Amber Dog across my legs.

Kim cracked a weak smile, reaching over to stroke Amber Dog's back. Her hand tightened in mine. Her fingers stroked my palm, sending heat surging through my aching bones.

"I wonder where she went," Griffin mused.

He didn't have to wait long for an answer. A small, open, black vehicle with four large black wheels zoomed into view. It pulled silently to a stop before us, Amber sitting behind the steering wheel.

"Get in."

She didn't need to tell us twice. We were on our feet in seconds with a renewed energy and sense of determination. Griffin propped a close-eyed Patrick in the back seat and squeezed in next to him. Kim slid in the back as well, leaving Amber Dog and I the passenger side. I flung open the door and patted the seat. Amber Dog jumped in and I followed. Amber jammed on the gas before I even shut the door.

I managed to pull it shut as we sped away from the building toward the shelter of the magnificent trees. The vehicle was small and low to the ground, the side and back windows free of glass. All of the bumps and dips sent us flying around in our seats. I glanced over my shoulder as the enormous building behind us grew smaller.

"Where did you get this?" I asked Amber.

She stared straight ahead, knuckles white on the wheel. She expertly steered between trees and onto a narrow dirt path. We skirted branches and leaves as we sped along.

"It's the grounds keeper's car," she replied as if it was no big deal.

"This will give us a head start," Kim commented. "They can't get their huge cars through these trees."

"Exactly," Amber replied. "We're driving 'til we run out of gas."

Peering over the dashboard, I spotted the gas dial hovering at a quarter full. I had never driven anything like this, but I hoped it was enough gas to get us very far away.

"Do you think she's following us?" Griffin asked. "Does she know we're out?"

"She knows we're out because our trackers probably disappeared from radar. And she will follow us," Amber answered. "But I didn't even think we'd get out of those doors. If we can get far enough away from this place, we can lose her."

"Do you know the area?" I asked. I hadn't been out of The City since I was a kid. The only things I was familiar with were the spiraling skyscrapers, run-down apartment buildings, and long crowded roads. I had scattered memories about nature from childhood in my brain, but it was nothing like this. This was real. I was inches away from structures that had branched out of the Earth itself. This wasn't created by some worker in The City. It was pure, almost untouchable. If it weren't for the branches scratching the sides of the vehicle, I might not believe they were real. It was like some kind of dream.

241

"No," Amber admitted. "I've been in that building most of the time. I know a little about the surroundings, but I've never been this far out. It was against the rules to leave the grounds unless on an order. Besides, I'm a scientist. I have no business out here."

"It's beautiful," I breathed. I fought the urge to reach out and try to grab onto a branch.

"It smells funny," Griffin snorted.

Something bubbled in my throat and a laugh rolled off my lips. I surprised myself, but didn't try to stop it. For some reason, despite the pressing situation and discouraging circumstances, I reacted with laughter. A response normally associated with happiness. Was I happy here? Running for my life?

A thick branch crashed through the windshield, shattering the glass and with it my thoughts. Shards of shiny crystal flew at my face. Instinctively, I covered my eyes and tried to shield Amber Dog. I felt a few flecks strike my arm, and then nothing. I moved my elbow away from my face. With the windshield gone, we were even closer to the trees. It also eliminated the shield we had from the wind.

Amber was un-phased by the incident, her brow set in a thin line of determination. Her knuckles were beginning to whiten from clutching the wheel so tightly. A roar erupted from the engine as she slammed down harder on the gas. The wind whipped at her face, but her hair was so short that it didn't hinder her driving. The headlights swung wildly across the trees.

The rush of air blew dust in my face. I squinted through the dirt, gripping the door to avoid sliding back and forth across the seat. My left arm draped over Amber Dog. She seemed nervous, whining as

242

the gusts thrashed through her fur.

"How's Patrick?" I shouted over my shoulder.

Griffin cleared his throat before answering. "It's hard to tell in the dark. And the fact that we're bouncing all over the place."

"He'll be okay though," Kim stated.

"I hope so," I murmured, my head slamming into the side of the car. It must have reopened my previous wound, if it had every closed at all. I could feel the warm trickle of fresh blood drip down my hair and neck.

"Are you okay?" Kim asked.

"Shit," I replied, holding my hand to the back of my head. In the hurry I had forgotten Kim's jacket. I considered using my own coat to blot up blood, but I wasn't sure if I could hold my hands steady along the rough terrain long enough to take it off. I also didn't want Amber Dog to go flying into Amber. Besides, the return of my pounding headache was a decent distraction from worrying about Patrick. Spots clouded my vision and I gritted my teeth to avoid crying out.

"Maybe you should ease up on the driving," Griffin suggested.

"Do you want to get caught?" Amber retorted.

"No," Griffin answered.

"Then don't criticize me," she hissed. She swung the wheel frantically to the right, narrowly avoiding a wide, looming tree trunk. The side of the car banged into another tree, jolting me into the door again. I was very thankful that my hand was between my head and the metal.

"I'm impressed we haven't crashed completely," Griffin confessed.

"It would be easier if we weren't forging our own

trail," Amber replied.

"Won't that make it easy for Angel to find us?" Griffin asked.

Amber spun the wheel again, dodging another tree. "Let's hope not."

"How are we doing on gas?" Kim asked.

I peeked over at the gas dial, which was now hovering above empty. "Have we really been driving that long?"

"When you're driving like a maniac, you burn gas faster." Amber's voice was steady and emotionless. "Besides, they put the crummy gas in these cars."

"Do you think Angel's coming after us?" Kim asked.

"She's looking," Amber answered.

"How good are her tracking skills outside of her empire?" I asked.

"The good thing is that her knowledge of this land is just as fuzzy as ours. She didn't deem it fit enough to include as part of The City. If we manage to lose ourselves out here, I think she'll lose us as well."

"I hope you're right," I said.

"She's been pretty on the ball so far," Kim pointed out.

"I hope that beast doesn't catch up with us," Griffin commented. "I can't believe she beat all of us in a fight."

"She didn't beat us," Kim hissed.

"Either way, I wouldn't mind having some of whatever drugs she's taking," Griffin said.

"Come on," I told him. I swiveled around, dropping my hand from the back of my head. The wound stung as I moved, but I tried to ignore it. Watching the front of the vehicle was making me dizzy. "You're not serious."

He shrugged. "I don't know. You've got to admit that being physically superior to everyone else would be pretty beast."

"There are always costs," Amber spoke up.

"What kinda costs?" he asked.

"Messing with people's bodies," she said. "It's not natural. All of the vitamins and drugs she pumps into herself, her experiments, and us are unnatural. They're genius, but there are side effects. They mess with the chemical makeup of our body. I've seen some pretty nasty responses to the life vitamins."

"Really?" I was surprised. "I've never heard of anything like that." My memory flashed back to the first set of Officials we'd met. Before we stowed away in the trunk, I remembered spotting the eerie glow of their silver skin.

"Angel would never let something like that out of the bag," she began. "She wants perfection. Screwed up mutations are not part of the plan."

"How does she deal with these mutations?" Kim wondered.

"She doesn't. We do."

"What do you do?" Kim pressed.

"Testing. We take samples of their blood, DNA, and such and try to find similarities. Things that could explain the reactions."

"And?" Kim asked.

"We have theories, but nothing is set in stone."

"What reactions are you talking about?" Griffin inquired.

"You don't want to know," Amber answered.

"I do," Griffin requested.

"There have been horrible rashes. Anything from flaking red skin to someone's flesh completely peeling off. Reports of people going insane, something

245

snapping in their brain and losing all sense of this world. Toes and fingers have broken off. Teeth have rotted and fallen out. Some people have attempted suicide or to kill someone in their workplace. People have stopped breathing. Some just die."

"That's nasty," Griffin said.

"It's sick," Kim agreed. "And everyone was just taking them because they thought it was good for them. Innocent people."

"How do you know that these were affects from the vitamins?" I asked.

"Because they all started on subjects of the experimental group," Amber said.

"You're saying you guys knew that these things could happen, but you sent the Life Vitamins out anyway?" I gasped.

"Like I said, we're messing with nature here. Angel was too impatient to wait. It took years to develop a near perfect product. Everything has its flaws, as much as she didn't want to admit it. Any substance put into the human body that isn't natural is going to have side effects, may they be mild or as serious as death."

"How were the scientists who created this okay with it?" Kim asked.

"Scientists can be pretty passionate about their work, no matter what it may be. They may not have supported what Angel was doing, may not have wanted to distribute the unfinished product. But they were running out of time, and I'm guessing they were curious. After slaving away for years, they had created something mind-blowing. A drug that was almost perfect. They couldn't wait to begin the master experiment."

We were quiet for a few moments, letting the

246

information Amber had just fed us sink in.

"Does Angel know that perfection doesn't exist?" Kim ventured.

"I think she knows, somewhere in her head. But she's messed up. After all of the trauma she has experienced, she's managed to convince her conscious mind that it does exist. That she created it, and as a result saved The City."

"It would be nice," Kim said thoughtfully.

"What?" I asked.

"Perfection . . ."

"How do you know?" Amber asked. "You've never experienced it. None of us has."

"But perhaps there are seconds of it?" Kim suggested. "We may not have a perfect society or a perfect life, but as we go about our day we can create our own moments. Moments where the world stops, the imperfections melt away, and for some amount of time we are truly happy."

"That's a nice thought." Amber slammed on the brakes, throwing us all forward in our seats. A huge brown object darted across the front of the car, slamming onto the metal and flying into the shelter of the trees. Amber Dog let out an alarmed bark.

"What was that?" I gasped, my breath catching in my throat.

"I think it was a deer." Amber's foot returned to the gas pedal.

"What's a deer?" Kim asked.

"An animal that lives out here in the wilderness. I think they're almost extinct. I've never seen one in person. But I'm pretty sure it matched the pictures I've seen."

"What else is out here?" I wondered. Suddenly the darkness and noises of the trees seemed a lot more menacing than beautiful.

"I don't know," Amber said. "Well, I might be able to identify something if we saw it."

"Are deer dangerous?" I asked.

"No."

"Are there dangerous animals?"

"Yes."

I shuddered and ran my fingers through Amber Dog's coarse fur for comfort. The longer we were out here, the more blatant it became that I knew nothing about my surroundings. I was defenseless against the unknown. Angel was scary, but what if there was something in these woods scarier than her? Was there anything more deadly?

The engine let out a sputtering noise and the car began to slow down. Amber kept pressing on the gas, but it continued to slow until we screeched to a halt. She slammed the wheel in frustration.

"What happened?" Kim's voice was high pitched.

"We're out of gas."

"Already?" Griffin growled. I felt a jolt in my back as he kicked my seat.

"I told you, even though these things are tiny, they run on crappy gas!"

"So what now?" I questioned, dreading the answer. My heart pounded in my chest, fueled by the anxiety building throughout my body.

"We need to put as much distance between ourselves and this car. Get as far away from Angel's Ring and The City as possible." Amber turned around to face us for the first time since she started driving. "I know we're all exhausted, but I'd rather be exhausted than dead."

"Agreed," Griffin remarked.

Kim sighed and nodded.

Amber's eyes rested on me. "Then it's settled. We'll walk until we can't walk anymore."

CHAPTER 15

The two sticks of lead attached to my torso grew increasingly heavy every second. My feet burned inside my tight boots, every step sending a painful explosion through my bones. Walking exasperated the pain in my back; it was a struggle to maintain a decent posture. I was hunched over and dragging myself along like an elderly man. My neck dropped, my head swaying from side to side. Struggling to keep my gaze ahead was too exhausting. I had settled on watching the feet in front of me. I didn't remember whose boots they were, but they continued moving so I forced myself to do the same. A robot slowly running out of battery, shuffling one foot in front of the other.

Noises echoed throughout the forest, fading in and out of my ears. Twigs crunched and cracked around me. Wind blasted through the trees, crinkling the leaves and scratching the branches. Unfamiliar hoots and chatters resonated through the trees, but whatever creatures the sounds belonged to chose to remain unseen. Shallow breathing escaped the lips of my traveling companions. We were silent aside from our wheezing.

Amber Dog was the only one with energy left, and even she was beginning to drag. What had started out as a brisk romp had slowed to a soft trot. She remained glued to my side, which was much better than her running ahead and circling us as she had at the start of our trip. I felt safer with her beside me, and hated the thought of her wandering too far into the dark. Without the headlights to light up the brush, we were ambling slowly and blindly. The canopy of branches and leaves overhead separated us from any light the moon and stars could provide.

My feet refused to lift more than an inch. I had to summon every bit of power inside me to hoist them over the tall tree roots and boulders. The spaghetti arms stretching from my shoulders were weak and floppy, but they sometimes assisted in lifting my legs. My fingers and cheeks were numb from the cold and stung with windburn. Every inch of my body was frozen or throbbing.

I wasn't sure how many seconds, minutes, or hours had passed. It felt as if we had been walking for days. Dried sweat covered my skin, a sickly odor seeping from my pores and drifting off into the cacophony of scents in the forest. My eyes kept threatening to close. Keeping them open was a chore and resulted in a harsh burning sensation. I kept blinking to keep my burning eyes open. The skin beneath my nose was raw and blistered from running so much. My socks were moist with sweat despite the chilly air. The skin on my legs rubbed against my pants uncomfortably. I couldn't think straight anymore, my thoughts clouding and melting into one another. Empty echoes

251

bounced back and forth, drowned out by the persistent chirping of the forest.

If I had been thinking straight, I might have stopped moving. The message of profound fatigue might have been successfully sent from my aching body to my brain. My muscles might have frozen and refused to budge. I wasn't sure what was moving them. I had run out of energy long ago. The adrenaline had dwindled after we had gotten outside. There was nothing left inside to keep me going, yet somehow I was moving. It was slow, but I was moving. I trudged along; alternating my feet in a movement I had taken for granted before. A movement that didn't used to be filled with agony. A movement that didn't make me want to cry. Good thing I didn't have the energy to make a noise. I just kept pushing through. Until I hit something.

The world spun momentarily, unbalanced by the collision. I managed to steady myself. The feet in front of me had stopped moving; I had banged into a person. The muscles in my neck screamed as I forced them to drag my head up. My eyes could make out the faint outline of short dark hair and a slim figure in front of me. Amber.

I tried to ask her why she had stopped, but my mouth was desiccated. I tried to swallow but my throat burned and sizzled, eager for water. Opening my mouth only made the sensation worse, the wind drying it out even more.

"Guys." The voice seemed warped and foreign. Maybe Amber's throat was in a similar condition as mine. Perhaps my ears were twisting the noise. Most likely it was a combination of the two. Either way, the noise startled me. Not only because it sounded odd, but because it was the only human sound I had heard

252

after eternal silence. It shattered the rhythm of the forest; all of the noises in the trees seemed to be stunned and interrupted by its presence. It didn't belong out here. It was foreign, intrusive.

Yet the voice was soothing. It allowed my eyes to move in their sockets, my eyeballs sliding to gaze out past the figure in front of me. My blurry surroundings slowly came back into focus. Blinking gradually cleared the images. I could see why Amber had stopped.

The scenery had changed drastically. We stood on the edge of the forest, the end of the trees. Beyond the line of trees stretched a long meadow, rich with grass and flowers. The stars and moon cast a blue light over the field, allowing me to acknowledge the incredible array of shapes and colors. The meadow stretched out over the horizon, its boundary uncertain. The stars overhead were brilliant and bright. Even though we could see the stars when the lights turned off in The City, it was nothing compared to this. If I thought the trees were the most beautiful thing, I was wrong. This was incredible.

"Look!" Amber raised a shaky arm.

I looked past to where she pointed. The shadow of a large cave rested among the trees to our left, branches and bushes growing around the entrance. Flowers were nestled among the edge of the rocks. Some kind of bird was perched outside on the ground, illuminated by the starlight. It raised its wings into the air and flapped them furiously, catching a gust of wind and taking off into the night.

"Shelter!" I croaked.

"I can't walk that far," Griffin groaned.

"We can sleep . . ." Amber seemed to want to continue the statement but ran out of stamina. She started towards the opening, crushing flowers beneath her boots.

I followed the path she was making in the high grass, dragging my feet as quickly as I could. Amber Dog had a renewed rush of energy, bounding ahead of me and then back to my side. A bark rose in her throat, splintering my eardrums. Before I could attempt to quiet her, she was off. She danced playfully in circles, nosing Amber's hands.

The slog to the cave seemed miles long, though it couldn't have been more than a hundred feet. It gradually grew larger as we drew closer and closer. The rocks were rough and dark, but they were inviting. It was a massive mattress with fluffy pillows beckoning us nearer.

Amber reached the rock first but I was close on her heels. Amber Dog had returned to my side, as if she was not eager to venture into the dark cavern on her own.

The stone felt hard and sturdy beneath my feet. There was a small man-made cave in one of the run-down City parks, but it couldn't hold a candle to this natural masterpiece. The edges seemed to glow in the moonlight.

Amber stumbled toward the entrance, hitting a button on her watch. A thin stream of light equivalent to a flashlight beam swung from her wrist, making a small dent in the blackness. She hesitated for a moment and looked over her shoulder.

I followed suit, making sure the others were behind us.

Kim's feet slammed down hard on the rock. She moved to Amber's side as if her boots were glued to the earth, sliding across the ground.

Griffin entered seconds later. His face was

contorted with pain and exhaustion, his back hunched heavily under Patrick's body. The second he reached the rock, his knees buckled beneath him. Patrick tumbled off his shoulder, landing on the ground. Griffin dropped onto his hands, letting out a long breath.

"Are you okay?" I reached down to touch his shoulder, but drew my hand back quickly as he cringed in pain. "I'm sorry."

He shook his head and coughed, his whole body shaking. His large frame seemed small and frail, threatening to collapse into the earth. Quivers shook his arms and legs as he struggled to hold himself up.

"I hear water!" Amber cried. Her voice was soft but excited.

Kim was at my side suddenly. She had come up so quietly I hadn't noticed her approaching. She reached out and grabbed Patrick's arms, dragging him through the cave's entrance.

I looked at Griffin, deciding to do the same. He shrunk away from me at first, but succumbed to my help when he realized that he could no longer move on his own. I didn't have the strength left to pick him up. I pulled him as gently as I could, slow and careful in my movements.

We followed Amber inside. The light from her watch skipped as she moved through the cave. A soft trickle caressed my ears. Amber was right; there was water in here somewhere!

The trickling grew louder until the light stopped on a rippling clear substance. She swept her wrist across the wall, briefly revealing a small waterfall leading into a thin stream. She let out a cry and threw her hands out in front of her, cupping them to catch the water sliding down the rock. She raised her palms to her mouth, taking a long drink and immediately going back for more.

I set Griffin down gently and imitated Amber's motions. The water dripped over my cracked lips and into my mouth. It trickled down my throat, freezing cold. Once I got a taste of it I couldn't stop. My hands dipped into the water again and again, filling my body with the ice cold refreshment until my stomach felt full.

Kim followed our lead. She stopped to try and make Patrick drink. The water trickled down his chin. I wasn't sure if any of it had gotten into his mouth and throat, but she continued trying.

I remembered Griffin behind me. Turning with a handful of water, I raised it to his lips. He looked uncertain, but then drank it eagerly. After finishing the water in my hands, he crawled over to the stream and began drinking next to Amber Dog.

I let out a sigh of relief as I slumped to the floor. Pain still reverberated through my body, but the water had eased it slightly. I was still incredibly tired and sore, but it had refreshed and replenished part of my being.

The others stopped drinking and we all paused to look at each other.

"Let's sleep here." Amber sat down next to the stream and sprawled out on the ground, making a pillow with her hands.

No one argued. We stretched out next to her, huddling together in a heap for warmth. Removing the pressure from my limbs shed light on how tired I really was. Relief flooded my body. After hours of running, I had never thought I would rest again. I was dirty, cold, and smelly. But I could finally stop moving.

256

At first I thought I wouldn't sleep. I was overtired and my appendages ached. The floor was hard and freezing, unfamiliar bugs crawling across my fingertips. But the events of the day caught up with me. I couldn't fight the exhaustion stretching over my body like a blanket. My eyelids drooped, closing fully. I drifted off into sleep.

*   *   *

I opened my eyes to light. It seemed strange after so much darkness, but I welcomed it. The sunlight cast warmth and shadows across the cave. A figure was perched on a rock at the entrance, looking out into the meadow.

I struggled to turn over, stretching out my arms and legs. All my muscles were sore. It was a thousand times more painful than the hardest weight lifting session of my life. Amber Dog moved when I rolled over, jumping to her feet and licking my face. I ran my fingers through her scruffy fur and used my other hand to press into the rock and lift myself to a seated position.

Amber, Griffin, and Patrick lay against each other. Their faces were calm and beautiful. They were still except for the slow rise and fall of their chests as they breathed. They looked so peaceful.

Patrick's color was gradually returning to his face. The grayness had disappeared from his hands and his breathing was close to normal. The vitamins Amber had given him had to be working!

I rose to my feet slowly. Each step hurt, but I wasn't going far. I padded over to the edge of the cave with Amber Dog at my feet. I rested my arm on Kim's shoulder.

She jumped slightly, swiveling in her seat. A soft smile spread across her face. Her eyes showed recognition, but there was an unfamiliar emptiness wavering behind her irises.

"Are you okay?" I asked, my throat hoarse.

She shook her head and burst into tears, burying her face in my chest. Her body quivered as she sobbed uncontrollably. I pulled her closer, wrapping my arms around her back and pressing against her. She allowed herself to fall into me, small and vulnerable in my arms. As her hair brushed my hands, I couldn't help but want to be closer. I knew she was upset but didn't know how to help her. All I wanted was to take her face in my hands and press my lips against hers, to show her with my body how much I cared about her. How I would do whatever I could to protect her.

She broke away, wiping her tears. Her eyes studied my face, resting on my lips.

My heartbeat accelerated in my chest. I was nervous, but I didn't want her to catch on. A lock of hair blew across her face in the breeze. A quick motion of my finger tucked the hair behind her ear. My hand lingered above her cheek, my fingers sliding across her jaw line.

Before I knew what was happening, I kissed her. My lips met hers and her lips met mine. Everything around me evaporated as I became lost in her body. I turned my head slightly and adjusted my mouth. She did the same, her tongue grazing the edge of my lips. Shivers ran down my spine, electrifying my body.

As suddenly as the kiss had begun, it ended. She pulled away, her eyes wet with fresh tears.

"I'm sorry," she mumbled. "I'm sorry."

I stood in a daze for a minute before snapping back

to reality. "Don't be sorry . . ."

"I'm sorry," she repeated, shaking her head. She walked away from me towards the edge of the rock, pacing across the opening.

"Kim." I took a step towards her. "Why are you sorry? That was amazing."

She continued pacing, sniffling and rubbing her face. Her ponytail swung back and forth as she walked

"Kim." I took another step and grabbed her arm. She stopped walking and looked at me. I didn't recognize the expression in her eyes.

"Kim. I love you." As soon as the words were out of my mouth, a huge weight was lifted off my shoulders. It was like I was flying, drifting up with the birds into the clouds.

I studied Kim's face, waiting for her reply.

She remained silent, her eyes dropping to the floor. She shook her head. "Vic, I love you too; I really do, but . . ."

The weightless feeling vanished, replaced with the sensation of being placed on the tracks before an oncoming train. Anticipation and fear rushed through my body, numbness sweeping through my limbs.

"I can't stop thinking about Adam!" Her words were rushed, and as soon as she finished she collapsed into a fit of tears.

I was speechless. I knew that Adam and Kim had known each other longer, but we had been through so much together in the past few days. The feelings I felt for Kim were undeniably strong, and I had assumed she felt the same way.

"I can't stop picturing him back there with her. What if she's performing some kind of sick experiment on him? Or the creature she has forced him into becoming?" Kim's voice was shaky and staccato.

"I'm worried about Adam too," I whispered. "But I just thought . . ."

"I know," Kim sighed. "I . . . I do love you. I think. Thinking of you makes me feel . . . incredible. But I also love Adam. And he's back there suffering right now. It just doesn't seem right."

The train mauled me. It flattened me against the tracks, accelerated, and dragged me beneath its wheels. I was crushed. I thought I had been in pain the previous night, but this was worse. I had taken a leap of faith and made myself completely vulnerable. And she had crushed me.

"I'm sorry." Kim looked away. She didn't say anything else.

Dejected and stunned, I returned into the cave. My stomach churned, but it wasn't from the lack of food. It was from the heavy blow that Kim had delivered to it.

Griffin, Amber, and Patrick were still asleep on the ground. I collapsed next to them, resting my head in my hands. I wanted to scream. I wanted to cry. But I was too upset to do anything. All I could do was sit there, hiding my face and shivering despite the sun's warm rays caressing my skin.

Eventually, I lifted my head. I couldn't sit like that all day. My back ached from leaning over, my spine still throbbing from the night before. My eyes caught on a silver container sticking out of Amber's pocket. I shouldn't have stuck my hand in her jacket; I shouldn't have invaded her privacy. But I did.

Curiosity got the better of me. I reached down and gently removed the silver container. She stirred slightly in her sleep, making me freeze. She rolled back over and buried her head in the back of Griffin's hair as if nothing had happened.

I breathed a sigh of relief and gripped the container tightly in my hands. I looked up across the cave. Kim was perched on the rock once more. She faced away from me, uninterested.

I turned my back to her, pulling open the container with shaking hands. Inside were the pills Amber had stolen from Angel's study. I thought for sure she had left them on the dashboard. What use could we have for them now?

Griffin's words echoed in my mind. *Did you ever think that maybe Angel was right?*

My eyes froze on three familiar white pills. I tapped the edge of the container so the tablets tumbled into my hand. The stamps across the capsules burned through my brain. LVs. I fingered the vitamins carefully, rolling them between my thumb and index finger.

The pain inside my heart was throbbing. The fact that we had escaped Angel and The City was meaningless now. Any sense of accomplishment I had felt had been washed away. The five of us had escaped alive; six counting Patrick, but the others had perished. Adam was lost. We had no food, no home, no idea where we were, and nowhere to go. We were cut off completely from civilization and had no safe haven. If we wanted to live, we would have to remain loners in the wilderness. Never again could we return to the place we once called home. And worst of all, the girl that I was in love with could not return the feeling.

It cut straight through me, a knife piercing my flesh and digging in until it struck and punctured all of my inner organs. The blood poured out of the cut and

261

drained the energy from my brain. The oxygen was dissipating, my head spinning. I was a pile of wood set on fire and left to burn into nothing more than ashes. The ashes would be swept into the wind and lost in the air.

The vitamins in my hand held the key to my painkiller. All I had to do was swallow them. Swallow three little pills. Once they entered my system, all the feelings towards Kim would fade away. With it, the pain of rejection would disappear as well. It was such an easy solution. Three little white ovals of salvation lay in my palm.

I raised them to my lips, hesitating. If I took them, they would also eliminate the feelings I had towards the others. I wouldn't care that Amber was my mother. I wouldn't care that Griffin was my friend, or that he had carried my other friend Patrick for miles to save his life. I would never get to exchange stories with my mother about how she had grown up or what I had done in my life. I would never again wrap Amber Dog up in my arms and let her shower me in kisses.

Then the pain returned. The agonizing, heart splitting aching threatening to rip apart my chest and bludgeon me to death. It was suffocating, terrifying, horrible. I couldn't focus on anything else. Only the throbbing pain. Kim didn't love me, or she loved Adam more. She couldn't love me without Adam being there, and couldn't love me if he was there. It hurt so badly. She had kept me going through everything. She had kept me fighting and running. And she rejected me. Like I was nothing to her. As if I had sacrificed nothing to save her. As if the fact that I cared about her more than anything in the world was unimportant.

So much pain. So much pain. All I had to do to make it all go away was take these pills. Three little pills.

About the Author

Lauren Kehoe is 20 years old. She lives on the Jersey Shore and just completed her Associate's Degree. Her hobbies include writing, reading, powerlifting, volunteering at the local animal shelter, and contemplating the meaning of life. One day she hopes to travel the world. She is currently working on her second novel.